THE MYSTERY OF MR DAVENTRY

Scandalous Sons - Book 4

ADELE CLEE

Books by Adele Clee

To Save a Sinner

A Curse of the Heart

What Every Lord Wants

The Secret To Your Surrender

A Simple Case of Seduction

Anything for Love Series

What You Desire

What You Propose

What You Deserve

What You Promised

Lost Ladies of London

The Mysterious Miss Flint

The Deceptive Lady Darby

The Scandalous Lady Sandford

The Daring Miss Darcy

Avenging Lords

At Last the Rogue Returns

A Wicked Wager

Valentine's Vow

A Gentleman's Curse

Scandalous Sons

And the Widow Wore Scarlet

The Mark of a Rogue

When Scandal Came to Town

The Mystery of Mr Daventry

The Mystery of Mr Daventry
Copyright © 2020 Adele Clee
All rights reserved.
ISBN-13: 978-1-9162774-2-7

Cover by Dar Albert at Wicked Smart Designs

CHAPTER ONE

M iss Sybil Atwood had seen many depictions of the devil amongst the literature in her father's library. The master of the underworld was often drawn as a monstrous creature with horns, a forked tail and huge wings capable of scooping up a damsel and carrying her off to the infernal regions of hell.

And yet Mr Lucius Daventry possessed none of those qualities.

As their gazes locked across the crowded auction room, Sybil couldn't help but notice the physical attributes that marked the gentleman as the most dangerous, most sinful man ever to make her acquaintance.

Like Lucifer, Mr Daventry's strength came from his muscular physique, from his coal-black hair and penetrating stare. For her to feel the full force of his wrath, he did not need to rant and rave or charge from the dais at the far end of the room—the place where Atticus Atwood's precious journals and scientific equipment were displayed in such a fashion as to attract the highest bidder. The firming of his sculpted jaw, the reprimanding arch of his brow, the clenched fists hanging at his sides created a volatile energy that he sent hurling her way.

Sybil swallowed past the lump in her throat.

Don't let him know you're intimidated.

Mr Daventry shook his head and appeared to mutter an obscenity.

The men occupying the rows of seats whispered amongst themselves and craned their necks to observe the person foolish enough to rouse the devil's ire. Some took advantage of the delay to dip into their snuff boxes, and the musty air was suddenly filled with the scent of spice and ground tobacco.

"It seems you have the measure of Mr Daventry's character," her friend, Mrs Cassandra Cavanagh, muttered as they lingered in the doorway of the private room hired by the scoundrel to conduct his devious business. "We're the only ladies here. Regardless of your connection, Mr Daventry would never sell your father's possessions to a woman."

No one had been more shocked than Sybil to discover her father had bequeathed his life's work to a man as immoral as Lucius Daventry. No one had been more shocked to discover Atticus Atwood had parted with his treasured journals a week before his sudden demise. Most shocking of all was the fact that a parent with a logical brain had made a terrible miscalculation. Dissolute rogues cared nothing for science. Dissolute rogues were not interested in society's advancement.

And Lucius Daventry was the epitome of dissolute.

"Mr Daventry believes women are incapable of under-standing scholarly works." Why else had he refused to extend her an invitation to the sale? What other reason could he have for being so rude and downright disagreeable?

Cassandra arched a brow. "Then Mr Daventry needs enlightening."

Sybil agreed. "The rogue suggested I take up painting to ease my boredom. Something less taxing. Only those immune to bouts of sentimentality should concern themselves with intellec-tual matters. Apparently, marriage and children would serve as a better means to occupy my time."

Cassandra snorted. "I assume he wasn't offering his services."

"I doubt Mr Daventry knows the first thing about art."

"I meant as a husband, not a painting master."

Sybil's stomach flipped at the thought of sharing the infa-mous man's bed. "Heavens, no. I imagine the rake quivers at the mere mention of matrimony." Even so, taming a man like Lucius Daventry was a challenge far beyond the realms of her capabilities. "He made it quite clear I lack the wherewithal required to tempt him."

In truth, he had been crude in his delivery, and took pleasure firing offensive remarks in Sybil's direction.

"You must be mistaken. Mr Daventry finds you far from lacking in that department. Benedict said he spoke highly of your physical attributes."

Sybil's heart skipped a beat at the thought of the intimate conversation. "Mr Daventry finds it amusing to tease me. He must have known your husband would tell you." Blood rushed to her cheeks when she stole a glance at the gentleman who roused lust in the breasts of women and fear in the hearts of men.

When a frail fellow with bony shoulders coughed into his fist and glared at them, it occurred to Sybil that they could not stand conversing in the doorway. She took hold of Cassandra's arm and guided her towards the row of empty seats at the back.

"Mr Daventry said you risk losing your virtue if you persist in this foolish endeavour," Cassandra murmured.

Risk losing her virtue?

That was a low blow.

Indeed, it was an idle threat. Nought but empty words. Once, when Sybil had found the courage to stare into Mr Daventry's unforgiving grey eyes, she had seen the devil's façade falter. She had seen a hint of compassion. It was enough to know that his intimidating remarks bore no real danger.

"Lucius Daventry may be a scoundrel, but he would never force a woman to act against her will. Why would he? He's not short of bed partners." His cruel words and actions were merely a means to discourage her interest in Atticus' work. The nagging question was why?

"He means to frighten you," Cassandra said, as if reading Sybil's mind. "Deter you from your current course. Nothing else makes sense. Perhaps your father didn't want you to have his journals. Perhaps Mr Daventry is simply following Atticus' instructions."

"Clearly they were well acquainted. Heaven knows how. They

are opposites in every regard." Atticus had been a warm, loving, generous father. Lucius Daventry was a cold-hearted beast.

"Mr Daventry said that if you were anyone else, he would have fondled your impressive ... well, it's probably best not to repeat exactly what was said. I speak only to draw attention to the fact that he has some respect for your family name."

Sybil clutched her pelisse to her chest as her mind ran amok, filling in the missing words. "If I were anyone else?" she mused as she tried to banish the image of the devilish Mr Daventry stripping her out of her stays.

It was then that she realised the hushed mutterings in the room had ceased. The thud of booted footsteps on the boards drew her attention to a stern-looking Mr Daventry who prowled towards her like a predator thirsty for blood.

He came to an abrupt halt beside her, grabbed the crest rail of her chair with his large hand and lowered his head. The spicy scent of his cologne filled her nostrils, and she ground her teeth in annoyance. No other man of her acquaintance had ever smelt so good. He was about to speak—about to say something inappropriate no doubt—when Sybil decided to steal the wind from his sails.

"Friend or foe?" She offered a beaming smile.

"I beg your pardon?" he snapped. Oh, he was dreadfully cross.

"Have you come to make an apology and invite me to bid in the auction, or will you continue to berate me in the brutish manner that is so wholly undeserved?"

He stared. Power radiated, dark and malevolent. "You expect to be taken seriously in that ridiculous hat?"

Was that the best he could do? The retort was rather tame compared to their previous exchanges. Perhaps verbally abusing a woman in public was bad for business.

Sybil drew her fingers along the peacock feather protruding from her short forest-green top hat. "I find it a rather captivating design. Most men say it draws out the emerald hue of my eyes."

The muscle in his jaw twitched. "Is that why you shroud yourself in black when you stalk me through the streets, Miss

Atwood? Do you fear I might recognise those green gems and that vibrant red hair?"

Hell's bells!

Though she suspected he had seen her following him on many occasions, this was the first time he had openly drawn attention to her amateur snooping.

Sybil raised her chin. "I wish to bid on my father's belongings." Lord knows why Atticus had trusted this devil with his valuable possessions. Had Mr Daventry's parentage been under question, she might have presumed a secret familial connection. But the gentleman had inherited the menacing look of his father, the Duke of Melverley, a man equally harsh and brutish. "You cannot prevent me from claiming that which should have been mine."

The rogue snorted. "Had Atticus wished you to have his journals, he would have bequeathed them to you in his will. Now, I suggest you cease with these petty games and accept defeat." He cast a suspicious glance around the room. Those gentlemen brave enough to watch the exchange averted their gazes and bowed their heads. He turned to her, leaned closer and in a sharp tone said, "Go home, Miss Atwood, before I shame you in front of these men."

He was so close she expected to smell brandy on his breath, expected the whites of his eyes to bear the spidery red veins of a night spent indulging in carnal pleasures. Neither proved true. The scent of clean clothes, shaving soap, and his intoxicating cologne marked him as a beguiling contradiction.

"My father trusted you with his prized possessions. You have betrayed that trust by the crude display on the dais." Having advanced this far on the battlefield, she refused to retreat. "A man's work is valued by those with common goals and shared interests. Yet you hawk his objects like a back alley pawnbroker, one ready to strike a deal with the first clueless ignoramus willing to part with his coin."

Mr Daventry reeled from the insult.

As the illegitimate son of a duke, he must be used to people drawing attention to his failings. Her criticism had nothing to do with the nature of his birth and everything to do with his vulgar manners.

"You think you have the measure of me," he said. "You don't. You will never understand my motives. Go home, Miss Atwood. I shall not warn you again."

Did she detect a hint of disappointment in his voice?

Surely not.

"Not until I have claimed ownership of my father's journals." If necessary, it would be a fight to draw first blood. "I'm prepared to pay more than any man here."

A wicked smile played at the corners of his mouth. Hard, flint-grey eyes pinned her to the seat as he called at the top of his voice, "Gentlemen, I wish to inform you that I've had a change of heart. As Miss Atwood kindly pointed out, it was never her father's intention to sell his work to the highest bidder."

Curse the saints!

It seems Mr Daventry would go to any lengths to prevent her from owning the journals.

Grumbles of disapproval grew into whining complaints. Men shot spears of scorn, spears that might have had her shrinking in her seat had she not learned to ignore public opinion. Confusion marred other men's brows. How had a mere woman manipulated such a merciless monster as Lucius Daventry?

One man found the courage to stand. Had there been other ladies in attendance, a collective sigh would have echoed through the room, for Lord Newberry was considered quite the catch.

"For weeks you've teased us, boasted of the contents of Atticus Atwood's private works." Lord Newberry's mouth thinned in disgust. "Is this a ruse to increase the bids? What reason can Miss Atwood have for being here other than to assist in your devious plan?"

"Devious?" Mr Daventry straightened to his full, intimidating height, and the air turned frigid. Indeed, some men drew their coats across their chests and shivered. "May I advise you to observe your tone, Newberry? In light of your disappointment, I shall permit one mistake, never two."

Lord Newberry shuffled uncomfortably. "Miss Atwood has no

understanding of what is at stake. Sentimentality forms the basis of her opinion."

Mr Daventry glanced at her, and wearing a smug grin said, "I happen to agree. The lady is ill-informed. Her logic is severely lacking."

Oh, the odious devil!

Sybil jumped up, outraged that men who professed to respect her father could treat his daughter so abominably.

"Atticus would be appalled." She lifted her chin and glared at the aggrieved, whose pouting lips and sulky faces spoke of their displeasure. "His modern views were often condemned. Condemned by men in this room, I might add." While she failed to identify anyone personally, the odds were favourable. "And so I can only conclude that you want to obtain his work so you can ridicule his claims."

"Curiosity is their primary motivation," Mr Daventry informed as his gaze journeyed from the tip of the feather in her hat slowly down to the hem of her dark green pelisse. The depth of his scrutiny brought heat to her cheeks. "But curiosity is a weakness, a weakness wrought with danger."

Sybil swallowed.

Was that a veiled threat?

"Please, do not insult me by pretending we share a common goal, sir. You stand with those who would rip my father's reputation to shreds."

Why else was he holding an auction?

Mr Daventry fixed her with a penetrating stare. "Know that I would never permit anyone to speak ill of Atticus Atwood. I would never give his enemies the means to trample over his memory."

"*Enemies?*" A shiver ran the length of Sybil's spine. "That's a strong word to describe those with differing opinions." Did men really fight over theories on magnetism and electrical currents?

Something strange was afoot.

Did Lucius Daventry know the real reason she had come? The reason that had nothing to do with sentimentality and everything to do with self-preservation?

"Men often commit evil acts to support their beliefs, Miss Atwood."

Sybil feigned a light laugh. "I hardly think books filled with scientific theories and some dusty old artefacts warrant a call for violence."

In truth, she knew nothing of the journals' contents. When at home, her father never discussed his work. But someone was desperate to discover the words written on the pages. So desperate, they had sent threatening letter after threatening letter, demanding she obtain the records of Atticus Atwood's theories.

Another peer came to his feet. Sir Melrose Crampton was a lean man of middling years with greasy black hair streaked grey at the temples. The angles of his skeletal features were as severe as his manners.

"I'll give you three thousand for the lot, Daventry." Sir Melrose removed his hat to push his lank hair behind his ears. "Three thousand is more than any man here will pay. Accept the offer and let's be done with it."

"I beg your pardon, Sir Melrose. Three thousand is not more than any woman might pay." Sybil pushed her fingers firmly into her kid gloves and with a grin added, "I'm willing to bid four thousand to secure my father's possessions."

A collective gasp rang through the room.

"Five thousand!" Lord Newberry cried before Sir Melrose made his counter-offer. The golden-haired Adonis flashed his perfect teeth. "You know I can settle immediately, Daventry."

Five thousand!

"Six!" Sybil blurted. Heavens, she would need to sell her mother's jewels should she have cause to bid again, and that was most definitely out of the question. "And I, too, can settle today."

Cassandra tugged Sybil's pelisse and whispered, "Have you lost your mind? You're gambling with your future."

The menacing tone of the anonymous letters *had* robbed Sybil of her facilities. If she stopped to consider the full implication of the threat, she would crumple to her knees a quivering wreck.

Indeed, numerous things had occurred to leave her nerves in

tatters. Twice during the last week, a stranger had followed her home. Someone had smashed a pane of glass in the kitchen window, though the culprit must have been starving as he stole nothing but a hunk of bread. Someone had delivered an ox's heart in a box, though Cook had not placed the order. Sybil had woken to find her bedchamber window open, the curtains flapping phantom-like in the wind.

"The items are of no use to either of you." Sir Melrose's croaky voice dragged Sybil from her haunting reverie. "Price should not be the only consideration. As an elected member of the Royal Society, you can trust Mr Atwood's work will be treated with the utmost reverence."

"And yet many are critical of the Society's approach to science," Sybil said. She read the broadsheets. How else was a woman to keep abreast of current affairs?

She turned to Mr Daventry, who appeared to have lost interest in the conversation. A sullen gentleman in the front row had captured his attention. The quiet figure cared nothing for the argument amongst the bidders. Indeed, he studied the equipment on display as if he could read their untold secrets.

"Seven thousand." Lord Newberry's bid sent the room plunging into shocked silence. "Take it now, Daventry, for I shall not make such a generous offer again."

The mention of his name drew Mr Daventry's attention back to the men with more money than sense. "Perhaps there is some fault with your hearing, Newberry. I've had a change of heart. The items are no longer for sale. Not today at any rate."

Sir Melrose's eyes bulged in their sockets. "Atwood would be mortified by this debacle."

"As Miss Atwood kindly reminded me, her father would want his possessions to go to a worthy patron. I suggest those who are interested in obtaining the items should send a written statement of how they intend to use the collection."

"This is outrageous!" Sir Melrose barged past those in the seats next to him. He lacked the courage to approach Mr Daventry and pursue his complaint. "You shall have my explanation as to why these items are of importance within the hour."

When Sir Melrose stormed from the room, other men rose

cautiously to their feet and ambled out behind him. Their whispered objections were inaudible, although one anonymous person blamed Mr Daventry's lack of breeding for his disgraceful conduct.

"Well, Daventry, you certainly enjoy causing a stir." Lord Newberry brushed the sleeves of his elegant coat and ran his fingers along the brim of his top hat. "I shall be at my club should sense prevail. I doubt you'll receive a higher bid."

"I'll have your written statement before I make my decision," Mr Daventry countered.

An arrogant smirk played on the lord's lips as he made to depart, but he stopped abruptly and focused his piercing blue gaze on Sybil. "Perhaps you would care to ride out with me tomorrow, Miss Atwood. Surely a lady with your adventurous spirit would enjoy a wild ride in a racing curricle."

Mr Daventry cursed beneath his breath.

Sybil might have been flattered—Lord Newberry was as wealthy as he was handsome—but suspicion flared. He had never shown the remotest interest in her before.

"Be careful how you use the term *adventurous*, Newberry." Deep furrows appeared between Mr Daventry's brows. "Just because the lady is outspoken when it comes to her father's personal effects, do not presume to know her character."

Good Lord!

Was Mr Daventry defending her reputation?

"I'm sure Lord Newberry meant no slight." She turned to the lord whose angelic features were so opposed to Mr Daventry's prominent cheekbones and sculpted jaw. "I'm afraid I have a previous engagement, my lord." It occurred to her that one of the bidders might be the vile person behind the threatening letters. Perhaps Lord Newberry would go to any lengths to achieve his goal. "Mr Daventry invited me to tea. With luck, I shall have an opportunity to examine my father's journals before they are shipped to the worthiest bidder. No doubt, I will find something interesting written in the volumes."

There, that set the cat amongst the pigeons.

Both men conveyed instant displeasure.

Both men acted oddly at her sudden declaration.

An uncharacteristic look of panic passed over Lord Newberry's fine features. Mr Daventry kept a stone-like expression, but she could almost hear his silent raging.

Perhaps the idea had merit. Perhaps it would help to know why so many men wanted access to her father's journals. Knowing Mr Daventry would never invite her to take tea, she would have to find a way of stealing into his home, find a means of examining the pages in those mysterious books.

CHAPTER TWO

Superstition proclaimed that bad luck came in threes.

The scandalous nature of Lucius' birth had been the first unfortunate event. He imagined a bitterly cold January day, a rather bleak period that served as a foundation for his childhood. Eight years later came his mother's disappearance—more an inevitability than bad luck when one considered the shouts and sobs echoing through the house at night.

Meeting Atticus Atwood had been his salvation, until the man pronounced Lucius head of their secret organisation, the Order of Themis, made him promise to protect his daughter and then promptly died under suspicious circumstances.

"I hardly think that's fair, Daventry," Newberry said in response to Miss Atwood's comment about inspecting her father's journals. "All potential purchasers should be allowed to examine the goods."

Lucius glanced at the lady in the jaunty green hat that marked her as the most original woman of his acquaintance. The lady who saw fit to turn his life upside down with her snooping and witless comments.

"Miss Atwood is mistaken if she thinks one bat of her lashes will bring me to my knees." He had held his desire in check for so long, she could flaunt her impressive breasts and he would still be immune.

As if hearing his thoughts, Newberry stole a glance at Miss Atwood's generous bosom, and Lucius imagined ripping the lord's eyeballs from their sockets and feeding them to the crows.

"Persuasion comes in various forms, Mr Daventry," said the lady who haunted his dreams.

His mind might have concocted a lascivious scenario, but he had conditioned himself to suppress dangerous thoughts of Sybil Atwood.

"Clearly you're accustomed to women using their attributes as common currency," she continued. "Heaven forbid a lady might employ logical reasoning to sway your decision."

"Nothing you could say or do would sway my decision, Miss Atwood." He hoped his razor-sharp tone conveyed his point. The lady's life was at stake, a life worth more than a selfish moment of pleasure.

Newberry snorted. "Then you're a stronger man than I, Daventry."

Lucius ignored the half-hearted compliment. "Should you still have an interest in the items, Newberry, I shall expect your letter this afternoon." He flicked his gaze towards the door as he had no desire to discuss the matter further.

Newberry did not incline his head but departed with a mocking snort and a comment informing them that he always got what he wanted.

Though still in the company of her friend, Mrs Cavanagh, the urge to tear into Miss Atwood burned in Lucius' veins. "Do you have the remotest idea what you've done?" he muttered through gritted teeth.

The lady cast him a beaming smile, which went some way to calm his temper. Once, from the shadows of Atticus' dark hallway, he had secretly witnessed her soulful cries, witnessed her crumple to her knees, grief-stricken. The harrowing sight had wrenched at his heart, and he would give anything not to see it again.

"I loved my father dearly and merely wish to reclaim his possessions," she said in the sincere way that confirmed she knew nothing about Atticus Atwood's real work.

The truth carried no shame.

But the truth would get one killed.

Indeed, he had to get rid of her. He had to send her home, had to hurt her enough that she would never dare approach him again.

"Frankly, your father didn't want you to have his journals. He told me so himself." It was not a lie. Atticus loved his daughter. Her safety had always been his primary concern. A concern Lucius had inherited, along with the written texts that people would commit murder to obtain. "Atticus may have been forward-thinking, but he wanted a *man* who understood his motives and principles to take possession of his life's work. In that regard, he found you lacking."

Fool! Lucius silently cursed. It would take more than that to hurt a woman with a backbone of steel.

"And clearly that *man* is not you, Mr Daventry," she countered. "You speak of principles, yet you have the morals of a sewer rat."

The harsh comment roused admiration rather than anger. He had never met a woman willing to call him out for his scandalous behaviour. Perhaps she would have a different view if she knew the truth.

"And your father would be ashamed to see you sneaking around town like an incompetent constable from Bow Street. Disguising yourself as a widow will not save your reputation." She always wore black when she spied on him. "He left you financially secure so you might do something worthwhile with your time." He twisted his mouth in a feigned look of disdain. "And yet here you are with your petty arguments about that which you know nothing."

The lady jerked her head back, affronted.

If he saw so much as a tear in her eye, he would falter. Lucius tore his gaze away, pretending to survey those men still sitting in the auction room.

Everyone had left.

Panic sent his heart shooting to his throat.

He looked at the empty seat vacated by the quiet gentleman with the pasty white face and thin lips. The ghostly figure who hid in the shadows, watching his home.

Damnation!

Lucius' gaze shot to the table. The scientific artefacts remained, but some light-fingered beggar had snatched the journal from the oak bookstand.

"Damn him to the devil!" Lucius dragged his hand down his face while he contemplated his next move. He rounded on Miss Atwood. "Must you persist in being such an annoying distraction?"

The lady blinked. "Evidently, you have no control over your temper, sir. Must you persist in being rude to the point of—"

"Good day, Miss Atwood."

Lucius had wasted enough time trying to make the woman see sense. Ignoring her shocked expression, he took to his feet and raced from the room. Barging past the few men conversing on the landing, he gripped the polished bannister and practically flew down the two flights of stairs.

"Mr Daventry! Wait!" His nemesis' frustrated voice trailed behind. "What on earth—"

"Go home, Miss Atwood!" he shouted as he skidded along the tiled hallway and shoved more than one man in the back in his bid to reach Gilbert Street.

As one would expect at eleven o'clock on a Monday morning—on a street so close to the museum—scholars laden with books and letter cases and portable writing slopes crowded the pavements. Tourists hurried from their lodging houses, eager to reach the building of wonders located on Great Russell Street.

"*Hellfire!*" Lucius cursed almost to himself. It was impossible to identify his quarry amongst a sea of black top hats.

"Mr Daventry?" Miss Atwood came to an abrupt halt next to him. She clutched her chest and gasped a breath. An action that drew his gaze to her heaving bosom.

Saints preserve him!

He must have wronged someone to deserve this fate.

Lucius forced himself to study the people on the street. "I've nothing more to say to you, Miss Atwood." He pitied Mrs Cavanagh, for the poor woman was left trailing behind her irate friend. For the last fifteen minutes, she had sat in silence, deep furrows a permanent feature on her brow. "Mrs Cavanagh has heard enough of our petty quarrels for one day."

"The j-journal," Miss Atwood panted. It took every effort not to steal another glance at her flushed cheeks and parted lips. "The one you displayed on the table. It's ... it's gone."

The distress in her voice was unmistakable. Part of him wanted to maintain the charade, make her think the object of her desire was lost, stolen by the fiend who had sat quietly throughout the proceedings and waited for the opportune moment to strike. Perhaps then she might put the past behind her and live the life Atticus intended.

But Lucius knew Miss Atwood better than that.

Besides, if there was one thing he couldn't bear, it was seeing pain and suffering in her eyes. Hearing grief in her voice at the loss of something precious would be like a barbed arrow to his heart.

"I suspect the fellow with the sallow complexion is the culprit." The truth hung like a heavy weight on his tongue. Honesty was his only option lest she take to her heels and chase after the blackguard. "There is something you should know, Miss Atwood." He could feel her penetrating stare long before he turned to face her. "The stolen book is not your father's journal."

Relief replaced the fear in her eyes. "Yet it looked so similar." The twinkling of those vivid green gems made it easier to raise his defences.

"My morals may be questionable on occasion, but I would never risk losing Atticus Atwood's work." That was far from the whole truth, but it would be enough to appease her.

"Only on occasion?" she challenged. "Is there a woman in the *ton* you have not bedded?"

The muscles in his abdomen clenched when the obvious answer sprang to mind. If she were anyone but Atticus Atwood's daughter, he would bed her in a heartbeat. "Opinion is not reality. Perhaps you should remember that when you make your veiled accusations."

He expected a witty retort, but instead, she narrowed her gaze and studied him with some curiosity. "Come now. Mrs Sinclair is your fourth mistress in as many months, is she not?"

The fact the lady had been monitoring his movements to such an extent proved flattering and terrifying at the same time. "You've been taking notes. When did you develop a deep interest in my personal affairs?"

"One can hardly help but take note. You engaged in an amorous clinch in Craddock and Haines' bookshop!" She gestured to Mrs Cavanagh, who was pretending not to hear their conversation. "We both saw you."

"A man might devour numerous pages in a book before he decides if tackling the volume will be worth the effort." Perhaps he should tell Miss Atwood that he had known she was there, that he had staged the interlude for her benefit. It was better if she believed he was the most dissolute man of the *ton*. Better for them both. "You saw me because you were following me around town dressed in widow's weeds."

"You stopped responding to my letters. How else was I to learn of the auction?"

The last comment raised an important question. "How did you know the auction was being held in Gilbert Street?"

He had been secretive in his arrangements. The process had involved men registering their interest—an important part of the plan in catching Atticus' murderer. He sent letters informing them where the auction would take place. He had changed the time and place twice. And still, his nemesis had appeared.

An arrogant grin played on her lips. "Can you not guess?"

"Do I look like a man who enjoys playing mind games?"

She shrugged her shoulders. "You have such a terrible temper I cannot imagine anything rousing your amusement."

"As always you base your opinion on very little evidence. Thankfully, your sex makes it impossible for you to take the bar. There are enough fools in wigs sending men to the scaffold."

Her mouth dropped open, and she snapped it shut. "One cannot help but form a judgement on what one sees."

"And that is the problem with the world, Miss Atwood." He was desperate to learn how she had known to come to Gilbert Street but would not give her the satisfaction of pressing her further. "For the umpteenth time, I bid you good day. Go home."

He moved to walk away, but she captured his gloveless hand

and held it in a firm grip. The sudden shock, coupled with the intimate tingle of awareness, sent his pulse racing.

"This ring was given as a mark of respect, though I have no notion why." She stared at the gold band on his middle finger, intrigue forming the basis of her enquiry. "My father must have seen something respectable in you, something that eludes the rest of us. He wore it for years. He could have given it to his cousin, but he gave it to you. Why?"

Every nerve in his body sparked to life, igniting the raging desire he'd thought he had buried beneath a mound of soil and a stone monument engraved with the words *rest in peace*.

"May I remind you that we are standing in the street." His cold tone was so opposed to the heat burning in his chest. He moved to pull his hand away, but she gripped it tighter. "Your reckless manner will be your downfall, Miss Atwood."

"This symbol meant something to my father," she said, tapping the ring. She spoke of the weighing scales etched into the red carnelian stone. "I noticed the same symbol on various documents, documents I presume you now possess."

The woman was too inquisitive. Dangerously inquisitive. Such an active mind would bring nothing but trouble. "Allow me to offer you advice, Miss Atwood." He did not wait for a response. "You should do everything in your power to conquer this inane curiosity. I have already suggested ways to cure your boredom." He glanced at Mrs Cavanagh, whose expression spoke of the weariness of being ignored for the last ten minutes. "Perhaps you might start with learning to be a better friend."

Miss Atwood swallowed deeply. She was so engrossed in her search for answers she had given Mrs Cavanagh little consideration.

"You're right," she said, releasing his hand and making her apologies to her companion. "Rudeness is a trait I despise, and I shall spend the rest of the day making amends. And what of you, sir? Are you able to take your own advice? Can you not extend the hand of friendship and assist the daughter of your mentor?"

Having sworn an oath to Atticus Atwood, he had spent the last year secretly playing knight errant. He had spent the last year training his mind and body to ignore this clawing attraction.

Being cold and callous and downright rude was a means of protecting her. A means of self-preservation, too.

"We are not friends, Miss Atwood." That would be a stretch too far. He was just a mortal man with a carnal craving. Prone to bouts of recklessness. Prone to bouts of weakness. "We will never be friends. Therefore, the same rules do not apply."

She swallowed numerous times. "What happened to you?" The words were but a whisper. "Have you no heart?"

Now it was his turn to swallow past the hard lump forming in his throat. "My heart is black." He refused to give her hope. "My father ripped it from my chest as a child and roasted it on a spit." Atticus had done everything in his power to repair the damage. "Now, I must return to the auction room before someone attempts to steal your father's scientific artefacts." They were worthless objects purchased from various pawnbrokers as part of the ruse.

"Something is dreadfully amiss, Mr Daventry, and I believe it has to do with my father."

Ignoring the comment, he moved past her, got as far as the door before her haunting last words chilled him to the bone.

"I shall never stop looking for answers. Not as long as blood flows in my veins."

CHAPTER THREE

Wrapped in her thick green cloak, and shrouded by a thin ghostly mist, Sybil found it remarkably easy to move unnoticed through the streets at midnight. A lady had to be careful where she walked. Thankfully, at this ungodly hour, the wealthy occupants of Brook Street were either tucked in their beds or making merry at a fancy rout or soirée.

With his dwelling situated on the south side of the street, one could access Mr Daventry's garden via the mews. Privacy when conducting illicit liaisons was not an important factor for a libertine who boasted of his conquests. But for a would-be snoop like Sybil, it gave her a means of entering the house undetected.

As arranged, Mr Daventry's valet had slipped out into the mews to meet her abigail. All Sybil had to do now was enter through the servants' quarters, and while the couple discussed their blossoming relationship, she would search the study for her father's books.

Simple.

And yet Sybil wasn't prepared for the rush of excitement she experienced upon entering the devil's lair. The hairs on her nape prickled to attention. Butterflies fluttered in her stomach. Absurdly, the urge to learn more about the man who was as mysterious as he was rude thrummed in her veins.

After mastering the basement's creaking staircase without

alerting the staff, Sybil crept to the room at the end of the dim hallway. In most grand houses, the study was a place where men struggled with the pressures of making financial decisions. Not that she expected Mr Daventry to use the room for such a purpose. No, she envisioned finding the rogue sprawled semi-naked on the chaise, Mrs Sinclair straddling his thighs while he feasted on mounds of bare flesh.

Sybil cursed her vivid imagination.

She had made sure Mr Daventry was not at home. He visited his mistress nightly, always before the stroke of twelve. Indeed, Sybil had sat hidden in a hackney on Davies Street for the best part of an hour, watching the entrance to the mews. The urchin she'd paid to spy on her quarry confirmed Mr Daventry's departure.

And yet the man's powerful presence still lingered.

The pang of apprehension did not act as a deterrent. Despite her heart hammering against her chest, she turned the doorknob and slipped into the dark room.

The thrill of invading dangerous territory left her weak at the knees. It took a moment to settle her ragged breathing as she stared into the gloom.

Mr Daventry's potent energy invaded the darkness. She narrowed her gaze and focused on the empty chair behind the desk. The rogue's unique smell reached her nostrils, although that was no surprise. She often woke at night and caught a whiff of his seductive scent.

Pushing aside her trepidation, she moved to the bookcase left of the desk. The glass doors were locked, the keys missing. A quick scan of the gold lettering on the spines confirmed Mr Daventry liked philosophy and law, though she would lay odds he never read them. Why would a man who enjoyed lascivious pursuits be interested in moral principles?

She turned her attention to the desk, to the quill next to the sheet of paper. While it was the height of bad manners to read a person's missive, she couldn't help but notice the single sentence scrawled in black ink.

Ignorance, the root and stem of every evil.

Strange.

It was one of her father's favourite quotes, yet it sounded more like a personal message. To some extent, she was ignorant. A quest for knowledge had brought her to Mr Daventry's home tonight.

Shadows of doubt held her rigid.

Had Mr Daventry discovered how she'd learned of the auction? Had the valet confessed to his friendship with her abigail? Was Mr Daventry aware of her plan and had faked his departure?

As her mind ran amok and her pulse soared, something else struck her as peculiar. So peculiar, she padded over to the fireplace.

The room was so warm one would expect to find flames dancing in the grate. But a quick prod with the poker confirmed someone had recently piled fresh coal on top of the glowing embers.

"A man visiting his mistress would have no cause to keep his study warm." Mr Daventry's rich, masculine voice echoed from the shadows. "That would have been your next logical thought, Miss Atwood."

Shock made her gasp.

The urge to flee quickly followed.

"Now you're wondering how I returned to the house without you noticing." He sighed. "You waited at least twenty minutes before entering the garden. Of course, you needed Ashby to unlock the gate, and the man can be somewhat tardy."

Sybil put her hand to her heart for fear the organ might burst through her chest. She peered into the darkest corner of the room—the gentleman's excellent hiding place.

"One would think a man besotted with a woman would be early for his secret rendezvous," she replied, stepping closer to the only person who roused her interest and her temper. "Not arrive ten minutes late."

As her eyes grew accustomed to the blackness, she noted the outline of his broad shoulders as he lounged in a wingback chair.

"Oh, I have no doubt Ashby thinks himself in love. How long did it take your shameless maid to lure him with her womanly wiles?"

"I assure you, sir, Miriam is far from shameless." An unmarried lady could hardly keep a maid with loose morals.

"Is she not frolicking in the mews as we speak?"

"Frolicking? They mean to marry."

"So I gather."

"I imagine they are discussing how they might keep their positions and still make a lifelong commitment. Of course, they will have to find lodgings."

"I'm sure a discussion of any sort is the last thing on their minds." From the realms of his secret lair, the devil snorted. "If Ashby is anything like his master, he will be stroking the tops of your maid's stockings by now."

Heat flooded Sybil's cheeks. "Not all men have your voracious appetite for sin. I'm surprised you bother fastening the buttons on your breeches."

"Passion is a potent drug, Miss Atwood." The teasing words drifted from the darkness to play havoc with her insides. "The clawing need keeps a man awake at night. Makes him restless. In desperation, he fantasises about all the erotic things he might do with the object of his desire, but that only intensifies the ache."

Heavens!

"Shouldn't you be berating me for stealing into your home, not educating me on the power of unsated lust?" Sybil preferred arguing with him than acknowledging the odd sensations thrumming through her body. "And I take umbrage at talking to a shadow."

The shadow rose to his full, imposing height and prowled out of the gloomy depths. Dressed impeccably, as usual, she couldn't help but wonder what he looked like in relaxed attire. Were his arms really that muscular? Or was his tailor an expert in exaggerating elements of a man's physique?

"People rarely surprise me, Miss Atwood. You do not strike me as a woman who would resort to manipulating the hired help. Yet you risked your maid's reputation merely to steal a glance at your father's books. One cannot help but be a little disappointed in your character."

"Disappointed in my character?" Sybil gave an unladylike

grunt. Still, the need to defend her position took hold. "One cannot fight a burning attraction."

The corners of his mouth twitched in amusement. "I'm flattered you find me remotely appealing. Every indication leads me to believe you despise me."

"You despise me just as much." Oh, he loved provoking her. "Besides, you know very well that I am speaking about Miriam and Ashby. They met a month ago when he was collecting your shaving soap from Floris."

Mr Daventry folded his arms across his broad chest. "You mean they met when you were following Ashby in order to satisfy your obsession with me."

Obsession?

Ha!

But Sybil caught herself. Perhaps the gentleman did dominate her thoughts too often.

She forced herself to look him in the eye. "At that point, I was trying to determine how a man like you gained my father's favour." At that point, she hadn't received the threatening notes or learned of his intention to sell the journals to the highest bidder. "I have witnessed your antics in the ballroom. The way you sneak away to dark corners with your mistress of the month. My father would never have approved."

"Nor would he approve of you gallivanting around town on a fool's errand. Your father's books hold a certain value, and men are willing to go to great lengths to obtain them."

Sybil knew firsthand how depraved these men were. The letters demanding she claim the books were meant to frighten and intimidate. Reading the theories might help her discover the villain's motive. Why else would she risk entering Mr Daventry's home in the dead of night?

"Yes, and you're desperate to be rid of the burden."

"The books are not the burden, Miss Atwood."

She ignored the sarcastic remark. "Will you let these men win? Will you bow down to these brutes? You don't strike me as the cowardly sort."

Something she said struck a nerve. Mr Daventry gritted his teeth and practically growled. He stepped forward, forcing her to shuffle back until her bottom came to rest on the edge of his desk.

"I bow to no one, Miss Atwood. Not to my father, not to those men who believe themselves superior, and certainly not to men who make idle threats."

"Which is why you should sell your books to a woman. Sell them to me. You must admit it is only fair—"

"For the love of—" Mr Daventry pushed his hand through his ebony hair. "I'm not selling the damn books. It is all a ruse to catch a murderer."

His sudden pained expression spoke of instant regret.

"To catch a murderer?" she repeated, aghast. Confusion reigned. "But I don't understand."

"You're not meant to understand. It was your father's wish you remain ignorant." Mr Daventry rubbed his forehead and looked to be in a dreadful quandary. "Please, Miss Atwood, go home. Invest your time mastering the usual ladies' pursuits."

Go home?

How could she rest when her mind was consumed with murder?

"Did someone close to you die? Is this an old case? Did my father write about it in his journals?" Sybil spoke so quickly she struggled to catch her breath. Her life depended upon discovering the answer. "Might there be a prosecution? Is that why so many people are seeking to obtain them?"

Mr Daventry shook his head. "The answer is no on all counts."

He was hiding something.

"You can tell me. You can trust me." She made the mistake of touching his arm, and he shot back as if she had scorched him with a hot poker. "But this has something to do with my father. Was he assisting you in—" Sybil stopped abruptly as another, far more terrifying, thought took root. "Lord, no! Tell me you don't suspect my father—"

"Forget my foolish words."

"But—"

"Forget the comment spoken in haste."

"You think someone murdered my father. Tell me I'm wrong."

Panic took hold and squeezed her throat until her voice lost its power. Her knees buckled. Lucius Daventry caught hold of her arm and kept her upright. Tears welled. Covering her mouth with her hand was the only way to stop herself from retching.

Mr Daventry dragged his handkerchief from his pocket and thrust it in her direction. "Don't cry."

He waited until she snatched the silk square before turning away. Clearly he had little tolerance for weeping women.

She grabbed his coat sleeve. "I deserve to know the truth." Water trickled down her cheeks. "If there are doubts surrounding my father's death, you have no right to keep them from me."

"Conjecture is not fact," he said while facing the fireplace. "A theory without sufficient evidence is worthless in a court of law."

"Then you must believe someone stole into our house to commit this vile deed."

She had found her father dead in his bed. Having struggled with a weak heart, it was presumed the organ had failed him during the night. That's what she told the coroner. A choking sob burst from her lips as she recalled his blue lips and grey complexion.

Mr Daventry sighed. With some reluctance, he turned to face her, and she saw another rare glimpse of compassion. "Ignore my theory. I am suspicious by nature."

"Suspicious only when you have just cause." She dabbed her eyes with his handkerchief, and the divine scent of his cologne had a bizarre soothing effect on her nerves. "You apply logic to every situation."

"I have a wild imagination, am prone to moments of fancy."

The lie rang as loud as a church bell. He was rude and obnoxious, but he always spoke the truth.

"No, I don't believe that. You're not the whimsical sort. You're a man who takes what he wants without compunction."

"Not everything I want."

Silence ensued.

Despite the host of questions swarming around in her head,

despite the excruciating pain that accompanied thoughts of her father's suffering, she couldn't help but wonder what treasure eluded a man as powerful as Lucius Daventry.

"If you do not confide in me now," she eventually said, "I fear terrible images will haunt me for the rest of my days." Sybil stared into the storm-grey eyes that often stole her breath. "I shan't sleep wondering what happened, wondering if there was something I could have done to help him."

"There was nothing you could have done." He glanced at the floor as she wiped tears from her eyes. "Your father kept his work private for a reason."

"It's the only part of his life he refused to share."

"As I said, for good reason." Mr Daventry's voice carried the wisdom of experience.

Sybil paused as she tried to assemble the pieces of the puzzle. "You assisted him in his quest for knowledge, didn't you?" It was the only explanation to account for her father's generous gift. Atticus might not have approved of Lucius Daventry's immoral pursuits, but he respected his opinion as a colleague and associate.

"I admire intelligence when used wisely."

Wisely?

She could hardly believe the word had fallen from Mr Daventry's lips. Was this not the debauched devil who sauntered through ballrooms committing sin?

"My father possessed many admirable qualities." Which was why someone had to fight for the supposed injustice. "If there is a hint of truth in what you suspect, then he did not deserve to meet such a dreadful end."

The tears brimmed again, and Mr Daventry muttered a curse.

"Rest assured. I am working to prove my theory." Even in the gloom, she saw a darkness pass over his features. "When I do, I shall exact the worst kind of revenge." He paused, let her absorb the menacing undertone that suggested he had no qualms killing a man. "But now I have another problem. A pressing problem that requires my undivided attention."

"You refer to me and my snooping. I can be persistent when I want something. But surely you understand my need to examine the books. What my father wrote in those journals might have cost him his life."

"Your snooping is akin to a signature on your death warrant. You're the most reckless woman I have ever known, and I have known many." He straightened and glared. "In coming to the auction you've given your father's enemies reason to believe you possess knowledge of his work."

"Not necessarily. Men think me sentimental."

"Men think you will stop at nothing to get what you want. You told everyone in the auction room you respect your father's vision."

"I do."

"No, you respect your father. You know nothing about what he did with his time. You know nothing of the risks he took. But I can tell you it had nothing to do with science."

Sybil blinked. Though loath to admit it, Mr Daventry was right. "I know he would never do anything nefarious."

Mr Daventry rubbed his jaw in frustration. "Doing the right thing carries greater penalties than some criminal acts."

The right thing?

She might have challenged his right to make the claim, but the gentleman strode over to the bell and tugged hard.

"Regardless of what you think of me, Miss Atwood, you will do exactly what I say without argument." He moved behind the desk, unlocked the top drawer with a key from his coat pocket and removed a pistol.

"Blessed saints!" Sybil gasped. "You do not need to threaten me with a weapon."

"Your father's enemies watch from the shadows. After the debacle today, they will have followed you here, and will assume you've examined his journals." He snatched a sheathed blade and slipped it into his boot. "Now they will attack us from all quarters."

A knock on the study door brought the butler.

Servants who held such a prominent household position were often past middle age and carried an air of refinement. Mr

Daventry's man looked as if he'd come from a prizefight in the rookeries.

"Bower, I'm going to escort Miss Atwood home in the hackney." Mr Daventry paused as if expecting her to protest. "You spoke to the jarvey and told him to wait on the corner of Brook Mews and Avery Row?"

"Yes, sir." Bower's voice was as deep as the scar cutting through his left brow. "The lady told him to wait on Davies Street where she'd alighted and paid half the fare."

Mr Daventry turned those gunmetal eyes on her. "If you must behave recklessly, Miss Atwood, learn to be less predictable. In this game, one cannot afford to make such a blunder. Oh and never trust the word of a starving boy looking to earn a penny." He switched his attention back to his servant. "You'll find Ashby in the mews with Miss Atwood's maid. Wait ten minutes before mentioning our departure."

The last instruction forced Sybil to say, "You cannot expect me to leave Miriam behind. She must come with us in the hackney."

Mr Daventry cleared his throat. "If you value your life and that of your maid don't argue." He scanned her attire. "Now remove your cloak."

"My cloak? Is that necessary?"

"Would I waste time asking if not?"

There was something salacious about the look in Mr Daventry's eyes as he watched her untie the ribbons and slip the garment off her shoulders. His jaw firmed when he glanced at her low décolletage.

With some annoyance, he snatched the cloak and threw it to Bower. "Wake Kitty and ask her to wear this. Make sure her red hair is visible but not her face." He continued to bark orders. "Don my hat and greatcoat. When Furnis returns from his ride around town, you and Kitty will take my carriage and escort the maid home."

It occurred to her that Mr Daventry and Bower were of a similar height. Both men had black hair. Both men had broad shoulders. Yet her host possessed an unnamed quality that marked him as unique. Memorable.

"Before venturing to Half Moon Street, visit Boodle's. The majordomo will approach the carriage. Pay him to take my message to Lord Newberry and wait for a reply."

"Yes, sir."

Clearly, Bower had prior knowledge of this secret message as he did not take receipt of a note, but merely inclined his head and left the room when dismissed by his master.

Mr Daventry gestured to the door. "We will leave via the garden. Will you be warm enough?" Again, his gaze drifted to the neckline of her dress. He didn't wait for a response but snatched the tartan blanket from the wingback chair and thrust it at her. "Cover your hair. It's so vibrant it's sure to catch a man's eye."

It came as a shock to hear concern in his voice.

More of a shock to hear a hint of admiration.

Sybil took the blanket and draped it over her hair like a shawl. The man who proved more confounding by the hour escorted her through the servants' quarters and into the garden.

"You accuse *me* of making a blunder," she said, hurrying to keep his fast pace. "Sneaking out of the back gate is the most predictable means of escape."

"Who said we are sneaking out of the back gate?"

"Oh! As we're marching through the garden, I assumed—"

"I've mastered the art of taking precautions, Miss Atwood. Trust me. When it comes to your safety, I have the situation under control."

CHAPTER FOUR

H *ellfire!*
        Lucius pasted a confident grin. With assured strides, he led Sybil Atwood to the summerhouse in the corner of the garden, though his heart hammered in his chest, and his mind whirled in turmoil.

Miss Atwood's prying would be the death of him, the death of the *ton's* most scandalous rogue. If some blighter didn't shoot him for defending the woman who placed herself in perilous situations, he would expire from the effort it took to keep his real emotions at bay.

At least twice in the space of thirty minutes, he had let his guard slip. He had watched her intently, drooling like a randy schoolboy as she slipped the cloak off her shoulders. Like the most creative playwright, his mind acted out a seduction scene— a full-blown drama involving a ravishing on top of his mahogany desk.

"Forgive me," the object of his torment began as she hurried to keep his pace, "but why are we going to the summerhouse? You said we were leaving here and taking a hackney."

"What reason might two people have for heading to a secluded shelter in the garden?" Indeed, his rampant mind envisioned Act II of the play entitled *The Desperate Desires of Lucius Daventry*. Perhaps *The Mystery of Mr Daventry* was a more apt title. Devil take it, he could not explain the force that drove him to crave Miss Atwood's company.

"Now you're teasing me, trying to scare me with empty threats to steal my virtue."

"What makes you think they're empty threats?"

"Because tonight you've had the perfect opportunity to teach me a lesson and instead you asked if I was warm and gave me a blanket."

The lady had a point. "You're right. I'm not about to ravish you in the summerhouse."

"Perhaps you're the one who should have a care," she blurted. "Perhaps I might ravish you to get what I want. Have you thought about that?"

Lucius laughed to prevent himself from imagining Act III. "Why would you do that when you despise me?"

"I don't despise you, Mr Daventry. If you had explained your motive for holding the auction, we might have avoided this unnecessary conflict."

The conflict was necessary if he was to keep his sanity.

"Miss Atwood, you're a woman governed by her heart." Damn. The comment sounded like a compliment. "You would never give yourself to a man you didn't love."

And that was his saving grace.

"Earlier you said I was reckless," she countered. "And loneliness is as dangerous as a curious mind when it comes to behaving inappropriately."

Lucius knew the anxious feelings that rose from isolation. He knew their destructive force, knew the way negative emotions played havoc with one's thoughts. The memory of Miss Atwood sobbing on the stairs flashed before his eyes, and he didn't want to dwell on all the ways they might ease each other's suffering.

Thankfully, they came to a halt in front of the summerhouse, preventing him from saying something he might regret.

He reached into his fob pocket and withdrew the ring containing four iron keys. "Follow me. Stay close." He sensed her hesitation as he led her behind the garden house and unlocked the wooden gate in the brick wall.

Miss Atwood remained so close he could smell the sweet

scent of her rose perfume. "I assume your neighbour knows you have access to his garden."

"Whether he does or not is immaterial considering I own this house, too." Lucius locked the gate behind them and pushed through the darkness. "Besides, I bought the section of land that runs the length of the row. Consequently, all the gardens are shorter, and I have a hidden escape route."

The lady stopped and observed the high hedgerow blocking the view of his neighbour's house. "So this is a secret alley?"

Lucius unlocked the gate leading to the next garden. "It provides a means of escape without alerting the spies watching my door." And it gave him an advantage when surprising hired thugs loitering in the mews.

He was about to step through into the next garden when Miss Atwood touched his arm. "You've taken some rather drastic measures in the name of safety." The words brimmed with concern. "Living cautiously must take its toll. I should know. Following you secretly through town these last few weeks has been exhausting. Have you lived like this since my father's death?"

He had lived like this since he was a boy of eight and believed a wicked devil had entered his home and stolen his mother away. He had lived like this since being hounded for his illegitimacy at school. Since joining the Order of Themis and gaining more enemies.

"Someone betrayed your father. I mean to stay alive long enough to string the blighter up on a makeshift scaffold."

"You didn't answer my question."

He glanced at the dainty hand resting on his sleeve. The soothing touch might easily tear a confession from his lips. "I suggest we stop talking lest we alert every resident in the street of our presence."

"Of course."

Her hand slipped to her side, and he felt the loss instantly.

They crept through the gardens until they reached the last house. From there, they entered the mews.

Wisps of mist reduced visibility by a sufficient degree for them to exit the mews unnoticed. Despite grave reservations, he captured Miss Atwood's hand. "Hold on to my arm. I intend to move quickly."

She offered no objection.

Every nerve in his body sparked to life when her fingers wrapped around his bicep, but he convinced himself that playing protector formed the basis of these confounding emotions. He owed Atticus Atwood his life, and though his mentor was beyond the grave, Lucius lived to make him proud.

A few brisk strides brought them out onto Avery Row. Seeing the hulking shadow of the hackney roused a modicum of relief.

"Evenin', governor." The jarvey—a fellow with ruddy cheeks and a bulbous nose—tipped his hat. "Back to Half Moon Street, is it?"

Lucius kept his attention trained on the hackney driver, looking for telltale signs that said a man was not who he claimed. "What street runs parallel with Soho Square?"

"What street?" The jarvey pursed his lips in contemplation. "To the east or west?"

"West."

"That would be Dean Street."

"Why are we going to Dean Street?" Miss Atwood whispered.

"We're not." The reasoning behind his question would soon become apparent. "And the street connecting London Wall and Long Alley?"

The jarvey frowned. "You mean Brokers Row?"

"Take us to the north side of Curzon Street." From there, it was a few minutes' walk to Miss Atwood's home. It would give Lucius an opportunity to know if someone trailed them from the shadows. "I'll rap the roof when we wish to alight."

Despite wearing a deep frown, the driver nodded.

Lucius threw the man a sovereign for the inconvenience and assisted Miss Atwood into the vehicle.

In the dark confines of the cab, he was acutely aware of the lady's penetrating stare pinning him to the seat. "You doubted the driver's identity?"

"A few simple questions can be the difference between life and death," he said as the conveyance jerked forward and picked up speed. "A thug from the rookeries would not have been so quick to answer."

"You must spend every waking minute fearing an attack." She lowered the blanket and patted the copper locks he imagined would slip like silk through his fingers.

"I fear no one, Miss Atwood." No one but her. She could unsettle him with a single glance. In her company he became forgetful, concentrating only on the sound of her breathing, on the way her lips moved to form words. "But I have a responsibility to guard the truth. And the truth can be dangerous."

Her beguiling eyes narrowed as she considered him with a level of scrutiny he found unnerving. "Then you must have considered the possibility that while we are journeying across town, someone is breaking into your house to steal my father's journals."

"Do you think I would keep my prized possessions at home?"

She released a lengthy hum. "No, I am beginning to see that you're far too clever to make such a foolish mistake."

Usually, compliments failed to penetrate his steely reserve. One could not disregard people's opinions only to coo with delight at the first sign of praise. And yet her good opinion was like a secret weapon to his battle armour.

"Have no fear. Your father's personal effects have never left the vault."

"The vault?" She blinked in surprise. "Sir, please tell me you have not placed your trust in a bank. My father often said one should be wary of all institutions."

A smile touched his lips. Atticus had said the same thing to him, many times. "No, I have not placed my trust in a bank. The vault is in a secret underground location. I could tell you where, but then I would have to find a way to ensure your silence."

The corners of her mouth curled in amusement. "What would you do, Mr Daventry, sever my tongue with hot pincers?"

"Nothing so Draconian."

She shuffled in the seat. "Women seem to have no problem doing what you tell them."

"There you go again, Miss Atwood, concocting a story based on what you suppose is true."

He should never have mentioned the vault.

He should have known it would feed her curiosity.

"You can trust me with a secret," she persisted. "After all, we share a common goal."

"And what goal is that?"

"To keep my father's work safe. To catch the villains who threaten our lives." A sudden rush of emotion fractured her confident tone, and he knew what she was about to say. "To find proof to support your theory regarding my father's murder and to exact a fitting punishment."

Knots wrung tight in his stomach as she dabbed the corners of her eyes with her fingers. He might have mocked her—as she knew nothing about his confidential activities—but she had made her point with surprising discernment.

It seemed the time for honesty was nigh.

The truth was the only deterrent.

Lucius sat forward. "I swore an oath to your father. An oath to protect the one thing he considered most important. I would rather die than break that vow."

Miss Atwood sat forward, too. Their knees brushed as the hackney rumbled along the murky street. "I have the utmost respect for my father's work and would have sworn the same oath."

"You misunderstand. While I go to great lengths to protect his journals, I promised to protect something far more valuable."

"What?"

"You, Miss Atwood."

"Me?" She jerked back as if they had bounced through a rut in the road. During the next few seconds, she shook her head and gave a half-hearted laugh as if it was the most ludicrous thing she had heard all season. "My father died almost a year ago and not once have you made a house call."

"A scoundrel does not call at the home of an unmarried lady." No, he hid in her garden and wrestled the thug trying to climb through her kitchen window.

"You could have written a note."

"And alert you to the dangers lurking outside your door?"

"You underestimate my ability to cope in difficult situations."

"Madam, I have the full measure of your character." She was wildly tenacious, spirited, would need a strong, virile man to hold her interest.

Her eyes grew wide, and she snorted. "You don't know the first thing about me."

This was where matters became awkward. "I know more than you think."

"But I'm a private person. You couldn't possibly—"

"You have a fondness for poached eggs in the morning." He sighed. "Insist on reading the broadsheets with your afternoon tea."

Miss Atwood gaped.

"You venture into town every Wednesday," he continued, "and while you admire the gloves in Hatcher's window, you never enter the shop to make a purchase."

"The assistant is snooty. I live in hope Hatcher will hire a replacement."

"You visit the circulating library weekly. Read gothic novels at a ridiculous rate."

"Where else might an unmarried lady find excitement?"

"I'm hardly the best person to ask." Although numerous suggestions sprang to mind. "Monsieur Messier designs your hats. You prefer the scent of roses to any other fragrance. You wear green, not because it enhances the vibrancy of your hair or because men tell you the colour makes your eyes sparkle like emeralds."

She swallowed deeply. "Why do I wear green?"

"Because it was your mother's favourite colour. When you feign a smile and move about in society, you feel as though she's with you. Should I go on?"

"No, Mr Daventry." She clutched the blanket to her chest as if finding herself shockingly exposed. "You have said more than enough."

"You're not the only person with a skill for snooping, Miss Atwood."

After a moment's silence, she said, "But you're rude or ignore me when I see you at a ball or soirée."

"Unlike you, I take a covert approach to work." Protecting

her had become more than a job to him. "I merely abide by your father's request to allow you freedom from fear."

"To take on such a dreadful burden, you must have respected my father a great deal."

"More than you know." Atticus Atwood had been a friend and mentor, and Lucius had dealt with his grief alone.

An air of melancholy filled the dark space. No doubt they were both consumed with memories of the past. Fond thoughts of a man who put the needs of others before his own. Angry thoughts at the injustice served by fate's cruel hand.

Miss Atwood's shoulders sagged, and she breathed a sigh. Numerous times she cleared her throat before saying, "Then I am at a disadvantage, sir. You have the measure of my character while I have made dreadful assumptions about yours."

No one knew the man behind the facade. No one knew of his hopes and aspirations. No one knew the effort it took to keep his promise to Atticus Atwood.

"People see what I want them to see, Miss Atwood. A selfish rogue obsessed with the next conquest." A man incapable of anything other than drinking and whoring his way around town.

She nodded, recognition flashing in her eyes. "You were right when you said I know nothing of the situation. It seems I am ill-informed on many counts."

"Take heart. Your ignorance stems from your father's need to protect you, protect you from the villains who disapproved of his work."

She firmed her jaw and ground her teeth. "Villains who must be made accountable for their crimes."

"It is not the thugs on the streets who pose a problem. Not the men who steal bread to feed their starving families. Men in positions of power wield the deadliest weapons."

Miss Atwood sat quietly for a moment before narrowing her gaze. "I'm beginning to see what my father saw in you, sir. You're remarkably perceptive."

"I had an excellent teacher."

Lucius peered through the window, noted they were approaching Curzon Street, and so rapped on the roof. He welcomed the distraction, welcomed a means of focusing his mind on anything other than her compliment. It was better if Miss Atwood disliked him, better if she found him rude and obnoxious.

The jarvey brought the hackney to a halt near Chesterfield House—a Palladian-style mansion with gardens that ran half the length of the street. With some reluctance, Lucius offered his hand and assisted Miss Atwood's descent.

"We should walk in silence," he said, trying to shift his awareness to something other than inhaling the perfume of her hair.

She walked next to the mansion's garden wall, and he fell into step beside her. He didn't offer his arm, for that would cause problems on many fronts. With the pistol weighing heavily in his pocket, he couldn't offer his coat to protect her from the chilly breeze but did insist she draw the blanket across her chest.

"I get the sense we're waiting for something," she whispered just as he became aware of faint footsteps padding behind.

"Yes, waiting for proof my theory is correct." He kept his voice low.

"What theory?"

"That having appeared at the auction house and declaring a desire to obtain Atticus' books, you have marked yourself as a potential target." He paused. "If I'm not mistaken, we're being followed."

Her eyes grew wide with alarm. She took ragged breaths, sending puffs of white mist to mingle with the night air. "You think he means to do us harm?"

"Keep calm. He will make his intention known."

Miss Atwood gulped. "As this is a night for honesty, sir, I should inform you that I've been followed home numerous times these last two weeks."

Fear almost rendered him immobile. He wanted to grab her upper arms, press her against the wall and demand to know why she'd not mentioned it sooner.

"Are you certain it wasn't an admirer?" he said, though concern weighed heavily in his voice. "Or Ashby hoping to catch a glimpse of your maid when he should be running errands?"

"Most certain. Particularly if one considers the threatening letters I received, letters demanding I obtain the journals."

What the devil!

Again, it took every effort to keep walking. Her butler mentioned she'd received upsetting news but couldn't find the evidence of her distress. What was the point of having a spy in her house if not to keep abreast of potential threats?

Lucius took hold of her arm and led her across the street. He brought her to an abrupt halt outside Mayfair Chapel.

"Move your mouth as though you're talking but don't speak," he said. It wasn't an indulgent request, but it gave him a moment to survey their surroundings.

Gazing beyond her luscious lips, he squinted through the gloom. A well-dressed gentleman passed beneath the street lamp on the opposite side of the road before turning left into Chester-field Street and disappearing into the night.

"Perhaps my fears were unfounded," he said, drawing her past the chapel towards Half Moon Street. "Still, when we reach our destination, I want to see these threatening letters, if I may."

"There's no need, I can recite the words from memory." Though she seemed composed, he heard the cracks in her voice, fractures of suppressed fear.

"You're good friends with Mrs Cavanagh. You should have approached her husband and spoken of your concerns."

"They've had their own problems to contend with. I didn't want to add to their burden."

He didn't like that she'd dealt with this trauma alone. Distancing himself from Miss Atwood was a mistake. But a scoundrel couldn't court a friendship with an unmarried woman without ruining her reputation.

"From now on, you will be my burden, Miss Atwood. Is that understood?"

The lady drew a sharp breath. "You may have inherited his possessions, sir, but you're not my father. I—"

"Trust me, Miss Atwood. I definitely don't think of you as a daughter. But you will inform me should you receive another note, should a devil follow you home or a thug break your kitchen window."

As soon as the last comment left his lips, he realised his error.

Miss Atwood came to an abrupt halt. "How did you know someone broke the kitchen window? I never mentioned it."

Lucius was considering how best to tackle the next revelation when a carriage turned into Half Moon Street. The vehicle slowed as it drew near, which would have been nothing unusual had someone not flung open the door and vaulted to the pavement.

"Grab the woman!" the coachman yelled before yanking a pistol from beneath the folds of his greatcoat and aiming it at Lucius.

CHAPTER FIVE

The attack happened quickly.

Fear wrapped its sharp fingers around Sybil's throat when the burly coachman took aim and fired his pistol at Mr Daventry.

A bright flash, a puff of smoke and a whiff of sulphur permeated the cold night air. Sybil screamed—her protector didn't deserve to die like this. She screamed again when a pair of sturdy arms grabbed her around the waist and hauled her backwards.

By God's grace, Mr Daventry anticipated the trajectory of the lead ball. With remarkable agility, the gentleman crouched, rolled and then sprang to his feet, unscathed.

"Hurry up, fools!" The driver tugged on the reins to slow the carriage. "Get her in the damn coach."

The brute, whose grip was as lethal as his foul breath, squeezed the air from her lungs as he lifted her off the ground. Unable to wriggle, Sybil kicked his shins, though he barely flinched. Then his accomplice jumped out of the trundling conveyance and grabbed hold of her feet.

"Get off me, you ugly brute!"

Mr Daventry drew his pistol and fired.

The coachman's sharp cry sliced through the chaos as the ball hit his upper arm. The shot spooked the horses. But despite his injury, the coachman captured the reins and brought the carriage to a crashing halt.

Mr Daventry ran, vaulted up onto the box and punched the driver hard in the face. A fight ensued. Vicious grunts and groans echoed along the deserted street.

The glow of candlelight appeared in the upper window of the house opposite. No one raised the sash and called for the watchman. No one came racing downstairs to offer their assistance. Not even when the brutes threw Sybil into the vehicle and clambered inside.

One thug rapped on the roof, but the conveyance failed to jerk forward and pick up speed. While they exchanged nervous glances, Sybil studied their faces, memorised every mark and blemish. Having seen Mr Daventry move with such athletic prowess, she had every confidence he would come to her rescue. And when he did, they would drag these felons before the magistrate.

"Go see what's 'appened to Fowler," the blackguard with the flabby chin ordered.

"I ain't goin' out there," snapped his bearded accomplice.

They continued arguing, but the decision was made for them.

The doors on both sides of the carriage flew open. Before her kidnappers could gather their wits, Mr Daventry thrust his hand inside the vehicle and pressed his blade to the bulbous neck of one fiend. Surprisingly, her butler appeared at the other door, wielding a hunting knife to keep the other devil in his seat.

"Move a muscle and I'll push this blade so far into your throat I'll pin you to the squab." Mr Daventry's eyes were feral, his tone brutal. He looked every bit as dark and as dangerous as the devil. With his free hand, he reached for her arm and beckoned her to move towards him. "Hold on to me, Miss Atwood, and step down to the pavement. Blake, if your man so much as murmurs, silence him for good."

When Blake nodded, it occurred to her that he bore a slight resemblance to Bower, Mr Daventry's butler.

Sybil shuffled backwards on her bottom. She took hold of Mr Daventry's strong arm and managed to climb out of the vehicle.

"We must discover who sent them," she panted, straightening her skirts. "These men hold valuable information."

Her footman appeared.

"Escort your mistress into the house, Harris. I shall follow shortly. Stand guard and don't open the door to anyone but me. Is that clear?"

"Yes, sir."

Since when had Lucius Daventry been on familiar terms with her staff?

And why were they so keen to follow his orders?

"Don't move, Harris," Sybil instructed. Had the man forgotten who paid his wages? "You can play escort while I fetch a constable. Great Marlborough Street is the closest office."

"No!" Mr Daventry barked. "I'd no more trust a constable than I would these filthy rogues. If you want to be of help, search the boot for a length of rope."

Sybil glanced at the empty box seat.

"The driver is unconscious and is no threat. But be quick."

Slightly alarmed, but pleased to be of use, Sybil climbed up to the box seat. The driver lay sprawled across the footboard, blood seeping from the bullet wound, staining the arm of his coat. With one eye trained on the lifeless rogue, she rummaged around in the skeleton boot until she found the rope.

Mr Daventry used his blade to shear the rope in two, and with the help of her butler bound the thugs' wrists.

Straightening, Mr Daventry turned his attention to her. In a voice surprisingly warm and brimming with concern, he said, "If you wish to be of further help, I ask that you wait indoors. I shall meet you there—you have my word—and then we shall decide how best to tackle our problem."

Perhaps it was the way he asked or his choice of words that called to her sense of reason. "My father trusted you, Mr Daventry, and so I shall afford you the same courtesy." She glanced at the thugs wrestling against their restraints. Despite knowing the gentleman could handle himself in a brawl and that the men were no longer a threat, she said, "Please be careful."

The muscle in his cheek twitched. She couldn't read the

fleeting emotion in his eyes, but he inclined his head and reiter-
ated his earlier instruction for Harris to guard her front door.

Once inside the house, Mrs Goodhope arranged for tea. It
came as no shock to the housekeeper that Blake possessed a
hunting knife or that he was more than capable of brandishing
the weapon.

"Your father hired Mr Blake because of his military back-
ground." Mrs Goodhope poured the tea as Sybil watched the
scene outside from her drawing room window.

"Strange that he never told me." Sybil took her tea from the
trestle table and hurried back to her snooping spot. "I presumed
he had always been in service." Blake had replaced the ageing
Hanley mere months before her father's death.

"He was in service before coming here, in service to Mr
Daventry."

"Mr Daventry?" Sybil whipped around to face the housekeeper, spilling her tea onto the saucer. "And no one thought to
mention the fact?"

Mrs Goodhope's brown eyes widened. "I would have
mentioned it, ma'am, if I'd known it was important."

For a year, Sybil had been living with a spy. A spy! Her disloyal
butler had been feeding Mr Daventry no end of tales. That's how
he knew about the broken kitchen window. That's how he knew
of her morning rituals.

Had she discovered this news before two thugs had bundled
her into a carriage, both Blake and Mr Daventry would have felt
the sharp edge of her tongue. Now, beneath the simmering anger
at being treated like a child, she felt nothing but gratitude.

"It's of no consequence. I just wish my father would have had
a little more faith in me," she muttered almost to herself.

Sybil turned her attention back to the window. Surely Mr
Daventry had tortured the information from the rogues by now.
The carriage had rocked so violently it was liable to snap a
spring.

What the devil was keeping him?

As if prompted by her thoughts, the carriage door swung
open, and Blake and Mr Daventry jumped to the ground. They
lifted the driver down from the box and deposited him inside the

carriage. Mr Daventry climbed inside and moments later handed Blake the driver's coat.

"What on earth are they up to?" Curiosity kept Sybil pinned to the window as Blake shrugged into the blood-stained garment. He snatched the coachman's hat from the footboard and thrust it onto his head.

Mrs Goodhope moved to stand at Sybil's side. "It looks like Mr Blake is sitting atop the box. Yes, he's taking the reins."

"Good Lord! That means he's going to drive."

Blake flicked the reins, and the kidnapper's carriage jerked forward, picked up speed and disappeared into the night.

"Well!" Sybil clenched her teeth. "The lying toad."

She wasn't sure what concerned her most. That Mr Daventry had broken his promise or that the gentleman was alone in the carriage with three violent criminals. What if they mounted a surprise attack?

"Ma'am, I'm sure Mr Blake has a good reason for darting off like that and forgetting his duties." Mrs Goodhope sounded just as panicked.

"I was speaking of Mr Daventry, not Mr Blake."

The rumble of a carriage outside kept Sybil at the window. Mr Daventry's plush carriage rolled to a halt outside the house. Bower, his butler, opened the door and alighted first. He assisted Miriam to the pavement, spoke to the other occupants, then escorted the maid to the iron railings and opened the gate leading down to the servants' entrance.

Sybil darted to the front door where Harris stood on sentry duty.

"Quickly, Harris, open the door."

"But, ma'am, Mr Daventry—"

"Mr Daventry is not your employer." Sybil opened the door herself and hurried out. Miriam was already at the servants' door with the butler following behind. "Bower!"

The burly servant looked up. "Just returning your maid home safely, ma'am."

"I need to take command of Mr Daventry's coach." Mr Daventry wasn't the only one who could break a promise.

Sybil informed Bower of the attack in the street, of his

master's sudden and swift departure. The servant seemed far from shocked by the dramatic turn of events and simply nodded.

"Then I'd best be on my way, ma'am." Bower climbed the stone stairs, and with hands the size of mallets closed the gate. The loud clang reverberated through the street. "I have my instructions."

Instructions?

But it had been a surprise attack.

Sybil was about to protest, but Bower was already climbing into the carriage. He glanced out from the conveyance and said, "Mr Daventry always keeps his word, ma'am," and then slammed the door shut.

"Well!" was all she could say as the coachman gave a quick flick of the reins and the carriage charged off in pursuit.

Tonight she had learned more about Mr Daventry and his relationship with her father. Yet the man still proved somewhat of a mystery. Indeed, it was as if Sybil had been whipped into a whirlwind and was still spinning.

Returning to the house in somewhat of a daze, she considered going to bed. But how could she sleep knowing Mr Daventry might be fighting his way through another vicious battle?

A battle of her creation.

A battle brought about by her desire to discover the secrets of her father's journals.

Besides, Bower's comment replayed over her mind. Mr Daventry had promised to return—and Mr Daventry always keeps his word—and so she would sit and wait patiently in the drawing room, indulge in a large glass of sherry to mend her tattered nerves.

⚜

Sybil sensed Mr Daventry's presence before she opened her eyes. She could feel his powerful energy thrumming in the air, could smell the alluring scent of his cologne.

So seductive.

So potent.

As her mind regained focus, she realised she was curled on the sofa and must have fallen asleep. Nerves forced her to keep her eyes closed a little longer. Had she kicked off her shoes? Had she removed the pins from her hair? Was she lying there in a state of dishabille?

The sound of his relaxed breathing suggested he had been in the drawing room for some time. How long had he stood quietly watching her?

Sybil opened her eyes slowly, only to meet Mr Daventry's intense stare. He was seated in the chair opposite, his elbows on the armrests, his fingers steepled, his muscular thighs straining against his buckskin breeches.

"Mr Daventry. You're back." She sat up and drew her loose hair over one shoulder. "What time is it?" The thick green curtains were drawn. The candle flickered in the lamp, and the fire still burned, yet she felt like she'd slept for hours.

"Almost dawn." His voice was a low, husky hum. Against the fire's amber glow, he looked more sinful than ever. "Forgive the delay. I called at Brook Street to wash and change."

Sybil noted his clean shirt and pristine cravat, noted he had taken the time to shave. "You should have woken me."

Heavens, how long had he been sitting there gaping?

"I needed a moment to gather my thoughts. And you were sleeping so peacefully it seemed a shame to disturb you."

"It's been an exhausting evening."

His gaze searched her face before drifting down to her white-stocking feet. "I considered letting you rest and calling tomorrow, but I gave my word I would return."

"And you always keep your word."

"Indeed."

Silence ensued.

A strange heat formed in her stomach when their eyes met. For some foolish reason, her tongue felt thick in her mouth.

After swallowing numerous times, she managed to say, "Did you discover who hired the thugs to attack us?" She wanted to ask what on earth possessed him to dart off into the night, to risk his life in such a reckless fashion.

"You mean who hired them to kidnap you and hold you for

ransom," he corrected. His jaw firmed. "I'm sure you can guess what they would have demanded in exchange."

"My father's journals." Guilt festered. Had she not attended the auction, this wouldn't have happened. If only he'd told her why he didn't want her there. "You're angry. I've made things difficult."

"It is not anger that holds me rigid in this chair, Miss Atwood. It is not anger that makes my stomach lurch at the thought of what they might have done to you."

"You're frustrated. You swore an oath to my father, and I'm making it impossible for you to honour your vow."

"Unbelievably impossible." He brushed his hand through his thick black hair and sighed. "Where you're concerned, *frustrated* is a word I would use to describe my current state."

If his suspicions about her father's death were correct, she wanted to help him not be a hindrance. "What can I do to ease your suffering?"

An amused snort escaped him. "Oh, I can think of a few things you might do, Miss Atwood. You can start by agreeing to heed my advice."

Sybil sat forward. "If you mean to tell me to find a husband and take up painting, save your breath."

"Have no fear. I doubt there's a man in the *ton* who can handle your wild temperament."

"No, sadly, I find them all rather lacking. Or, more to the point, they find me lacking. Who wants a wife who gallivants about town like an incompetent constable from Bow Street?"

"Who indeed?"

The air thrummed with that strange energy again, and she found it almost impossible to hold his gaze.

"Thankfully, you have returned unscathed," she said to ease the nervous fluttering in her chest. "And what of the men foolish enough to mount an assault? I assume you didn't deposit them at Bow Street."

"No. I would need to accuse them of a crime, and we have enough to contend with at present."

"We?" Her heart leapt in excitement, and she clasped her hands to her chest. "So you agree I might assist you in this case?"

His expression turned solemn. "Numerous men are trying to obtain your father's journals. Once they have proof of the contents, they will presume we are party to the incriminating information. Then they will kill us, kill us both."

Perhaps it was his grave tone or the hard look in his eyes, but Mr Daventry had a way of striking fear into her heart. After the incident in the street, she believed his concerns were not unfounded.

"Whether I like it or not, our paths are entwined," he continued. "Though it goes against my better judgement, we have no option but to remain together until we resolve this matter. Until we eradicate the threat."

Remain together?

What on earth did he mean?

"You cannot stay here." She swallowed at the thought of meeting him on a dark staircase in the middle of the night. "While my father was a champion of women's rights, there are limits to what he considered acceptable. Even under such dire circumstances."

"Agreed. Besides, I cannot catch a murderer when confined to this house."

"Oh!" Surely he didn't expect her to stay in Brook Street, in the home of a known seducer. "If people discover I'm living in Brook Street, they will assume I'm your new mistress of the month." And Mrs Sinclair would certainly have something to say about that.

He watched her through dark, sensual eyes. "And who would want the inconvenience of being labelled a mistress without receiving any of the pleasure?"

Pleasure!

The word caressed her mind, worked its way slowly down through her body—as smooth and as rich as the finest cognac—to ignite an internal flame.

"Who indeed?" she breathed.

Mr Daventry's gaze brought tingles to her skin as he studied her from the comfort of his chair. "Every nerve in my body tells me it is unwise to draw you into this partnership. Logic says there is no other option."

"What do you suggest?"

A weary sigh escaped him. "I'm going to take you away, to a secret place ten miles from here. We will conduct our investigation from there. Only venture to town to implement parts of the plan."

She should have been nervous at the prospect of leaving town with the scandalous son of a duke. But her father had trusted this man. When she took a few seconds to examine her heart, it came as some surprise to find she trusted him, too.

"Don't look so glum," she said, trying to lighten the mood. "It is only a temporary measure, and I can be entertaining company."

"That is my fear."

"What? Can you not enjoy the company of a woman you don't want to bed?"

"Who said I don't want to bed you?"

Sybil laughed to suppress a pleasurable shiver. No doubt the man was extremely skilled between the bedsheets.

"Mr Daventry, if we are to become colleagues, you must cease with the teasing." Her heartbeat pounded in her chest though she had done an excellent job of hiding the wild rush of emotions.

The gentleman stood and straightened his coat. "I shall return for you tomorrow at midnight. In the meantime, Bower will remain here and keep watch. I ask that you tell no one of your plans. Not even your maid."

"I cannot bring my maid?"

"No."

Sybil stood though her legs were shaking. "Are you going to tell me where we are going?"

"No. The house is large and draughty. Bring warm clothes." He spoke with the cold indifference she was used to. "When we arrive at our destination, I will explain how I came to know your father, and why these men want to kill us. I will let you read what he wrote in the books."

CHAPTER SIX

L ust wasn't meant to be a complicated emotion.

Lucius knew what it was like to be held in the grip of desire. But he feared his obsession with Sybil Atwood went beyond satisfying a craving.

He'd lived with the hunger for years, long before Atticus' demise. He'd done everything to banish the yearning. The confusing part was that he found gratification in ridiculous things—in her smile, her laugh, in the way her cheeks flushed red when he'd spoken of pleasure, the way she inhaled the scent on his handkerchief before drying her tears.

He might have analysed the last point further, had the rumbling of an approaching carriage not drawn him from his reverie.

Sitting astride his black stallion and hidden deep amongst the shadows of beech and oak trees, Lucius kept his gaze trained on the narrow woodland road. On such a gloomy night as this, he was invisible to passersby. But Miss Atwood would be perched on the edge of the seat, gripping the overhead strap, her gaze pinned to the window, wondering when he would appear.

He waited for the unmarked carriage to pass as it climbed up towards Bronygarth. Perhaps he should have warned Miss Atwood she would be travelling alone. Perhaps he should have explained the need for detours, for changing vehicles, for his absence.

Doubtless, the lady would take pleasure in berating him, which would calm the rush of longing he'd experienced since deciding they would sleep in the same house.

Lucius hung back in the darkness to ensure hired thugs weren't trailing behind. Once confident they had eluded their pursuers, he edged his horse onto the muddy track and headed for the seventeenth-century castle near the edge of the woods.

Samuel—a young groom whose golden hair was as bright as his temperament—stood near the steps leading to the castle's studded oak door.

Lucius dismounted. He waited for the boy to hang the lit lantern on the metal crook in the ground and then gave him the reins. "Have your father ride Phaedrus down to the toll road and then scout the perimeter."

"Aye, Mr Daventry, sir."

Father and son had been loyal servants ever since Atticus had saved the boy from being sentenced to ten-years transportation.

Lucius left his horse in Samuel's care, mounted the stone steps and cleaned his boots on the iron scraper. In truth, he would prefer to wait until morning to discuss matters with Miss Atwood. Daylight carried an air of respectability. Subdued lighting, dark corners and the need of a warm bed roused lascivious thoughts.

Miss Atwood was standing before the huge stone fireplace in the hall when he entered, warming her hands on the heat from the flames. She heard the clip of his boots on the checkered tiles and merely cast him a sidelong glance.

"Welcome to Bronygarth," he said cheerfully to defuse the pricking tension. "I'm sorry if the journey was unpleasant, though I'm sure you understand the need for caution."

"Bronygarth?" Her shoulders relaxed beneath the heavy material of her dark green cloak. "It's an odd name for a castle situated ten miles north of London. Did your mother's relatives descend from Wales?"

"Not that I'm aware, but then I know nothing about my mother's family." Nothing except that the maternal grandmother he had never met had named him sole beneficiary in her will. The inheritance wasn't a huge sum by society's standards, but it was enough to make wise investments and earn him a small fortune. "I bought the house as a ruin. Some parts are still in need of renovation."

"Is it haunted?" Miss Atwood glanced at the lofty ceiling, at the broad staircase rising between vast gothic arches, at the hanging cobwebs, faded tapestry and the suit of armour in need of a polish.

"No doubt ghosts wander the halls at night." He dismissed the image of her hurrying along the cold corridors in her flimsy nightdress, looking to throw herself into his comforting embrace. "Though I have yet to meet a phantom on the stairs."

"What of your servants?" She straightened and looked around as if waiting for the butler to appear to take her cloak. "Surely they've heard eerie whispers, seen strange shadows."

"Not to my knowledge. Besides, the house runs on minimal staff." Lucius trusted only a handful of people to keep his secrets. He stepped forward and offered to take her cloak. "As there are no maids, you will need to fetch your own water, dress yourself, style your hair."

"I am more than capable of washing and dressing," she said, slipping the garment from her shoulders and handing it to him. "Though had you mentioned it earlier I might have put more thought into packing."

He frowned. "More thought?"

"Front fastening stays would have been preferable."

"Fear not, Miss Atwood. I'm adept at untying laces and ribbons."

"I'm sure it is one of your greatest talents." She turned to warm her hands on the fire. "Am I to clean out the grate, too?"

"Jonah attends to most household chores. He's a footman-of-all-work, if you will. And Tomas prepares meals."

She looked at him and arched a brow. "Poor Mrs Sinclair. How does she tong her ringlets without help?"

Did he note a hint of jealousy in her tone?

The possibility roused both hope and fear.

Lucius stepped closer. "You're the first woman I've brought

to Bronygarth." He hadn't wanted to feel a feminine presence in the house, or more to the point, feel its sudden absence.

Silence ensued as their gazes locked—the same silence that vibrated with a potent energy whenever they were alone together.

"The hour must be close to two," he continued. "Sleep beckons. I can show you to your room, and we can discuss your father's work in the morning. Or I can take you to see the journals."

She glanced at the dim staircase, at the feeble glimmer from the candles flickering wildly in the standing candelabra. "There's an air of loneliness here, a sense of isolation. I'm not sure I will sleep if left alone on a wing."

Lucius shuffled uncomfortably. "You won't be alone. You will sleep in the room adjoining mine." Devil take it. His tongue felt clumsy as he formed the words. "We must take every precaution, and there are few chambers in the house I would call habitable."

Miss Atwood swallowed deeply. "Oh, I see."

"You can lock the adjoining door and take the key." He didn't mention he had a spare.

She opened her mouth to speak, and the slight tremble of her bottom lip belied the confident tilt of her chin. "Will I be able to sleep after learning about my father's work?"

"I expect learning more about him will rouse old memories. The truth is often hard to hear." Lucius' stomach sank as an old memory burst into his mind. He recalled the day he begged the duke to tell him about his mother. The day his father uttered the words "she's dead".

Miss Atwood gave a weak smile. "Knowing more about my father's secrets might bring comfort. And talking about loved ones can be a huge help."

Talking? How did one begin to unravel the knot of questions plaguing one's heart and mind?

"Then I shall start by showing you the vault." No one but Atticus had seen the secret room, and he hoped he wasn't making a mistake trusting the man's daughter. "You will need this." He felt an inner chill when he returned her cloak. "It's bitterly cold out tonight."

She slipped the garment around her shoulders, fiddled with the ribbons, struggled to tie a bow. "So cold my fingers are numb."

"Wind blows over the battlements, sending draughts through the east wing. Here, allow me."

A nervous smile touched her lips when he stepped forward to attend to the task. "So, you're skilled at tying ribbons, too?"

"Dressing a woman can be a sensual experience."

"And you have had no end of practice."

"Not as much as you might think." He stood so close her essence threatened to consume him. As soon as the ribbons were secure, he stepped back, keen to maintain some distance. "The entrance to the vault can be found near the lake."

"Near the lake?" Excitement danced in her eyes. "How intriguing. Lead the way, Mr Daventry, and I shall follow."

"Lucius," he said as they descended the front steps. He took the lantern hanging from the metal crook. "I think we have progressed beyond the need for formality."

"Lucius," she repeated with a warmth that surprised him. "I presume you're named after a relative."

"My mother chose it. That's all I know." He hadn't meant to speak so sharply, but it was the reason his father still called him *boy*.

"Well, you will probably protest, but I would rather you call me Sybil," she said, dispelling any awkwardness. "You always sound so cross when you refer to me as Miss Atwood."

"That's frustration, not anger." Still, he wasn't quite ready to use her given name. "You're as stubborn as you are curious."

"And as reckless as I am stubborn," she teased. "How do you tolerate my company?"

"I have a hardy constitution."

Navigating the garden at night proved hazardous. Miss Atwood tripped over the protruding root of an oak tree and had no option but to hold his arm. Every touch brought a profound sense of familiarity.

The storm clouds hung thick and low, the blackness creating a suffocating tension that mirrored his internal dilemma. Had they walked beneath a sky of twinkling stars—their path lit by the silvery light of the moon—he might have felt more optimistic about revealing the life he kept secret.

Lucius brought Miss Atwood to a halt before the lake that glistened like shiny black glass in the dark. Beneath the still water lay the truth that might one day change opinion. But those keen to possess the journals wouldn't rest until the books were burning on a bonfire.

"Are we to swim to that island?" She laughed as she pointed to the grassy mound in the middle of the lake.

"Not in these temperatures. But you will need to take my hand. The stairs are steep. Moss makes them slippery underfoot." He held the lantern aloft and motioned to the low stone wall hiding the narrow flight of steps. "This used to be an escape route for the tunnels running beneath the house."

Again she looked at him—not in the salacious way women usually did—in the way that said she found him fascinating, found more to like than a handsome face and a tongue that could bring untold pleasure.

She accepted his outstretched hand without hesitation, clutched his fingers tightly as they descended the worn steps. With some reluctance, he released her to draw a key from his coat pocket. Lucius unlocked the iron door at the bottom, locked it behind them once they had stepped into the old stone tunnel.

"Is the vault located beneath the lake?" she said as they climbed down another set of old steps. The sound of dripping water must have unnerved her, as she asked, "Is it safe?"

"Your father assured me it is."

Lucius explained briefly about the design and what he knew of the castle's history. The story of a priest who hid in the tunnels for months, of a recluse who believed the end of the world was nigh and spent most of his time underground, too.

She listened with interest. "Remarkable. What is even more remarkable is the breadth of your knowledge. As your conquests are well noted, I assumed you cared about nothing other than satisfying your cravings."

That was his intention.

"Miss Atwood, my work has led me to associate with certain

people I would ordinarily avoid. I'm no saint. And you're right. I have used my *conquests* to satisfy fleeting cravings. Equally, gaining information has always been my primary goal, as you will soon discover."

He gestured for her to continue along the arched tunnel leading to the next solid iron door some five inches thick.

"You see," she began, waiting for him to lead the way, "had you used my given name it wouldn't have sounded like a reprimand."

"It wasn't a reprimand, merely a means of providing context. Now, I need to concentrate on the next task. We can discuss my failings later."

He extracted another key from his fob pocket. The brass implement was cylindrical, and he pushed it into the same shaped hole in the door. To the left was a wooden plaque filled with tiny brass cogs. Each cog had an unusual shape cut into the centre—a star, a hexagon—and he moved them in the specific sequence ingrained in his memory. The correct combination released the pulley system, which allowed him to turn the door handle and enter the underground chamber.

"I assume someone else knows the combination," she said.

"I am yet to name my successor. Pray I don't end up a bloated corpse in the Thames."

"That would be a tragedy on many levels."

"Why? Would you miss me, Miss Atwood?"

"I believe I might."

The lady followed him into the chamber, a small room that looked more like a wine cellar than an underwater storage facility. After glancing numerous times at the ceiling, she walked towards the first in a row of wooden chests resting on a two-foot-high plinth. She raised the heavy lid and pulled back the red velvet cloth covering one tome.

"This can't be my father's journal." She scanned the spine, ran her finger over the date embossed into the leather binding. "1756. This one refers to the Seven Years' War."

Lucius closed the iron door, and the loud clunk made Miss Atwood jump. "Those are your grandfather's journals."

She swung around to face him. "My grandfather's journals? Did he record his scientific theories, too?"

Lucius braced himself. He had an awful lot of information to impart.

The question was where to begin.

"Follow me." He closed the lid of the chest and led her to the metal trunk sitting on a plinth at the far end of the chamber. "This is a transcript of a trial." He delved inside the trunk and removed a black letter case. "The boy was twelve years old when threatened with transportation for a crime he didn't commit."

Miss Atwood looked between him and the letter case and frowned. "My father was always interested in law. He fought to abolish the severe punishments handed to children."

"He did more than that. He was head of a secret organisation called the Order of Themis. A small group of men who share the same ideals."

"Themis?" She edged closer, so close every nerve in his body sprang to life. "The goddess from Greek mythology."

"The goddess of fairness and law."

She glanced at his ring, at the symbol carved into the carnelian stone. "Themis carries the Scales of Justice. My father believed the poor often commit crimes out of necessity."

"Indeed. And affluent members of society look for scapegoats when committing evil deeds. As members of the Order, we hunt for evidence to cast doubt on the witness statements in some prosecutions." It was more complicated than that. "Samuel was one such boy, wrongly accused of larceny. Your father secured his release, and now he lives here as my groom."

"You speak of the cheerful boy in the stables? He looked at me as if I were an angel descending from heaven, not a weary woman clambering out of an unmarked carriage."

"You're Atticus Atwood's daughter."

"And you have taken my father's place as leader of the Order."

"I have." Relief rushed through him. He'd never thought to confide in anyone, anyone outside the Order. "Your father also uncovered corruption amongst privileged society. These files and journals contain evidence of trials, of bribery, of the underhanded way the rich abuse the poor. They are truthful, accurate records of events."

She glanced at the leather-bound book in his hand. "And so someone named in one of these books murdered my father to hide his crime."

"I believe so. And now the felon will use you as leverage." Guilt bubbled like bile in Lucius' throat. He had failed to save Atticus but would do everything in his power to save his daughter. "Some men believe they are bidding on important scientific theories. One man is bidding because he knows the truth." Lord knows how.

"And you held the auction merely to see who would bid?"

"Yes. The auction was a means of gathering information. Had you not arrived, I would have found an excuse not to sell."

"Then you should have thanked me for my timely intervention."

"Perhaps."

"Is Lord Newberry a suspect? He was desperate to win the auction."

"His conduct suggests he is hiding something. The same is true of Sir Melrose. Your father was working on various cases before his death. Complicated proceedings involving negligence and fraud."

Lucius didn't mention that the runner working on the same cases was found dead in the Thames. Or that it meant he had lost two close friends in the same month.

Her gaze drifted as she became lost in thought. Eventually she looked at him. "You've yet to tell me what happened to the thugs who attacked us on Half Moon Street."

Lucius decided on the short, concise version, not the version involving torture, threats to gut the brutes, or the struggle to hold their heads in a water barrel until they kicked and flailed and fought for breath.

"The solemn man who stole the journal from the auction room hired them to kidnap you. They were to take you to a warehouse near the docks. We waited there, but the devil failed to show. I know he speaks with a Scottish accent. But that is all."

Miss Atwood put her hand to her throat. "And what happened to the men?"

"I have an associate who owns a shipping company. The men are on their way to Portsmouth having taken work aboard a vessel bound for Calcutta." He never explained his actions, yet he found the need to say, "I gave them the chance of honest work. I couldn't leave them to continue their criminal activities on our streets."

Her green eyes grew vibrant as she studied him. She placed her hand on her abdomen and exhaled. "Sir, you are more complex than I ever imagined. I'm puzzled by your motivation. I'm in awe of your strength and determination. Baffled by your behaviour in the ballroom."

"I would hate to be predictable."

She glanced around the chamber and smiled. "Your mind is a source of wonder. You control all of this. You're responsible for protecting my father's legacy, for documenting the truth. And yet my innate curiosity is desperate to know if you're happy."

"Happy?" He almost choked on the word.

"What brings you contentment? When you've sought your revenge, what then? Will you continue to live a life where you have to sneak through your neighbours' gardens?"

Part of him wanted to confess his worst fears, wanted to explain how the past made it impossible for him to feel truly content. Part of him wanted to get rid of this woman, for she asked questions he could not answer.

"Miss Atwood, I have been raised on a diet of disappointment, a menu of misfortune. Had it not been for your father's intervention, I would be the scoundrel seeking to numb my pain in dark corners of the ballroom." He gestured to the wooden chests. "Guarding this gives me the only stability I have ever known."

Pity filled her eyes. "And what if it is all washed away? What if water floods this chamber to rot the foundation upon which you've built your life?"

"It won't." Still, the thought sent a bolt of fear straight to his heart. He lived to protect Atticus' work, had no other purpose. "I have taken every precaution."

"You cannot thwart every threat. You cannot prevent a natural disaster."

The urge to steer the emphasis away from him took hold. "What will you do when we've brought your father's murderer to justice?" he countered. He wasn't the only one who clung to Atticus' memory. "Will you continue to hound and harass me, desperate to know why your father trusted *me* with his work, not you? Will you still feel so desperately inadequate?"

She sucked in a sharp breath and drew back. Hurt swam in her eyes and left him fighting the urge to pull her into an embrace.

The few seconds' silence felt like a lifetime.

"It's late," she said coldly.

"Yes." He placed the case in the trunk and closed the lid. "I'll show you to your room. In the morning, you can return here and examine the journals."

She nodded but said nothing.

Lucius secured the room and led her back through the old stone tunnel. She took his hand when climbing the worn steps, and despite the frosty atmosphere, he felt the thrumming energy of her life force mingling with his.

Neither spoke on the walk back to the house.

Neither spoke as they mounted the broad staircase.

For months he had behaved badly, been rude, blunt. It was different then. He was keeping an oath, protecting her life. Now, standing outside her bedchamber in a corridor lit only by a wall lantern, he found he couldn't walk away and pretend he didn't care.

"I spoke out of turn. Forgive me." He never apologised for his conduct. "When under attack, one draws on their opponent's weaknesses."

Miss Atwood swallowed deeply. "It wasn't an attack. I loved my father, but I saw how work took its toll." She gave a light laugh. "Of course, I believed he was suffering from anxiety over solving a scientific equation."

"Righting the injustices of the world was important to him, as it is to me."

Miss Atwood nodded, though her downturned mouth still

spoke of concern. "I'm sure many people welcome your intervention." Then she did something that heated his blood, something that tormented his heart and teased his cock. She placed her hand on his coat sleeve and said, "Thank you, Lucius. I know you wish it were otherwise, but I am so grateful for your honesty tonight."

There was another awkward silence.

He had to walk away before his imagination took to forming another act in the play entitled *The Desperate Desires of Lucius Daventry*.

"Good night, Miss Atwood." He turned on his heel and strode down the corridor. A large glass of brandy awaited. He could not enter his bedchamber until satisfied she was asleep.

"Mr Daventry," she called. "May I ask you something?"

He came to an abrupt halt, held himself rigid as he glanced back over his shoulder. "Yes."

"Will you dismiss Ashby?"

The question surprised and delighted him. Their lives were in danger and she was worried about his servant.

"Dismissing a man for falling in love would make me the heartless cad who saunters through the ballrooms." A man just like his father.

"But men are rarely tolerant when it comes to betrayal."

"Is it betrayal to follow one's heart? Should loyalty always prevail? It is a complicated dilemma." One he knew only too well. "Good night, Miss Atwood."

"You haven't answered my question."

"Perhaps because I find the puzzle somewhat perplexing."

CHAPTER SEVEN

Locating the dining room was easy when all one had to do was follow the smell of coffee and cooked bacon. Sybil entered to find Mr Daventry reading the newspaper while tucking into a hearty breakfast. A man with his strength and stamina must have quite the appetite. He was so engrossed in reading the article he failed to hear her enter.

"Good morning, Mr Daventry. Please, don't get up."

Last night, she had spoken his given name with ease.

In the cold light of day, the word felt too intimate.

On the subject of intimacy, and their cozy sleeping arrangements, she wondered if he knew he'd called her name during the throes of his nightmare? The painful cries had tugged at her heart. It had taken all her strength not to unlock the adjoining door and rush to his aid.

The gentleman looked up from the absorbing article. Those intense grey eyes spent an age surveying her copper curls hanging loosely over her shoulders.

Sybil tucked her hair behind her ears. "I'm far too impatient to style it myself, and there's no one here to object." When he failed to respond, she said, "I presume you have no complaint?"

"No, no complaint. Your hair is as wild and as temperamental as your character. When restrained, it makes me a little nervous."

She smiled, pulled out the chair opposite and sat down. Her stomach rumbled as she caught a whiff of bacon. "So you do have some weaknesses, sir."

"Some."

"I heard you last night." The man lived for the truth, and so there was little point avoiding the subject. "You called out in your sleep."

From the firming of his jaw, he knew what she had heard. "My demons appear when I'm at my most vulnerable. Perhaps I should have given you some warning. The problem occurs whenever the environment is unsettled."

Well, he did not appear embarrassed to speak openly. "Your demons sound rather wild and temperamental, too." She scanned the cut of his expensive dark blue coat and the crisp folds of his cravat. "Though you present yourself as quite the opposite."

"Does that make you uneasy, Miss Atwood?"

"On the contrary, I fear seeing you relaxed and unrestrained would make me a little nervous."

Again, his penetrating gaze studied every facial feature. "My demons are well behaved during daylight hours. They get a little restless after dark, but I keep them on a tight leash."

"Unless brutes attack you in the street," she said, recalling the expert way he had fought the beasts. "Then you let them loose."

"Then I let them cause untold havoc," he agreed. He rose from the chair and moved to the platters on the sideboard. He lifted the china covers and began filling a plate.

Sybil took a moment to survey the dining room. Dark oak wainscoting and dull blue wallpaper made the space feel rather bleak. The cold flagstones added to the austere atmosphere. There were no paintings of sour-faced relatives hanging from the dusty picture rail. Nothing to indicate the owner's history. If anything in the room embodied the master's complex character, it was the Elizabethan-inspired fire surround—tall and dark with intricate carvings and fascinating detail.

Mr Daventry appeared at her left. "Tomas makes a perfect poached egg," he said, placing the plate in front of her. He was so close she felt the same tingling awareness she had last night. "Coffee?"

"Please."

Mr Daventry leaned closer as he poured her beverage, and she was captured again by his alluring scent. "Can I get you anything else, Miss Atwood?"

Something in his tone made her pulse race. Sybil glanced at the table and looked for the rack and butter dish. "Toast?"

He moved to the sideboard and returned with toasted bread cut too thickly and butter in a chipped china keeper. "No one here has time to polish silver."

"Butter is butter regardless of how it is served."

"Most ladies would frown upon our unrefined ways," he said, returning to his seat.

"I am not most ladies."

"No," he mused. "I've been aware of that for some time."

Sybil cleared her throat to mask her rumbling stomach. "Should I take that as a compliment or a criticism?" she said as she buttered her toast.

"You're an intelligent woman, Miss Atwood. Do you think I'm a man who cares for custom and convention?"

"I think you are a complete mystery, Mr Daventry. Today, I'm an intelligent woman. A mere week ago, I was a foolish chit with a brain fit for nothing but painting and playing the doting wife."

Mr Daventry studied her over the rim of his coffee cup, his intelligent eyes brightening with mild amusement. "The important thing is not what I said but what you believe."

"I am aware of my worth." Yet few men admired ladies with such strong opinions. "What you said speaks more of your failings than mine."

"Indeed, it does." He raised his coffee cup in salute. "But public opinion creates dreams and nightmares. The truth matters not, which is a point your father was eager to address."

He seemed keen to steer the conversation towards her father's work, but the mention of nightmares focused her thoughts in another direction.

Sybil swallowed her coffee to bolster her courage before asking, "Last night, when thrashing about in your sleep, you cried, 'don't leave me'. I cannot help but wonder if your quest for the truth stems from a personal need to lay your demons to rest."

Silence ensued.

A heavy silence.

A suffocating silence.

She had heard the gossip about his mother. The Duke of Melverley was known as a cruel man with a wicked temper. No one blamed his mistress for packing a valise and fleeing into the night. There had been other whisperings, too, nasty suspicions that the woman had never left Bideford Park, that her remains might be found in an unmarked grave in the garden.

Mr Daventry dabbed his mouth with his napkin. His eyes were like granite. Cold and hard. Impenetrable. "We are not here to analyse my mind, Miss Atwood, or to determine my motives for acting as I do."

It was as if someone had opened a window and an icy wind had swept in from the north. So, he could admit bad memories plagued his dreams but refused to give any insight as to the root of the problem. Surely it had something to do with his mother.

"Forgive me," she said, retreat being the best course of action to prevent him from erecting a wall between them. "Curiosity drives me to pry. I cannot help but find you somewhat of an enigma. And like my father, I cannot walk past a puzzle without examining the pieces."

"There is no puzzle to examine, no mystery to solve," he said bluntly. "My mother left when I was eight, and I have not seen her since. My father sent me to school, made an effort to pay the fees but had time for little else except playing tormentor."

Her heart lurched.

She cut into her poached egg, for he would see pity if she looked into his eyes. "And how did you meet my father?"

"He came to school to give a lecture. It was supposed to be an education in philosophy—few masters see the value of science —but it turned into so much more."

The urge to ask a hundred questions burned in her veins, but Mr Daventry held a world-weary air, a look that begged her not to press him further.

Sybil gestured to the newspaper on the table. "I see something caught your interest in the broadsheet. Reform is the topic of the day. Peel is determined to grant the judges power to give lesser sentences for some crimes where the death penalty is mandatory."

Mr Daventry snatched the paper and pushed it across the table. "I only wish your father had lived to witness the fact. But I found this in his journal, a sheet taken from an old newspaper. There was a riot at Smithfield Market two years ago. He'd made some notes at the top in pencil, though they've faded."

Sybil took the paper and read the article while Mr Daventry finished his meal. The riot started over an argument between a customer and a butcher. A crowd gathered to support the customer who complained the meat was rancid. The rioters took umbrage and smashed carts and overturned stalls. Fights ensued. Someone opened the gate to the livestock pens, and the animals stampeded through the market, trampling over people amid the chaos.

"Five people were pronounced dead at the scene," Mr Daventry said gravely. "One with a stab wound. Two suffered broken necks in the crush. Two from internal injuries. Your father was interested in the man with the knife wound to the chest."

"Mr Cribb," she said, finding the name at the bottom of the article.

"They found the butcher guilty of causing and encouraging a riotous assembly. A felony punishable by death. Despite a description and witness reports, the customer complaining of the rancid meat disappeared."

Sybil absorbed the information, though she wasn't sure what it had to do with her father. "Was my father championing a repeal of the Riot Act?"

"Your father believed someone murdered Mr Cribb and arranged the riot to cover the crime. He questioned witnesses and recorded evidence in one of his journals."

A hard lump formed in Sybil's throat. "And you think whoever killed Mr Cribb killed my father to prevent anyone discovering the truth."

"Perhaps." He glanced at his plate for a few seconds before adding, "Another member of the Order worked on the case with your father, though he is also dead."

Sybil's cutlery slipped through her fingers and clattered on the china plate. Somewhere in the back of her mind, she'd hoped Mr Daventry's suspicions were wrong, that her father's heart had given out, and he had died from natural causes.

"How did the man die?"

"I found him in the Thames."

She sensed the scene was probably more gruesome than that.

"Mr Proctor used to work as a runner," he continued. "He was an expert interrogator. His skill at reading people, at picking apart statements was second to none. Hence the reason your father recruited him to the Order."

An image of Atticus scribbling away behind his desk sprang into her mind. Her heart ached when she thought of the many secrets he'd kept hidden. The stress of righting injustices must have taken its toll.

She studied the handsome gentleman sitting opposite. He seemed so different from the arrogant rogue who'd had a string of mistresses. Was this the first time he had let anyone see the real man behind the façade?

"Losing a colleague must be difficult. I get the sense Mr Proctor was also a friend."

"Proctor was an honest man, one who had witnessed first-hand how money and position create their own version of the truth. His stories of corruption are the reason I trust no one at Bow Street."

The need to reach out to Mr Daventry came upon her from nowhere. It boggled the mind to think that this strong, confident man needed comfort. And yet she couldn't banish the thought of cradling him in her arms and stroking his hair until he slept without being haunted by memories of the past.

"How many men did my father recruit to the order?"

"Seven. The men are masters of their craft, men who share the same vision. A mathematician, physician and enquiry agent, to name a few. There are two empty places. Places left by the death of two exceptional men."

"Yes," she said, speaking of her father. And yet the more time she spent in Mr Daventry's company, the more she found him rather exceptional, too.

Hunger led her to gather her cutlery, slice the bacon and pop a piece into her mouth. After swallowing her food, she said, "And so our main objective must be to find the person responsible for Mr Cribb's murder."

"I visited Cribb's last known address, spoke to the other tenants. No one recalls anything unusual about the gentleman."

"And what of the other members of the order? Do you trust them?"

"With my life. Only Proctor knew of your father's most recent cases."

"Cases? You mentioned there was more than one."

Mr Daventry pushed out of his chair and moved to the sideboard. He opened the top drawer, delved under napkins and removed one of her father's journals. "Read this while you eat your meal, and then we will discuss my plan."

Something told her Mr Daventry was keen to exclude her from the investigation. Eager to hear his thoughts on the matter, she took the journal and read the neat script while Mr Daventry ate a second helping of bacon and eggs.

Judging by the date recorded, it seemed her father was investigating a case involving a collapsed mine near Wigan that had killed almost thirty people. The company who owned the mine evicted the surviving miners from their cottages and sold the land. From what Sybil could ascertain, there was a suspicion the collapse had been deliberate.

"It states all records relating to the owner of the coal mine and those relating to the sale of the land have either been lost or were destroyed in a fire."

Mr Daventry exhaled deeply. "Atticus discovered that three men owned the mine. One lives in India, though your father was still waiting for a reply to his correspondence. The second, Lord Talbot, has since died. The third man remains a mystery."

"And there is no connection between the two cases?"

"None."

Sybil heaved a weary sigh. With every new piece of information, the plot thickened.

"Someone betrayed your father. For years, we have kept our work secret, dealing only with a handful of professional men we trust. But someone learned of his current investigations. Though I received numerous bids from men who weren't at the auction, Sir Melrose, Lord Newberry and the solemn stranger dressed in black are at the top of my suspect list."

"And so what is our next course of action?"

The gentleman cleared his throat and seemed to think carefully before saying, "You will remain here and examine the books. Jonah and Tomas will ensure your safety until I return."

She was about to object when he raised a hand to stall her.

"My father is sick and has taken a turn for the worse. My intention was to settle you here and then return to London to visit him. Sir Melrose has invited me to attend his ball tonight. I'm sure you will agree it's not because he craves my company. But it will afford an opportunity to snoop around the man's home and study. I have it on good authority Lord Newberry will be in attendance."

While she relished the thought of studying her father's notes, of hearing his voice burst to life in the words, her need to assist Mr Daventry proved stronger.

"I'm sorry to hear about your father's ill health."

"Don't be. He's the devil, and I'm his spawn."

Now wasn't the time to discuss his father or delve into the whys and wherefores of their strained relationship. If she was to help Mr Daventry banish his demons, she would have to take a leaf out of his book and work covertly.

"Will Mrs Sinclair accompany you to the ball?" From what she had witnessed this morning, the man had a huge appetite, and the dark-haired temptress knew how to satisfy hungry men.

"Mrs Sinclair merely helps me maintain my disguise."

Sybil snorted. "I'm sure she does a lot more than that."

Strangely, the thought of him escorting the widow home and slipping beneath her bedsheets made Sybil feel nauseous. Indeed, the sickly sensation mingled with burning jealousy to send her pulse soaring.

"I cannot concentrate on solving this case if I have to worry about your welfare," he said, steering the subject away from his mistress.

"You mean you're a man of your word and must keep your oath to my father."

"I mean I don't want to see you hurt."

"Then I shall come with you. You can sneak around Sir Melrose's abode, and I shall entertain Lord Newberry." She might discover the real reason the lord had asked her to take a drive around the park. "The Cavanaghs will play chaperone. Afterwards, we will return here, to Bronygarth, and discuss our findings."

"No."

"No? Sir, I have lived alone for the best part of twelve months. What possible danger—"

"And I have thwarted numerous attacks on your person. How do you think I know about the broken kitchen window?"

The revelation caught her unawares. "I presumed it was a boy looking for bread."

"That's what I wanted you to believe. The thief was looking for the journals. The unnamed gentleman who hired him told him to search the drawers in your father's study. And while we're on the subject of threats, you were supposed to give me the letters."

"Letters?"

"The ones you received demanding you find the journals."

"I—I can't. I threw them into the fire."

He frowned and cocked his head. "Why would you do that?"

"Because I found them distressing."

"Now I have no way of comparing the handwriting with the examples I have of Newberry's and Sir Melrose's penmanship." His cheeks ballooned, and he sighed. "Can you recall what the blackguard wrote?"

She shrugged. "Always the same thing. I am to obtain my father's journals. When I do, I am to take them to a coaching inn called the Black Swan on the Great North Road. I'm to ask to rent room five and wait for the villain to make contact."

Mr Daventry shot to his feet so quickly the chair almost

toppled over. He threw his napkin onto the table. "Devil's teeth! Did you not think to mention this before?"

Sybil gulped. "I've spent the last two weeks doing my best to ignore the threats. My only focus has been obtaining the journals so that I could understand the devil's motives."

"Asking to meet at a coaching inn is hardly a threat."

Sybil shivered as she recalled the terrifying words scrawled at the bottom. "He promises to gut me from neck to navel if I do not comply."

Mr Daventry's face turned ashen. He dragged his hand down his face, closed his eyes and shook his head.

"That's why I was so desperate to attend the auction, why I made such an extortionate bid. Stealing into your home was the only course of action left open to me."

Mr Daventry muttered a curse. "And you've dealt with this worry alone."

"Since my father's death, I've had no one to turn to for help." Sybil could feel the tears brimming, feel the ache in her throat as she struggled to keep her emotions at bay.

"Please. Don't cry." He strode around the table.

Nerves forced her to stand, too. The tortured look on his face, the guilt flashing in his eyes, left her unsure what he would do.

Mr Daventry took hold of her hands and gripped them far too tightly. "You will come with me to London. The sooner we catch this blackguard, the sooner we can resume our normal lives."

From what she had witnessed, chasing the truth was part of a normal day's work for Lucius Daventry. "So you see the sense in me attending Sir Melrose's ball, in using the opportunity to question Lord Newberry?"

Mr Daventry swallowed deeply. "No, I see the sense in keeping you close when the Black Swan is but a few miles north of here."

CHAPTER EIGHT

A chaotic mind was of no use to anyone. A body plagued with crippling emotions was just as much of a hindrance. Every nerve, every fibre of Lucius' being wanted to gallop to the Black Swan, race to room five and lie in wait for the cunning bastard.

But the basis of any wisdom was patience.

Atticus had quoted Plato so many times the words were etched into Lucius' memory. And so he had Miss Atwood write a note. Robert and Jonah accompanied her to the Black Swan, where she rented the room and left a letter saying she was in the process of obtaining the journals and would deliver them soon.

Tomas and Samuel took their positions in the taproom where they were to keep watch for the next few hours and note all who entered the coaching inn. Jonah returned to Bronygarth to guard the vault, while Robert drove Lucius and Miss Atwood to Bideford Park, one of the many residences belonging to the Duke of Melverley.

Melverley's steward, Mr Warner, an educated ponce who thought himself above the duke's illegitimate offspring, intercepted them in the hall.

"You will have to wait. It's simply not convenient. Sir Herbert is examining His Grace and may be some time. Carter will attend you in the drawing room until you're summoned."

Lucius considered grabbing the man by his high-collared shirt and driving an upper-cut to his elongated chin. Instead, he patted the steward hard on the chest and said, "I'll show myself upstairs, Warner. Miss Atwood will take tea in the drawing room."

Lucius mounted the grand staircase with haste, ignoring the steward's pitiful pleas. Lingering brought back painful memories of restless nights when his mother's shouts and sobs disturbed his peaceful slumber.

He met Sir Herbert on the upper gallery, discovered that the duke was suffering from paralysis due to cerebral apoplexy. He had regained consciousness, but the prognosis was grim.

"This could well be the last time you'll see him." Sir Herbert's jowls wobbled as he shook his head in disbelief. "Best say what's needed now. He can hear you but will struggle to respond." With a grave expression, the physician patted Lucius on the shoulder before ambling away with his bulging black medical bag.

What was there to say to the father he despised?

Lucius had come to torment the duke, not spout sentiment.

The duke's bedchamber was as dark as his heart, the atmosphere as stuffy as his opinions. Thick red curtains kept the daylight at bay. Bowls of dried lavender lay scattered around the room, though they did nothing to disguise the pungent smell— the smell of death and the rotten stench of a liar.

Lucius used the fading candle in the lamp to light the wall sconces, although the noticeable brightness failed to lighten the bitterness in his heart.

"For the first time in my life, I can speak without interruption." Lucius moved closer to the imposing figure with sallow skin, resting against a mound of pillows. The man whose core was as putrid as a month-old apple. "Sir Herbert tells me you're not long for this world, though I cannot say I give a damn."

Glassy, bewildered eyes stared back.

"No doubt this is another one of your devious schemes," Lucius continued. It felt strange not closing his ears to the constant criticism. "Despite hovering on the brink of death, you had to find a way to shut me out, to keep from revealing the truth about what you did to my mother."

The duke seemed to squirm at the mere mention of Julia Fontaine.

"What's the point of taking a secret to the grave?" Lucius moved closer and perched on the edge of the bed. "All you have to do is blink if the answer is yes." He paused. The thought of asking the question made his stomach wrench. "Did you kill her in a jealous rage?"

The duke lay still, frozen in stasis.

Lucius repeated the question with more vehemence.

Nothing.

"Blink, damn you. I know you killed her. I heard the piercing cries at night." He had done everything to banish the sickening sound from his memory. "Is that why you sent me away? Did you fear I would discover your wicked deed? Do I remind you of her? Do you hate me that much, too?"

Still nothing.

Lucius thought to throttle the answer from his father's lying lips. "Tell me!"

Frustration quickly turned to despair. He scrubbed his hand down his face to ease his inner turmoil. Focusing on one's breathing was said to bring inner peace. It was easier said than done.

Lucius stood. Hatred and loathing consumed his heart. "I pray you have left me a legacy. For if you have made even the smallest bequest, know that I will look for every lost and lonely boy, every boy left to cry himself to sleep in a dark school dormitory, and I will fund his escape. Your money will educate the next generation of doctors and solicitors. Men who will carve a new world. A world of equal opportunity."

The duke's breathing grew raspy and his mouth twisted into an ugly grimace.

"No amount of money will repair the damage." Money could not atone for those years spent without his mother. Money could not fill the hole left by an absent father. "Before you're cold in your grave, before your coxcomb of a cousin inherits, I will dig up every inch of this garden, and I'll not stop until I've found her remains. Do you hear?"

Bony, gnarled fingers clutched the coverlet.

Behind Lucius, the bedchamber door clicked open. He'd hoped to see Miss Atwood, driven upstairs by Warner's pathetic whining, but the sour-faced steward entered as if he had every right to intrude on the last moments between a father and son.

Warner marched over to the bed. He fussed with the coverlet and pressed his hand to the duke's damp brow. "Your presence here is detrimental to His Grace's health."

"Get out!" Lucius growled through gritted teeth. "You will give me a moment's privacy, or there'll be hell to pay."

Warner straightened and brushed his sleek red hair from his brow. "I answer only to His Grace, and he is not in any fit state for lengthy visits."

Lucius squared his shoulders and stepped forward. "I answer to no one and will decide how long I want to remain at my father's bedside."

"His Grace finds your hostile manner distressing."

"Hostile? You expect to see warmth and generosity from the son of that cold-hearted bastard?" Lucius pointed at the helpless figure in the bed. "Now, get the hell out before I rip those ruffles from your shirt sleeves and stuff them down your throat."

"Mr Daventry," a soft feminine voice called from the doorway.

Lucius remained rigid and glared at the pompous steward, begging him to issue another lofty command.

The patter of footsteps preceded the gentle touch of a hand on his shoulder. "Let your father rest," Miss Atwood said softly. "We have other matters that require our attention and can return on the morrow."

Miss Atwood's calm tone had the power to temper anger's flames, until Warner muttered, "It seems your strumpet is the only one with any sense."

An unholy rage surged through Lucius' veins. He flew forward and threw a punch that knocked the arrogant toad on his arse.

"Call me what you will." He was so livid he struggled to speak coherently. "But slander Miss Atwood's good name and I shall beat you until your chin is the size of a normal man's."

Warner lay sprawled on the floor, clutching his jaw in shock.

"Mr Warner has a right to his opinion." Miss Atwood tugged Lucius' arm. "Just as we have the right to tell him he's an obnoxious weasel."

Lucius let Miss Atwood pull him back towards the door. "Don't fool yourself into thinking my father gives a damn about you, Warner. You're the hired help, nothing more. When I return, I suggest you make yourself scarce. Trim your nibs, for soon you'll be hunting for a new position."

Warner scrambled to his feet but remained silent as he brushed dust off his black coat and breeches and continued fussing with the bedsheets.

The need to escape the stifling memories saw Lucius grip Miss Atwood's hand and practically pull her down the broad oak staircase. He couldn't bundle her into the carriage quick enough. He couldn't rap the roof hard enough.

"Well, that was a rather unexpected encounter." Miss Atwood panted as she flopped into the seat. The vehicle jerked forward and crunched along the gravel drive. "I thought you kept your demons on a tight leash. The beasts were snapping and snarling at your heels the moment we stepped over the threshold."

Lucius took a few measured breaths. "I cannot abide self-righteous prigs."

"Are you referring to your father or Mr Warner?"

"Both."

"I see." She clasped her hands in her lap and watched him as he jiggled his leg and fidgeted in the seat. "So, restraint is something you're still trying to master."

"I never professed to be a saint." God, he was desperate to rip Warner's head from his shoulders. "Discipline requires patience. Some emotions are difficult to control."

Like his sudden urge to calm his temper by claiming Miss Atwood's delectable mouth. He would coax her warm lips apart, delve inside and sate his raging hunger. In anticipation, hot blood pooled heavy in his loins. He knew beyond any doubt, he could lose himself forever in her embrace.

"You admire Plato," she said. "Does the philosopher not say that a man's greatest victory is conquering himself? Some things are meant to be a struggle."

Bloody hell!

Why couldn't this be a time of recklessness, not reason? Could she not have beckoned him to the opposite side of the carriage, flashed the tops of her stockings and said to hell with oaths and vows? Could she not have told him to take whatever he needed to relieve the infernal ache?

"Trust me, Miss Atwood, a man has his limits."

"Then we should replay the events of the morning to distract your mind. Devise a plan for this evening. We cannot be seen whispering together in a secluded corner of Sir Melrose's ballroom."

It was not his mind that needed distracting.

Still, he had to do something to rein in his rampant thoughts. "Perhaps you should tell me again what happened when you gave the innkeeper your name and said you wanted to rent room five."

Miss Atwood straightened. "Well, it was as if he was expecting me. He nodded and simply gave me the key."

Lucius fired his logical brain into action, a task that soon dampened his ardour. He couldn't fantasise about bedding Miss Atwood while exploring critical aspects of the case. "The inn sits on the busiest stretch of road heading north out of London. Is it not odd that the room was available?"

It was odd that the blackguard's chosen inn was so close to Bronygarth. Worrying, when one considered few people knew Lucius owned the house. Somewhere in the process of being discreet, he had made a mistake.

"The villain must have paid for the room in advance," Miss Atwood said.

"And so you left the letter on the bed," he said, recapping what she had told him not two hours earlier. "No one approached you or made contact, not even a maid."

"I was there but ten minutes. Numerous people passed me on the stairs, but no one spoke other than to bid me good morning."

"Only good morning?"

She gave a half shrug. "The lady in the room opposite was entering as I was leaving. She said if I was taking supper to avoid the stew and dumplings. I thanked her for the warning, and we parted ways."

Lucius mulled over the snippets of useless information. A conversation about dumplings was hardly a veiled threat. "The innkeeper must be in contact with our quarry. How else would the devil know to come to the inn? But if I interrogate him, it will only arouse his suspicions."

"Unless our quarry is a resident. When on his travels, my father often stayed at the same inn for a month or more."

A fond memory filled Lucius' mind. "Yes, Atticus once bought me dinner at the Duck and Partridge near Wetherby. I shouldn't have left the dormitory, but your father was quite persuasive, and I was going through a difficult phase."

A disobedient and destructive phase was a better description.

"Wetherby?" Miss Atwood frowned. "You went to school in Yorkshire? One would think you'd have gone to Harrow or maybe Charterhouse, what with your father's seat being in Surrey."

"One would think so," was all he could bear to say on the matter.

Since the day Lucius' mother disappeared, the duke had deliberately kept his distance. He rarely ventured to Surrey, rarely left Bideford Park. Perhaps he feared someone might stumble upon Julia Fontaine's grave.

Silence descended, and they stared out of the window. There was no urge to speak, no urge to converse idly about the weather or the excessive tolls. Though nothing more was said about the duke, Lucius suspected Miss Atwood had the measure of the situation.

As the bustling streets of London came into view, and the carriage swayed to avoid carts and reckless riders, the lady turned her attention to their appointment at the home of Sir Melrose, and of their late-night rendezvous.

"So, you will arrive with Mrs Sinclair," she began, though there was a thread of tension in her voice, "and I shall—"

"I'm not attending with Mrs Sinclair."

"Oh. Is the widow out of town?"

Having spent time alone with Miss Atwood, he couldn't bear

the widow's company. And he had the sudden need to appear as more than a scoundrel hellbent on pleasure. Yes, society would be all agog. The worst of rogues rarely reformed. But they could all go to Hades.

"Mrs Sinclair and I have parted ways." He had broken the news to the widow on his way home from the docks, once he had decided there was no other course of action but to take Miss Atwood to Bronygarth. "Your father disapproved of my methods of gaining information, as you were wont to remind me."

She shuffled in the seat and lifted her chin. "A man with your intelligence can surely find other ways to gain the knowledge you seek. Mrs Sinclair's wisdom extends to the purchasing of fripperies, and you're worth so much more than that."

"Am I?" The compliment touched him so deeply he had to smile to hide the rush of emotion. "And I thought you despised me."

Her gaze drifted to the ebony lock he brushed from his brow. "Opinions change. Indeed, having discovered more about you, I find the opposite is true." Her eyes softened. "I have the utmost respect for your kindness and loyalty."

Good Lord!

Lucius was prone to bouts of fancy where Miss Atwood was concerned, but he knew the glint of desire in a woman's eyes. He knew the radiant glow, the faint hunger.

The muscles in his abdomen clenched. His stomach grew warm as the intense longing he had only recently put to bed stirred from its slumber.

"But how will you slip into dark rooms without a mistress in tow?" said the lady whose mouth was a constant torment. "Won't it look odd if you're seen sneaking about alone?"

"People often see me walking the corridors. Most presume there's a lady waiting for me somewhere."

"So Mrs Sinclair knows nothing about the Order?"

"Of course not. The woman would sell her soul for an hour of pleasure. She thinks I'm as morally depraved as she is, that I live to commit sin. Mrs Sinclair is a renowned gossip and was once Lord Talbot's mistress."

"Lord Talbot. One of the men who purchased the mine in

Wigan and sold off the land after the collapse." Miss Atwood arched a brow. "I see your logic in pursuing a liaison."

"Everything I do stems from a need to help the Order."

"Everything? Are we friends purely because I am a terrible snoop with an insatiable curiosity?"

He smiled. "We are friends because we share a common goal. We have the intellectual capacity to keep each other entertained." And because he liked her far more than he cared to admit.

"You really are a mystery." She shook her head, although still seemed amused. "On the day of the auction, you said we would never be friends."

"Opinions change. Having discovered more about you, I find the opposite is true." Having her as nothing but a friend would come at a hefty cost to his sanity. Was that not why some men turned to drink, wrote morbid poems or developed an opium addiction?

She smiled—a smile that could make a man forget his troubles. "It comes as a surprise to find I like you, Mr Daventry."

"It comes as no surprise to find I like you, Miss Atwood." When she frowned at the apparent discrepancy, he added, "You are Atticus Atwood's daughter."

"Yes," she said and gave a satisfied sigh. "Now, we've spent the entire time talking and have not made plans regarding our return to Bronygarth this evening."

The thought of sleeping in the next room to hers for another night filled him with excitement and dread.

"Furnis will come to Half Moon Street at midnight. This time he will take you to the Wild Hare. Robert will meet you there and ferry you to Bronygarth."

She nodded. "And you will arrive a few minutes later."

"Yes, after ensuring no one followed you from town. Now, Blake and Bower will accompany you to the Cavanaghs, and you're to send word if your friends cannot attend tonight."

"They will attend. Having given them a clue that helped solve a terrible problem, they are desperate to repay the debt."

Ah, she spoke of Mrs Cavanagh's staged ruination. "Make sure you remain with them for the entire evening, that they escort you home before midnight. Trust I shall be there, watching from the shadows."

She nodded. "And when I dance with Lord Newberry, for he is sure to ask if only to probe me for information about my father's journals, is there anything specific you wish me to discover?"

Lucius' heart sank to his stomach. Newberry would take every advantage. A man would need his wits to ensure Miss Atwood's safety, which was yet another reason he could not be hampered by the insipid widow.

"Limit your time with him to one waltz, nothing more." God, he was starting to sound like a protective parent. "Say you've heard your father's books may contain information other than scientific theories. Say you wonder if Atticus wrote about his interest in justice, in prison reforms, and judge his reaction."

Miss Atwood pursed her lips and hummed. "Might I enquire about the note you sent to Lord Newberry at Boodle's? If he mentions the matter, I would prefer not to gape like a dull-witted dunce."

"Newberry failed to send the written statement I requested. I merely gave him a two-day extension. My real motive for sending Bower to Boodle's was to check that Newberry was at his club and had not followed you to Brook Street."

"Oh." A flush crept up her cheeks. She exhaled deeply as the carriage turned into Half Moon Street. "I'm sorry. My impetuous nature has caused you no end of trouble."

"Had I trusted you with the truth, we might have avoided any unpleasantness. After all, who wants to be embroiled in midnight chases? Who wants to sleep in a haunted castle with a rogue plagued by nightmares?"

A smile played at the corners of her mouth. "Who indeed?"

CHAPTER NINE

Most ladies lived to attend the next ball or rout. They spent days mithering their modistes, scouring fashion plates from Paris, searching for the perfect gown to attract a wealthy husband. Draped in jewels and drenched in perfume, they sauntered through the ballrooms, flicking their fans in the flirtatious way that was sure to gain a gentleman's attention.

Sybil found it all rather tedious.

A lady living alone should be happy to spend an evening in the company of like-minded people. But she preferred sitting by the fire reading gothic novels, preferred donning widow's weeds and spying on the elusive Mr Daventry.

So why had she spent an age picking the right gown to flatter her figure? Why did it feel as if grasshoppers were leaping about in her chest? Why did her heart dance in her throat when she entered Sir Melrose's crowded ballroom? Indeed, her hands shook, and her cheeks flamed as she scanned the throng looking for the enigmatic owner of a haunted castle.

"Come," Cassandra said, gesturing to the far side of the ballroom, "let's find a quiet place by the alcove, and we can discuss your intentions."

"My intentions?" Sybil craned her neck and searched the room once more before following the Cavanaghs through the crowd.

"What do you intend to do about Mr Daventry?" Cassandra spoke as if Sybil had a problem hearing above the din. "Might you come to an understanding?"

What was she to do about Mr Daventry?

The question brought to mind numerous answers. None of which ought to enter the head of an unmarried lady. While curious about her father's work—astounded at the lengths a man would go to in order to save the innocent—she found herself more intrigued by the new master of the Order.

Perhaps she had inherited her father's need to help the tormented. Perhaps she just wanted to know what it would be like to be captured in the scoundrel's arms and have her mouth pillaged and plundered.

"Let me deal with Daventry," Benedict Cavanagh said, directing them to a secluded spot near the terrace doors. The Earl of Tregarth's illegitimate son was just as handsome as Lord Newberry—hence the permanent grin on Cassandra's face. Both men had golden hair, though unlike Lord Newberry, Benedict possessed a natural charm that gave one confidence his manner was equally pleasing. "I shall negotiate terms on your behalf."

"Terms?" While the idea of being any man's mistress was abhorrent, she liked the thought of late-night walks through the garden of Bronygarth. She liked the thought of bidding Mr Daventry good night, conversing over breakfast. She liked the confusing roiling in her stomach whenever those stormy-grey eyes met hers.

"Lord knows why your father left Daventry such an important legacy," Benedict said. "Surely it's only right the books belong to you."

"Oh, by terms you mean negotiate a price for my father's work." Heavens, for a lady who professed to have a logical mind, her brain had turned to mulch.

Cassandra frowned. "Are you unwell? You seem distracted. Perhaps that dreadful argument at the auction has affected your nerves."

Sybil reminded herself that Cassandra knew nothing about her stealing into Mr Daventry's home, about the abduction attempt, or about her staying at Bronygarth. And while she wasn't ready to confess her sins, the need to defend Mr Daventry pulsed in her veins.

"Mr Daventry will do the right thing," Sybil said, daring to take another glance around the ballroom. "My father had the utmost respect for him. And so I shall have faith in Mr Daventry's character, too."

Cassandra's frown deepened. "Are you sure you're all right? I understand the need to nurture positive thoughts, but we are talking about the man you despise to the core of your being."

Oh, she did not despise Lucius Daventry—not anymore.

"Being angry hasn't helped. So I have decided to take a different stance."

Benedict arched a brow. "I advise you err on the side of caution. Annoy Daventry at your peril. He will think nothing of ruining your reputation."

Goodness, her stomach was tied in knots with the need to correct their misconceptions. She wanted to grab them by the shoulders, wanted to shake them and explain how Mr Daventry had risked his life to protect her. She wanted to sing his praises from the rooftops, tell them how remarkably logical he was, how his loyalty knew no bounds.

"Have no fear. I have the measure of Mr Daventry's character."

"Thank heavens." Cassandra released a weary sigh. "Who would want to find themselves in a compromising position with a man like that?"

"Who indeed?"

"Besides, since your meeting at the auction, Lord Newberry seems to have you in his sights." Cassandra nodded discreetly to a point beyond Sybil's shoulder. "He hasn't taken his eyes off you since he noticed you walking through the crowd."

Sybil didn't want to look at Lord Newberry. She didn't want to catch any man's eye other than Lucius Daventry's, but she had not come to the ball to sip ratafia and gossip in the retiring room.

"Lord Newberry strikes me as a man with many secrets." Sybil stole a quick glance at the handsome lord who was watching her intently. "I'm not sure he is entirely trustworthy."

Benedict snorted. "Newberry is equally renowned for his conquests. It's said that when he's done sowing his oats, he will marry Lady Margaret, daughter of the Earl of Langley."

Benedict Cavanagh seemed to know a lot about those in the *ton*. Perhaps he might know something relating to the incidents her father was investigating. But how to broach the subject without arousing suspicion.

Sybil smiled. "Regardless of his intentions, I could never love a man like Lord Newberry. Something tells me a devil lurks beneath that angelic smile." She stepped closer and whispered, "I heard tell he hides a terrible secret."

Cassandra frowned for the umpteenth time. "What sort of secret?"

"I cannot recall if it was something to do with his friend Lord Talbot, or his association with Mr Cribb."

"Mr Cribb?" Cassandra looked at her husband. "I have never heard the name."

Benedict shook his head. "No, I can't say I have. As for Talbot, they belonged to the same club, but I would hardly call them friends."

With a nonchalant shrug, Sybil said, "Oh, well. Perhaps I should pay more attention to retiring-room gossip."

"If it's gossip you seek, you should visit Mrs Crandall." Cassandra's eyes brightened with amusement. "The madam owns many secrets. I'm surprised she sleeps at night. A desperate man might resort to drastic measures to secure her silence."

Owning secrets was a dangerous game. "Am I correct in thinking Mrs Crandall is a courtesan?"

"Was a courtesan," Cassandra corrected. "Now she arranges private parties for the demimonde at her address on Theobolds Road. Debauched parties." Cassandra giggled. "Parties where people forgo numerous items of clothing and frolic in the dark. Mr Daventry often attends."

Did he indeed?

Mr Daventry failed to mention that during one of his *truthful* talks. And yet lately Sybil had no problem imagining the gentleman frolicking in the dark without his coat and cravat.

"I wouldn't say often," Benedict interjected. "But Daventry

frequents the place on occasion. As for Mrs Crandall, she receives anonymous threats weekly, but no one is brave enough to chain a ball to her ankle and throw her into the Thames. She makes it known the secrets are stored safely, that the truth will out should she suddenly meet a grisly end."

An image of the underwater vault at Bronygarth passed through Sybil's mind. Keepers of the truth gathered many enemies. Someone murdered her father to ensure their secret remained hidden. Perhaps Atticus should have adopted Mrs Crandall's attitude and made his suspicions known. But he would never have risked the lives of family and friends.

Cassandra's sudden gasp drew Sybil from her reverie. "Quick. Straighten your shoulders. Your new gentleman friend is heading this way."

"Mr Daventry?" Sybil's heartbeat pounded in her ears, drowning out the music of the orchestra.

But a quick assessment of her emotions said Cassandra wasn't speaking of Lucius Daventry. The energy in the room changed when he was near. Nerves mingled with exhilaration whenever she sensed his presence. Now, she felt nothing but a clawing apprehension.

"Not that rogue. I speak of Lord Newberry. Honestly, do you think about anything other than Mr Daventry?"

Benedict Cavanagh studied Sybil through narrowed eyes. Clearly he sensed something was amiss—Sybil knew it the moment he said, "Are you expecting to meet Mr Daventry this evening? You won't persuade him to your cause. Not when his only interest lies in seeking pleasure."

Sybil might have challenged Mr Cavanagh's opinion had Lord Newberry not barged in between them and insisted he lead her in a waltz.

Sybil forced a smile. The moment the lord clasped her hand and drew her close, she knew there was something dark lurking beneath his cherubic façade.

"So, did you take tea with Daventry?" The lord wasted no time coming straight to the point. "I pray Mrs Cavanagh wasn't your chaperone. When a lady has no option but to marry

Tregarth's son, one can hardly regard her as a paragon of virtue."
He snorted as if in awe of his superb wit.

Every bone in Sybil's body longed to knock this man off his
lofty pedestal. "Do not concern yourself with my reputation, my
lord. Besides, Mr Daventry withdrew his invitation after I
caused such a terrible ruckus at the auction."

"Daventry is a master of manipulation. It wouldn't surprise
me to find he invited you to the auction as an excuse to raise the
bids. I take it you can't match my figure of seven thousand."

The arrogant devil.

He looked so smug she was liable to say something deroga-
tory. "I hope my written statement will be sufficiently persuasive.
The journals belonged to my father, and I have a rightful claim.
Have you submitted your statement, my lord?"

"Daventry doesn't care about statements." His tight smile
conveyed a hint of doubt. "He merely enjoys belittling his betters."

His betters!

Anger brought a boulder-sized lump to her throat. Pompous
oaf. She had the urge to stamp on his toe. But if she couldn't
keep a tight rein on her emotions, she would ruin her one chance
to question the lord. Besides, mere days ago, she had thought the
worst of Mr Daventry's character, too.

"Ah, you refer to his illegitimacy," she continued.

"What else?"

"I thought perhaps you were alluding to his immoral pursuits.
Then again, most of the peers in the *ton* keep a mistress. It
would be hypocritical to judge Mr Daventry."

"Madam, are you always this free with your tongue?" The lord
drew her a little closer and gave a salacious chuckle. "When I
offered a wild ride in my curricle, I meant it."

Sybil squirmed "Are you always so forward in manner, my
lord?"

A sudden shift in the air captured her attention. She was so
busy thinking of a way to lure Lord Newberry into her trap that
she failed to notice Lucius Daventry enter the ballroom. She
glanced around covertly but couldn't see him in the crowd. Yet
every tingling nerve in her body said he was close.

"You're an intelligent woman, Miss Atwood, not one of the dim-witted ones. I'm sure you know how it works."

"Of course." Her father said the truth was one's greatest friend. She wondered if Lord Newberry would agree. "You want to bed me before you finally settle and marry Lady Margaret. You want to bed me because I am Atticus Atwood's daughter. You hope, after a night of pleasure, I might reveal his secrets."

Lord Newberry's head fell back, and he laughed.

It was then that Sybil saw Mr Daventry amongst the crowd. Dressed in black, he prowled the perimeter of the dance floor like a panther stalking his prey.

Her heart skipped a beat.

Weak knees caused a misstep.

Lord Newberry firmed his grip and must have presumed he had a powerful effect on her senses. "Perhaps a delicate little lamb lurks beneath your wolf's disguise, Miss Atwood."

Aware of Mr Daventry's penetrating gaze, Sybil stuttered, "And ... and perhaps a devil lurks beneath your angelic mask, my lord. My father was a keeper of secrets. He liked to observe the actions of immoral men. The study of people is a science, too, is it not?"

The lord's expression turned serious. The light vanished from his bright blue eyes. "I see nothing remotely fascinating about the study of the human psyche."

"Do you not?" The need to hurry—for the dance would soon be at an end—and the need to speak secretly to Mr Daventry forced her to say, "Few peers care about science. Which begs the question, what possible interest can you have in my father's work?"

The question seemed to unsettle the arrogant lord. His mouth opened and closed, but he failed to find the answer.

"No doubt you couldn't write a statement declaring your intention," Sybil continued smugly. "My father cared about the poor, about prison reforms, about men in power abusing their positions. As you're not poor or in prison, I must assume you have an interest in the latter."

There was nothing angelic about the way the lord's features contorted and twisted to reveal the ugly truth behind the mask.

He gripped her hand so tightly he was liable to break a bone. It took all her strength not to whimper.

Through gritted teeth, he snarled, "Be careful, Miss Atwood. A man can only tolerate a snoop for so long before releasing the hounds." And then he pasted an amiable smile which he shared with those dancers nearby.

Fear should have seized Sybil by the throat and held her in its frigid grip, but Lucius Daventry was seconds away and would soon put this bully in his place. While Mr Daventry took a covert approach when investigating, she preferred reckless and direct. What had she to lose? Her life was already in danger.

"I have read what my father wrote in his journals—detailed evidence of fraud and deception. What interests me is how you know. And you must know. Why else would you make such an extortionate bid for what people believe are nought but scientific theories?"

The lord's jaw firmed.

The earlier comments about Mrs Crandall crept into Sybil's mind. There were ways of protecting oneself from devils like Lord Newberry.

"Should anything happen to me, my lord, know that I have made notes on my father's work. Notes that will pass to the appropriate authorities should I meet my demise."

The dance ended before the lord could muster a reply.

With a firm hold of Sybil's upper arm, Lord Newberry led her from the floor. "Your threat changes nothing," he whispered through gritted teeth as he escorted her back to the Cavanaghs. "No one will believe the scrawled notes of a woman committed to an asylum for the insane. Once I obtain the journals from Daventry, you might find yourself spirited away in the dead of night, never to be seen again."

"You do not scare me," she lied as a bleak image of a ragged woman sitting in a dank cell entered her mind. Rich lords had the power to manipulate any situation. Wasn't that the reason her father had formed the Order?

"Then why are you trembling, my dear?"

"Perhaps it has something to do with the breeze blowing in

from the terrace," she countered, forcing yet another smile as she rejoined the Cavanaghs.

Lord Newberry did not give Sybil a moment to gather her wits before saying, "I must insist on another dance, Miss Atwood, and simply won't take no for an answer."

No doubt women scrambled to please this gentleman. Sybil was of a mind to refuse, but the need to gather more information convinced her to say, "Of course. But if we are to discuss our mutual interest in my father's notes, we will have to dance the last waltz."

The lord gave a spurious smile. "I shall await our conversation with bated breath, Miss Atwood." And with that, he flicked a golden lock from his brow and strode away.

"Well, you certainly have a lot in common with Lord Newberry." Cassandra's gaze burned with curiosity. "I took a quick peek, and you never stopped talking the whole time you were dancing."

"Conversation is an excellent way to gauge a person's character."

Cassandra laughed. "That all depends on whether one's partner is spinning a yarn."

"As you can imagine, Lord Newberry is rather frank when giving his opinion." His warning rang of desperation. Only frightened men threatened women. Lord Newberry was guilty of something. She just had to discover what.

A sudden shiver ran the length of Sybil's spine, though it had nothing to do with her fear of Lord Newberry. This was a different sensation. And it came as no surprise when Mr Daventry appeared and bid the Cavanaghs good evening.

"Mr Daventry?" Sybil feigned surprise. He looked splendid in his black evening coat, though his trousers didn't grip his thighs the way breeches did. "Have you reconsidered your position, sir? Have you come to say you'll accept my offer of six thousand pounds?"

"Six thousand?" Benedict Cavanagh sucked in a sharp breath upon hearing the extortionate sum. "I'm sure Daventry understands that the books belong with their rightful owner. Morally, money shouldn't matter."

"I came merely to tell Miss Atwood that I have decided to keep her father's books." Mr Daventry's confident stance and arrogant grin made him look just like the disreputable rogue whose list of mistresses could fill a journal. "The last thing I need is her stalking me in the dark while I am otherwise engaged."

"I am standing here, sir." Sybil rather liked this game. Yes, she hated being dishonest, but the truth could endanger the lives of her friends. "Can you not address me directly?"

Mr Daventry's jaw firmed as he met her gaze. "Wearing that gown, Miss Atwood, you risk me making good on my earlier threats to steal your virtue. For your safety, I believe it is better if I direct all conversation to your friends."

She had made a deliberate effort tonight and was glad he'd noticed. Yes, the scooped neckline was a little low, and the pearl choker added an air of decadence. Not to mention her gown was the perfect shade of green to complement her unruly copper curls.

Cassandra inhaled deeply. "Sir, if it's a deterrent you seek, it will take more than a threat to Miss Atwood's virtue. I'm afraid she doesn't frighten easily."

Lucius Daventry's intense grey gaze drifted from Sybil's hair slowly down to the valley of her breasts. "Perhaps Miss Atwood wishes to court my attention for some reason other than an interest in scientific theories."

"You approached me, sir. Perhaps you wish to court my attention for some reason other than to tell me you won't sell." While she tried to sound amused, her tone held a flirtatious note that was sure to rouse the Cavanaghs' suspicions.

Heat swirled in her stomach when Mr Daventry moistened his lips and said, "I'm a man who takes what he wants, Miss Atwood. Cavanagh will tell you. I could offer a crude retort, but it would only incite you to retaliate. And I like a good fight as much as I like a good—"

"Did you catch the thief?" Cassandra said in a panic. "Did you find the man who stole the fake book?"

Mr Daventry turned his attention to Cassandra, though the air continued to thrum with excitable energy. "No, madam, though I believe he is of Scottish descent."

"Scottish? I imagine quite a few people would want to steal important scientific theories and take praise for their discovery."

"Who can say what motivates the criminal fraternity."

Silence ensued.

Sybil found it difficult not to stare at Lucius Daventry's broad shoulders or the errant ebony lock falling over his brow, though a glance at Benedict Cavanagh caused a pang of alarm. The tilt of his head and the odd shooting glances said he was mentally assessing their interactions.

"Well, don't let us keep you," Sybil said, quick to avert suspicion. "I'm sure Mrs Sinclair is pining for your company."

Mr Daventry arched a brow. "A man must have some means of relieving his frustrations." He inclined his head. "I wish you all an enjoyable evening."

Mr Daventry turned on his heel and stalked through the crowd, who quickly parted to create a wide walkway. Some men shuffled nervously as he passed. Some gave a curt nod, while various ladies stroked the necklines of their gowns in open invitation.

Sadness touched Sybil's heart.

People thought they had the measure of his character.

People were wrong.

"Daventry is up to something." Benedict Cavanagh's comment captured Sybil's attention. "I've known the man for years, and that's the first time he has ever approached a lady in a ballroom."

Heat flooded Sybil's cheeks. She tried to appear indifferent, but she was equally intrigued. Why had he felt the need to approach her in public? Was there any truth in his heated gaze?

She swallowed past her growing need for his company. "I caused him no end of trouble at the auction. He's tired of my snooping and wished to issue a veiled warning." There, was that not a reasonable explanation?

Mr Cavanagh pursed his lips and hummed. "There's something different about him, something I cannot name."

"I have to agree." Cassandra seemed determined to add fuel to the fire. "While Mr Daventry was as crude as expected, there was a slight warmth to his tone and manner that I failed to notice at the auction."

Sybil screwed her nose in protest. "But he was as rude and as obnoxious as ever."

Benedict Cavanagh shook his head. "If I'm not mistaken, I believe Lucius Daventry is hunting for his next mistress." His tone sounded grave. "And I cannot help but feel he has you in his sights, Miss Atwood."

"Me?" The thought roused a nervous excitement. "Don't be ridiculous. The man likes to taunt me that is all."

Heavens, her words rang with insincerity. She was an appalling liar and needed to make a quick escape. A few minutes in the retiring room would give her ample opportunity to gather her composure.

The sudden arrival of Mr and Mrs Wycliff, good friends of the Cavanaghs, distracted her chaperones momentarily. Indeed, Sybil slipped away quietly and was soon lost in the crowd. Locating the retiring room should have been a priority. But she caught sight of Mr Daventry sneaking upstairs and had the overwhelming urge to follow.

CHAPTER TEN

For twenty minutes, Lucius had listened to Sir Melrose Crampton's constant barrage of questions. Had Lucius received the written statements? Could he not see the logic in selling the journals to the Royal Society? What the devil did Newberry want with scientific theories? When would Lucius make his decision?

He would have enjoyed tormenting Sir Melrose, picking the man's mind apart, establishing if his reasons for bidding were genuine. But Lucius' only focus had been the vivacious woman in green silk, dancing the waltz in Newberry's blasted arms.

Miss Atwood had looked happy and radiant as she twirled about the floor, but the sick feeling in Lucius' gut said something was wrong. He studied her when she rejoined the Cavanaghs, watched her interaction with Newberry, saw the pain behind her smile.

Despite agreeing to keep his distance, he'd been compelled to approach. And so he had conversed with the Cavanaghs, played the disreputable rogue while Miss Atwood acted the disgruntled nemesis. Through her confident façade, he had noted the throbbing pulse in her neck, the tremor of suppressed fear in her voice.

Damn Newberry to hell!

Lucius mounted the stairs to the first floor, hunting for the lord who had entered the mansion house with an arrogant swagger and who would leave shuffling on his arse with two broken kneecaps.

Locating Newberry wasn't his only reason for venturing upstairs. After a brief conversation with Mrs Cockborne—a notorious widow who rode her conquests so hard those in the demimonde referred to her as Mrs Cockburn—Lucius discovered that Sir Melrose Crampton had a private office and a library on the first floor.

Both the office and the library were locked, which might have posed a problem had Lucius not designed a skeleton key capable of bypassing warded locks. But the stifling heat in the ballroom had forced a host of guests upstairs, seeking refuge in the family's private drawing room. Lady Crampton—a woman half her husband's age—sat in a wingback chair near the window, holding court with an entourage of admirers. Consequently, Lucius only managed to unlock the library door before hearing the pad of footsteps on the stairs.

Returning to the task of finding Lord Newberry, Lucius headed towards the other three rooms on the floor. Those doors were locked, too. Perhaps the fop had ventured up to the maids' quarters in the attic. Discovering the peer in a compromising position with a servant girl would give Lucius a perfect excuse to throw a punch.

"Lucius."

He was about to mount the stairs to the upper floor when he heard the feminine voice call out to him. A choking panic rose to his throat. Miss Atwood knew better than to repeat his given name in public. She knew better than to follow a rogue upstairs. Although on reflection, he knew it to be Larissa Sinclair's sibilant hiss.

"Lucius. Darling." The widow called him again, and he had no option but to turn around lest Newberry learn of his impending arrival. She glanced at the upper staircase. "Don't tell me you've cast me aside to frolic with the maids."

Lucius forced a smile and strode towards the woman who looked keen to flex her jaw and swallow him whole. Strands of black hair had escaped her coiffure. Swollen lips suggested she had recently enjoyed a wild romp in a bedchamber.

"Larissa. I wasn't sure you'd be here tonight." He hoped to avoid her. "As for casting you aside, ours was only ever a temporary arrangement."

The widow's dark, sensual eyes devoured every inch of his body. "If it's a temporary arrangement you want, I'm not doing anything for the next hour."

Lucius cleared his throat. "I'm otherwise engaged. On a matter of business, not pleasure."

She glanced at the upper staircase again. "Does your business involve bedding Lady Crampton or one of her maids? As the lady is currently pandering to a host of sycophants in the drawing room, one must suppose the latter is true."

"I'm not interested in bedding Lady Crampton or her maids." Truth be told, he had no interest in bedding anyone but Miss Atwood. Perhaps the infamous Lucius Daventry would have to live life as a monk.

"I understand. You want me to wait until you've concluded your business." Larissa stroked her fingers over the swell of her breasts, breasts that were in no way as magnificent as Miss Atwood's. "Perhaps you might come to me later so I might ease the tension in those muscular shoulders."

He stood and stared.

His motivation for keeping company with Larissa Sinclair stemmed from a need to find Atticus' murderer. Having spent the last two days in Miss Atwood's company—being himself— he found he no longer had the stomach to play games. Indeed, the thought of locking lips with the widow made him nauseous.

Hellfire!

The truth hit him squarely on the jaw, and he mentally reeled. Yes, the copper-haired beauty in the captivating green dress was the only woman he wanted. Until now, he'd been able to ignore the cravings, ignore the internal ache, ignore the intense longing that sometimes woke him in the dead of night.

Not anymore.

He didn't want to be cruel—although Larissa had no problem

shedding her skin and starting anew. "I don't want you, Larissa. I cannot lie to myself anymore."

Larissa laughed. "Of course you don't. You've got someone else in mind." She placed her hands on his chest, fiddled with the gold buttons on his waistcoat. "Although I guarantee she lacks my experience and stamina in the bedchamber."

Lucius snatched the widow's hands, for he found her touch repulsive. But then his senses alerted him to movement at the end of the hall. Numerous people milled about, but he knew Miss Atwood's energy the moment it came within twenty feet of his own.

For a brief second their gazes locked, though Miss Atwood looked away as quickly as he did. The guilt rising like acid in his gullet must have been evident on his face. He knew how it looked—like a rake stealing an intimate moment with his mistress.

What the devil was she doing upstairs?

Knowing Miss Atwood's curious mind, she had come to spy on Lord Newberry. So much for the Cavanaghs playing chaperone.

Lucius was aware of her quickly trying the office door before moving to the library and stealing inside. In a bid to distract Larissa's attention, he backed her into the doorway of the room she had just vacated.

"You're not interested in me, Larissa." Lucius reached behind her, turned the doorknob and forced her back into the room. "You cannot abide the fact I'm not fawning over you."

Fawning was not his style.

"Oh, poor darling. Newberry told me who's taken your fancy." Larissa gestured to the arrogant lord standing in the corner of the dim bedchamber, tucking his shirt into his black satin breeches. So that's where the devil was hiding. "You want the clever little virgin with the large breasts."

Anger flared.

When tasked with protecting Miss Atwood, this was precisely the problem he wished to avoid. He should have left her at Bronygarth. But it was easier to rescue a ruined reputation than save her from an unforeseen attack.

"Perhaps you need to assess your skill between the sheets, Newberry," Lucius said, desperate to change the subject. "It's been five minutes since your passionate encounter, and Larissa is already seeking satisfaction elsewhere."

Larissa sniggered. "Newberry did spend more time asking questions about some stuffy journals than he did pleasuring me." She turned to the handsome lord. "Didn't you, darling?"

Lucius imagined grabbing the lord and throttling an explanation from his devious lips. But removing Miss Atwood from the library was his pressing priority. If the lady had any sense, she'd have snuck back to the ballroom.

"A woman hates feeling exploited, Newberry," he said, keen to start a row between the pair. "Larissa can't be happy that you used her to gain information about me."

Newberry scowled.

"I knew you had an ulterior motive." Larissa turned on the devil. "You said you were hunting for a mistress. That we might suit."

"Newberry wants answers, not a mistress," Lucius countered. "He wants to know if I've spoken about the contents of Atticus Atwood's journals." Perhaps it was time to add a pinch of spice to the cooking pot. "And he wants to know if Lord Talbot told you about his investments in Wigan."

Newberry's mumbled curse punctuated the tense atmosphere. "What the devil are you talking about, Daventry?" In a panic, he crossed the room and captured Larissa's hands. "Can't you see he is trying to cause an argument, sweeting?"

Larissa glared at the lord. "But you did ask questions about Talbot."

Newberry huffed. "I asked if he was a good lover, not about his personal investments."

"And you asked if I had ever stayed in Brook Street, if I'd ever seen those old tomes."

While the conversation might prove useful in the investigation to find Atticus' murderer, saving Miss Atwood's fall from grace was his primary concern. And so Lucius backed out of the room and left the couple to their heated discussion.

In the drawing room, the sycophants were still gathered

around Lady Crampton, laughing and nodding and hanging on her every word as if she were the next Messiah.

Lucius crept past, opened the library door, slipped inside and eased it closed with both hands. The moment he entered the dark room, he knew Sybil Atwood was still inside. The sweet scent of her rose perfume hung in the air. His heart hammered against his chest as every nerve in his body sprang to life.

"I know you're here, Miss Atwood," he whispered into the gloom before locking the door. "I saw you enter."

Silence.

"Sybil?" Desperation forced him to use her given name. Oh, but he loved how it sounded. "Sybil. We shouldn't be alone in here."

The curtain twitched. The mere sight of her peering through the gap in the material sent blood racing through his body at a rapid rate.

"What the devil are you doing upstairs?" He kept his voice low. "We agreed you would remain with Mrs Cavanagh for the entire evening."

She slipped out from behind the curtain, and he rather wished she hadn't. The muscles in his abdomen clenched at the sight of that damned green silk clinging to every lush curve.

"I saw you mounting the stairs and wished to snatch a moment alone." The silk swished as she moved towards him. "But you were engaged in a clinch with your mistress, and so I thought to wait in here."

"I was not engaged in a clinch. And Mrs Sinclair is no longer my mistress."

"So why did the widow look like you'd ravished her in the alcove?" Jealousy weaved through her tone.

"Newberry ravished her in a bedchamber." Though it must have been a rather quick affair. Nothing like the long hours he'd spend lavishing Miss Atwood's body. "He used the opportunity to question her about the journals, about Talbot, about us."

Us.

The word settled in his chest, so warm, so damnably satisfying.

"Us?" She swallowed deeply, drawing his eye to that teasing

pearl choker and the milky-white column of her throat. Lord, how he longed to settle his mouth there, longed to feel the rapid beat of her pulse against his lips.

"Mrs Sinclair believes I have cast her aside because I have set my cap elsewhere." Her essence reached for him like sensual fingers in the dark, gripping his coat, pulling him forward, forcing him to close the gap between them. "That I've cast her aside because I want to bed you."

"Me? What gave her that idea?"

Lucius couldn't help but smile. He was to blame. Sometimes lust was hard to hide. "Not what, but who. Newberry must have mentioned our conversation at the auction. I defended your character far too quickly."

She pursed her lips. "Only out of respect for my father."

"Out of respect for you." Respect was the only thing preventing him from speaking openly about his need for this woman.

Her emerald eyes twinkled in the darkness. "You *were* prowling around the dance floor like a wolf assessing his prey. Lord Newberry doesn't know that you promised to protect me. He must have assumed you were jealous."

Jealousy had flooded his body with bitter poison. "I sensed he made you uneasy."

"Lord Newberry is an odious creature." She shuddered. "Threatening women comes naturally to him. He did his utmost to frighten me."

"Frighten you? How?" He made a mental note to pounce on the lord in the darkness. To teach him the true meaning of terror.

"He suggested someone might kidnap me from bed and lock me away in an asylum."

"Kidnap you?" Suspicion flared. Perhaps Newberry hired the solemn-looking Scot to assist in his duplicity. "Kidnap you because you have an interest in your father's books?"

The moment her gaze dropped to her slippers, he knew she'd given Newberry some provocation. "I said I had read my father's journals. I said they contain more than scientific theories and practically accused him of deception and betrayal."

What the devil?

"Have you lost your mind?" It took strength not to raise his voice and punch the air. He stepped closer, and she shuffled back against the row of bookcases. "If Newberry is guilty of a crime, you can be damn sure his next task will involve getting rid of you."

"What is the point of firing a measly arrow at the castle walls? I thought it better to load the trebuchet and hurl a fireball over the battlements."

"A fireball!" His mouth dropped open.

Miss Atwood smiled and tapped him under the chin. "There is sense in my madness. This way, we will force the villain to attack. It is far better than waiting like sitting ducks."

Sitting ducks?

Her comment hit a nerve.

Did she think he wanted to play the rational investigator? Did she think he enjoyed being the pragmatic one? No, he wanted to throw caution to the wind. Take risks. Dance with danger.

He braced his hands on the bookshelf above her head, locking her in his masculine prison, pressing his body closer than he had ever dared before. "Being vigilant doesn't make me a damn duck."

Miss Atwood laughed nervously, her hot breath breezing across his cheek. Oh, she was so achingly close. "Your promise to my father has made you too cautious. This matter calls for a little recklessness. It calls for the devil-may-care attitude you display in the ballroom."

Oh, so she wanted reckless.

"I'm the *ton*'s most scandalous rogue. I can be irresponsible." Indeed, his ropes of restraint were already frayed. A hint of encouragement from Miss Atwood would snap the bindings in two. "Don't taunt me about being impulsive when we're locked in a dark room. Not when I'm as randy as the devil. Not when I'm fighting against taking what I so desperately crave."

Long lashes fluttered against her porcelain skin. "But you don't find me attractive in that way."

Damn, how could an intelligent woman be so blind?

"Madam, I find everything about you so damnably appealing." He moved closer until those magnificent breasts were squashed against his waistcoat. He was already harder than he'd been in his life. Mother of all saints. If he didn't kiss her now, he might die. "If you don't say no, Miss Atwood, I'm going to devour your mouth. I'm going to plunder you senseless."

She stared at his lips as her breath grew short and shallow.

"Say it, Sybil. Say no. Say it now before we enter into something neither of us—"

She pressed her mouth to his in a soft, sweet kiss. So innocent. So sensual. A rush of euphoria robbed him of rational thought. The rehearsed skills needed to seduce a woman abandoned him, too.

This was something new.

Something exquisite.

Something precious.

Abruptly, she broke contact and pressed her fingers to her lips in shock. "Forgive me. Heavens. My insatiable curiosity got the better of me."

"Is that all it was—a quest for knowledge? If all you want is an education, I'm afraid I cannot oblige."

Silence ensued, though it did nothing to dampen his ardour.

"I can't seem to control these strange feelings when I'm in your company." She struggled to hold his gaze. "I don't know what it means, but I wanted to feel your mouth on mine."

He wasn't sure what it meant either, but it didn't stop him saying, "Would you care to feel my mouth on yours again?" She replied by leaning forward and tilting her chin, but he tapped his finger on her lips. "It's my turn to kiss you."

When she nodded, he pinned her to the bookcase, let her feel the power of his body as he angled his head to feast. He rocked against her as he coaxed her lips apart and slipped his tongue slowly into her wet mouth.

Holy mother Mary.

The smell of roses filled his head. She tasted of innocence mingled with hidden secrets and untamed passion. Her powerful essence penetrated his steely composure, seeping into his body to stir Lucifer's lust. A ravenous hunger surfaced. He tried to maintain control—tried to drink with care—but he had no defence against her potent allure. Not when she arched her back and moaned into his mouth. Not when her hands snaked inside his coat and clutched his hips.

Passion's fire blazed.

Retreat proved impossible.

He needed to strip her naked. He needed to indulge every wild and wicked fantasy. He needed to stroke her sex and cradle her as she shuddered and cried his name.

Before he knew what was happening, they were writhing against the bookcase with reckless abandon. They couldn't open their mouths wide enough to feed the flames, couldn't taste each other deeply enough to ease the heavy ache.

The bookcase shook. Volumes fell to the floor with a thud. Their ragged pants filled the air as they clawed at each other's clothes. He stole under her gown and gripped her thigh. The need to push deep into her body left his cock throbbing. He wanted to touch her, fuck her, love her.

"Say no." He forced the words from his lips before kissing her neck just below her choker, before inhaling the perfume of her hair. "Say no, Sybil. Say no now." He was stroking her thigh, caressing her bare buttock. "I don't have the strength to stop."

"I can't stop, either," she panted.

"I don't think you have the measure of the situation." The words kicked logic from its lazy slumber. Still, as her head fell back against the bookcase, he couldn't resist settling his mouth to the sweet spot just behind her ear.

"What was that?" Her sudden gasp startled him.

He groaned against her neck. "Loath me to point out the obvious, but I'm aroused to the point of madness."

"Not *that*," she said, pushing gently on his chest. She seemed comfortable touching him now. "That clicking sound."

Panic forced him to snatch his hand from her thigh as his gaze shot to the door.

"It wasn't the door, but something on the bookcase behind me."

He almost said to hell with the damn bookcase, but she forced him to ignore his throbbing erection and examine the shelves. While numerous volumes had fallen to the floor during their amorous encounter, the ones on three shelves were all positioned at the same odd angle.

Sybil placed her finger on the headband of a red leather volume. "*Confessions* by Rousseau. How apt." She attempted to push it back into position, but the whole row of books moved. "There it is again, Lucius, that odd clicking sound."

His curiosity piqued, Lucius ran his hands over the volumes. What looked like a row of books to the naked eye was nothing more than false spines.

Placing his hands flat against them, he pressed hard and heard the click again. A quick tug on the spines resulted in the whole panel swinging forward to reveal a secret cupboard.

They both peered into the hidden compartment containing an odd assortment of objects—silk gloves, powder and rouge, a miniature portrait of a woman in a white gown, a small red box. The only items that might belong to Sir Melrose were official-looking papers and a brown leather pocketbook wallet.

"So, this is where the Cramptons hide their valuables," Lucius said. He removed the wallet and discovered vowels to the value of five thousand pounds belonging to a Mrs Dunwoody.

"Dunwoody?" Sybil muttered, glancing at the crisp notes in his hand. "I don't know anyone of that name."

"No." Lucius closed the wallet and returned it to the shelf. He took the papers and read the first few pages. "These are the deeds to a property in Dumfriesshire." Again, it meant nothing. But then it occurred to him that the solemn man hailed from Scotland.

Coincidence perhaps?

Sybil took the portrait and studied it while Lucius fiddled with the lock on the red box. "I must say, the lady in the miniature has a rather masculine jaw."

Lucius stole a quick look at the portrait. "That's because it's a man dressed in women's clothes." Indeed, something about the feminine objects told him they didn't belong to Lady Crampton.

"It's a rather odd thing to hide in a secret cupboard."

"It's an odd thing to own, but exactly the thing one would hide from prying eyes."

Lucius picked the lock on the box with the thin metal implement he'd taken from his pocket. He raised the lid expecting to find pearl earrings or a diamond brooch, not pencil sketches of naked men.

Shock rendered him speechless.

Sybil gasped and clutched his arm. "Why would Sir Melrose keep sketches of naked men?"

"Why indeed?"

Lucius removed the expert sketches drawn on the back of invitation cards. On the reverse were the words *Gorget's Garrett*, but no date or address. He flicked through the drawings until one large anatomical feature caught his attention.

"Devil take it. Look closely at the image." He handed the sketch to Sybil. "Tell me what you see."

"Is that supposed to be funny?" A crimson blush stained her cheeks, and he knew she couldn't resist scanning the entire drawing. "Well, the large chin makes him look somewhat like Mr Warner, your father's steward, though I'm sure he would be mortified by the similarity."

"Interesting." Lucius took the image and slipped it into the inside pocket of his coat. Then he returned the box to the cupboard and closed the door.

"You think that is Mr Warner, don't you?"

"The likeness is uncanny." Too uncanny to be a coincidence. "As such, it might prove useful in our quest to find a killer."

"Collecting odd items doesn't make a man a murderer," she said. "We've found nothing to suggest Sir Melrose is guilty of a crime. There's nothing to prove they belong to him."

"While you could argue these items belong to Lady Crampton, I doubt it." Lucius gathered the fallen books and placed them back on the shelves. "We'll discuss our next course of action when we return to Bronygarth. Can you persuade the Cavanaghs to leave early?"

"Lord Newberry insisted I dance another waltz."

"Newberry can go to hell."

"Then I shall tell Cassandra I feel hot, a little faint."

Lucius arched a brow. "It's said I have that effect on women."

With a sudden gasp, she patted her hair. "Do I look like you've ravished me in the library?"

He tucked a loose tendril behind her ear, fought the need to kiss her again, to cover her with his naked body. "No one will notice. Your hair is always a little unruly. Come." He moved to the door and unlocked it with the skeleton key. "We shouldn't leave together. I shall exit first, distract anyone hovering in the vicinity. When you hear me cough twice, you'll know it's safe to leave."

Though Sybil nodded, he knew nerves formed the basis of her tight smile. Guilt should have gnawed away at his insides, but he was not sorry. He would risk the noose to spend another few minutes locked in her passionate embrace.

Sybil hid in the darkness while he eased the door from the jamb. He might have taken a surreptitious glance along the corridor had the imposing figure of Damian Wycliff not stepped forward to block the doorway.

CHAPTER ELEVEN

"Leave now while the corridor is empty." The deep masculine growl reached Sybil's ears, yet it was not Lucius Daventry who spoke.

Panic held her rooted to the spot.

She daren't peer around the jamb.

"Follow me downstairs, Daventry," the angry gentleman continued, though his voice was almost drowned out by the laughter spilling out of the private drawing room. "My wife will attend to Miss Atwood and escort her back to the ballroom."

Sybil waited for Lucius' steadfast denial, his bitter retort, but he simply said, "Very well." He stepped back from the doorway, looked at her and whispered, "Remain calm. I shall meet you downstairs once I've dealt with Wycliff."

Wycliff?

Oh, Lord!

"Now, Daventry."

Sybil's breath quickened upon hearing Mr Wycliff's murderous whisper. People said he was as skilled in combat as Lucius Daventry, said he bore the scars from numerous battles, said he thought nothing of meeting a gentleman on the common at dawn.

A sickening dread shot to her throat when Lucius left the room. A few seconds later Mrs Wycliff entered, her ebony hair fashioned in the latest style, her sapphire and diamond necklace complementing her midnight blue gown.

"Miss Atwood," the lady began in the compassionate tone of a woman who had survived many scandalous situations. "I see your obsession with Mr Daventry is still very much your focus."

Two weeks ago, Sybil had sat with the Wycliffs in Cassandra's drawing room and told them about spying on Mr Daventry, about her urgent need to attend the auction. Then, she had thought Mr Daventry a heartless devil, too.

"It is not an obsession," Sybil corrected.

"No, you're just desperate to purchase your father's journals from a man who enjoys playing games."

"Mr Daventry has no intention of selling the journals and has expressed his deep regret over the misunderstanding."

A smile played at the corners of Mrs Wycliff's mouth. "Regret so deep he had to lock you in a dark library to make his point."

"It's a complicated situation." One of a secret society, of murder, treachery and a sworn oath. "One you wouldn't understand."

Mrs Wycliff's smile deepened. "I know what it's like to fall under a rogue's spell, Miss Atwood."

"Mr Daventry is not a rogue."

"And neither is Mr Wycliff." The lady tugged her long white gloves up past her elbows and then offered her hand. "Now, while the men talk of threats and violence, let us speak calmly and honestly. Walk with me."

Sybil hesitated. But what choice did she have?

She linked arms with the lady—once known as the Scarlet Widow throughout the *ton*—and they descended the stairs.

"Mr Daventry will never commit to one woman," Mrs Wycliff said, leading Sybil through the hall towards the supper room. "The man lacks integrity. His only interest is his latest conquest."

Sybil stiffened. "Did people not say the same about Mr Wycliff once?"

"They did," the lady had to admit.

"And yet I have never seen a man as loyal or committed."

Mrs Wycliff gave a satisfied sigh. "Damian is everything a woman could ask for in a husband."

"And do you not credit me with your intelligence, Mrs Wycliff? I am capable of discerning Mr Daventry's character and deciding if he is suitable company."

If only she could offer examples of his resounding loyalty.

If only she could explain how he strived to keep his vow.

"Are you in love with him?" Mrs Wycliff asked bluntly. "Everyone believes you hardly know one another. I'm not convinced. As Mr Daventry strode towards the stairs with my husband, he said that protecting you was his priority."

Sybil shrugged. "What can I say? The man you think you know is nothing like the real man behind the façade. Mr Daventry saved my life."

Mrs Wycliff snatched two glasses of champagne from the footman's tray and handed one to Sybil. "You didn't answer my question, Miss Atwood. Are you in love with Mr Daventry?"

The memory of Lucius' hard body pressing her against the bookcase left her breathless. The memory of him stalking around the dance floor, all dark and devilish, sent delicious shivers to her toes. She trusted him implicitly. Admired his mind. Lusted after his body.

But love?

"I don't know. Love develops over time," she answered truthfully before sipping her champagne. "But I have the utmost respect for him, would defend him with my last breath."

That seemed to satisfy Mrs Wycliff, whose assured smile remained constant even while drinking her champagne. "Love can happen in an instant. For me, it happened over the course of three days. I knew I loved Damian the moment I realised I saw him as no one else did. The road was rather bumpy after that, but one cannot fight against the power of true love."

Mrs Wycliff's words struck a chord with Sybil.

"Now," the lady continued, placing their glasses on the supper table. "Let us find the men before one of them is carted off to Newgate and charged with murder, but not before we have eased Cassandra's fears."

A pang of guilt made Sybil sigh. "I shouldn't have slipped away, not without offering an explanation, but ..."

"But you simply had to speak to Mr Daventry, and Benedict would never have let you go alone."

"Something like that."

"He sent Damian to search for you. It would have roused suspicion had they been seen scouring the upstairs rooms looking for their charge."

"After what happened to Cassandra at Lord Craven's ball, I should have had more consideration for her feelings, but ..."

"But when your mind is consumed with thoughts of Mr Daventry, you can think of nothing else."

Mrs Wycliff was extremely insightful.

"Something like that."

They found the Cavanaghs waiting near the terrace. Sybil offered a sincere apology, though made no mention of the illicit encounter in the library. Cassandra was simply relieved she had been found safe and well. Mrs Wycliff insisted she would play chaperone, and they left the couple to enjoy a waltz.

"How do you know Mr Wycliff and Mr Daventry are outside?" Sybil said as Mrs Wycliff led her back into the grand hall.

"Neither man wishes to make his grievance known. There is only one place they might conduct a secret conversation at short notice—Damian's carriage."

A storm was brewing. The temperature had plummeted, and so they retrieved their cloaks from the liveried attendant and headed down the steps onto Maddox Street. Rows of carriages lined the pavements, but Mrs Wycliff directed Sybil towards the mews.

"With so many people here tonight, I'm surprised Sir Melrose granted your husband use of the mews."

Mrs Wycliff smiled. "Damian would never be without access to a vehicle. He paid Sir Melrose's coachman handsomely for the pleasure of keeping it here."

They headed through the cobbled yard lit by braziers and hanging lanterns. From the shadows of the stables, grooms and coachmen watched them hurrying towards the black unmarked carriage.

Mrs Wycliff glanced up at the box seat. "I presume my husband is inside the vehicle, Alcock?"

"Aye, ma'am." The sturdy woman sitting atop the box in coachman's garb doffed her hat and said, "Mr Wycliff's got another gentleman in there with him." She leaned forward and whispered, "I've not heard the shouts for a few minutes now. Happen one of 'em is dead."

Mrs Wycliff tutted at her servant. "I can assure you they are both very much alive." She ushered Sybil to the carriage door. "Forgive my coachwoman. Alcock often expects the worst where my husband is concerned." The lady rapped on the window. "It's me, Damian."

"Enter," came the terse reply.

Mrs Wycliff opened the door, and her husband dropped the step.

Sybil climbed into the vehicle and settled next to Lucius.

He forced a smile, though his storm-grey eyes looked ready to unleash a violent tempest. "Did anyone see you leave the library?"

"Not that I'm aware." While she longed to see the flames of desire dancing there, she found the dangerous gleam surprisingly attractive. "People were too busy playing blind man's bluff in the drawing room to notice."

Mrs Wycliff closed the carriage door and gripped her husband's thigh as she moved to sit beside him. "Well, I'm glad to see no one has suffered an injury."

"No visible injury," Lucius snapped, his voice barely masking his rage, "yet I find myself reeling at your blatant interference."

"Do not speak to my wife in that tone," Mr Wycliff protested. "She is merely trying to defuse the tension."

"And Mr Daventry was merely inferring that we had the situation under control," Sybil said, feeling an overwhelming need to defend the gentleman.

Mr Wycliff snorted. "When it comes to mastering control, Miss Atwood, I believe you fall dreadfully short."

"Do not speak to her in that tone," Mr Daventry countered.

"She is merely providing clarity. Say what you will about me, but do not dare make assumptions about Miss Atwood's character."

Mr Wycliff's eyes grew wide, though he appeared more intrigued than offended. He folded his muscular arms across his chest. "Tell me, Miss Atwood. Is everything Daventry said about your father true?"

"Clever bastard," Lucius muttered beneath his breath as he lounged back and draped his arm across the back of the seat.

Sybil wasn't sure how to respond. Lucius would have told some semblance of the truth, but he would never mention his work for the Order.

"That would depend on what Mr Daventry told you, sir," she said to give her time to form an appropriate reply.

Lucius cleared his throat. "I have explained our reason for attending the ball tonight. I have told Wycliff about my suspicions regarding your father's death. That on occasion, Atticus liked to play Bow Street investigator."

"I see." She took a moment to choose her words carefully before turning her attention back to Mr Wycliff. "Everything Mr Daventry said is true. My father fought for reform. He believed the law served the rich, not the poor. Certain cases in the newspaper drew his attention, and he often conducted his own investigations. It was a hobby of sorts."

Mr Wycliff stared through coal-black eyes. "While commendable, that's a rather dangerous hobby, Miss Atwood. Still, I fail to see the connection between a distinguished man of science and a scandalous rogue."

"Is that really any of your business, sir?"

A glint of admiration flashed in the gentleman's eyes. "You have gumption, Miss Atwood. I'll give you that."

"Enough gumption to decide whether I want to spend time in a locked library with Mr Daventry." The memory of their illicit encounter brought heat to her cheeks. It didn't help that Mr Daventry took the opportunity to stroke her nape.

"Cassandra was worried," Mrs Wycliff said calmly. "You know what happened to her at Lord Craven's ball. She would never forgive herself if something happened to you while in her care."

Sybil's heart sank. The last thing she wanted was to hurt Cassandra. Her poor friend had suffered enough.

"We were desperate," Lucius interjected. "While I hate to sound dramatic, our lives are in danger. Under normal circumstances, I cannot imagine Miss Atwood would ever neglect her friends."

Mr Wycliff turned to his wife. "Do you see what's happening here?"

The lady smiled. "With astonishing clarity, which is why I think we should offer our assistance."

Lucius lowered his arm and straightened. "We have managed well enough on our own."

"From what you've told me, Daventry, Atticus Atwood passed almost a year ago and you're still searching for the culprit."

Lucius sucked in a sharp breath. "Months passed before I could examine Atticus' notes. Months before I began piecing the information together. Other matters have slowed proceedings, matters I am in no position to discuss."

He spoke of protecting her, protecting the men who served the Order. Preventing them from suffering the same fate as poor Mr Proctor.

"So, the bastard son of a duke is out to avenge the death of an eminent scientist," Mr Wycliff mused. "I'm still baffled by your connection."

"They met when Mr Daventry was at school," Sybil said. Admiration filled her chest when she glanced at Lucius. "My father was an excellent judge of character. He came to respect Mr Daventry a great deal."

Lucius swallowed deeply. "Atticus was my friend. The only person who visited me at school during my lengthy and harrowing ordeal in Yorkshire."

The atmosphere in the carriage shifted.

All tension dissipated.

The Wycliffs looked at each other, understanding and pity swimming in their eyes. The gentleman brought his wife's hand to his lips and pressed a kiss to her knuckles.

"Well," Mrs Wycliff began when her husband finally released his grip. "I know what it is like to sit alone in a seminary and have no one come visit. Your actions stem from loyalty, loyalty to the one person who cared."

"School can be an unpleasant place for the illegitimate sons of the aristocracy." Mr Wycliff clearly spoke from experience. "Do you stand by your earlier declaration?"

Lucius cast Sybil a sidelong glance. "I will do whatever it takes to protect Miss Atwood."

Mr Wycliff seemed to find something amusing when he said, "And if marriage is the only means of saving her reputation?"

Marriage!

"Sir," Sybil began, laughing at the absurdity of the question. Lucius Daventry was already married, married to the Order. He'd openly admitted that work was his life. "There is no need to—"

"Yes," came Lucius' steadfast reply. "Should the need arise, and Miss Atwood is willing."

Sybil's mouth dropped open. Yet while she found the notion ludicrous, the possibility of sharing her life with such a passionate, intelligent man roused a strange longing.

"Good," Mr Wycliff replied. "Let me make you aware of our resources should you need assistance. You've heard of a gaming hell called The Silver Serpent."

"Dermot Flannery's establishment."

"Dermot is as close as kin and can be called upon when needed."

Lucius seemed impressed. "Flannery has the respect of the rogues in the rookeries, and the lords whose vowels he holds."

"As such, he is extremely resourceful." Mr Wycliff paused. "As you know, Mrs Crandall is fond of Cavanagh and is willing to negotiate when it comes to trading secrets. Assuming you have a secret worth trading. And you know my father, I'm sure. Blackbeck is a fountain of knowledge when it comes to the history of those in the upper echelons."

Sybil narrowed her gaze. "And why would you help us, sir?"

Mr Wycliff smirked. "As sons who've suffered as a result of our illegitimacy, Daventry and I share a kinship. And I like honest men, Miss Atwood."

Silence ensued, though Sybil could almost hear the cogs turning in Lucius' mind. Eventually he said, "A man died during a riot in Smithfield Market, a Mr Cribb who lodged above the china dealer in Saffron Hill. I've spoken to his neighbours, but like his death, the man's life is a mystery. If Flannery could use his connections to discover anything pertinent, it would be an immense help."

"Consider it done."

"And I'm curious whether Flannery has ever heard of the term *Gorget's Garrett*."

Mr Wycliff inclined his head. "I shall visit Flannery tonight and make enquiries."

"Can I ask that you escort Miss Atwood home?"

Panic tightened Sybil's chest.

Surely Lucius still planned for her to stay with him at Bronygarth.

"There's every chance Cassandra will visit me in Half Moon Street tomorrow," she said, attempting to remind him of their prearranged plan. "Perhaps you need to offer the Wycliffs more information regarding my whereabouts."

Lucius grimaced but gave a curt nod. He glanced at the gentleman seated opposite. "Hired thugs tried to kidnap Miss Atwood some nights ago. Consequently, she is staying at a secret location. Should anyone call after midnight this evening, they will not find her in Half Moon Street." He paused. "I assume I can trust your discretion in this matter."

"You can," Mrs Wycliff quickly replied when a disapproving grumble escaped her husband. "And yes, we will see Miss Atwood home."

"May I ask that you remain with her until my coachman calls?"

The lady smiled. "You may, and we will."

Sybil silently groaned. Midnight felt like days away. Perhaps Mrs Wycliff was right. Perhaps she was a little obsessed with Lucius Daventry. Surely it wasn't normal to ache for a man's company.

"Then you have my utmost gratitude," Lucius replied. "Miss Atwood's safety is extremely important to me."

Mrs Wycliff glanced at her husband. "I think that is plain for all to see."

CHAPTER TWELVE

Minutes had passed since Damian Wycliff's burly coachwoman flicked the reins and guided the carriage out of the mews. Yet Lucius stood, staring through the soft glow from the lit braziers, trying to make sense of the internal chaos.

He held his fists clenched so tight it would take effort to unfurl his fingers. His ragged breaths sent puffs of white mist into the night air—the smoke of fury's flames. Grooms and stable hands working in the cobblestone alley froze when Lucius blurted a vile curse.

No one dared utter a word.

No one dared approach.

Not since his youth had he been forced to account for his actions. What he did with Sybil Atwood in the privacy of a locked library was his own damned affair. And yet fragments of logical thought said he should be grateful, grateful there were people who cared for Sybil's welfare.

To make matters worse, the Wycliffs had offered their assistance—as if they possessed more skill than those working the murky streets solving crimes. But having access to a man as knowledgeable as Dermot Flannery was worth the trouble of dealing with Damian Wycliff's arrogance.

Lucius might have spent the next few minutes considering why Sir Melrose had trinkets hidden in a secret cupboard. He might have considered Newberry's vile threats. Might have spouted another vicious profanity. But the only event that demanded his consideration was the passionate kiss he had shared with Sybil Atwood.

Merciful Lord. It had taken every ounce of strength he had not to settle between her soft thighs and drive long and deep into the only place he belonged. During sleepless nights, when woken by a nightmare, he'd often imagined taking her in his arms and delving into her warm, wet mouth.

Nothing prepared him for the reality.

Even now, her captivating scent clung to his clothes, obliterating the acrid aroma of damp stables, piss and wood smoke. When he moistened his lips, he could still taste the sweet essence that drove him wild.

Upon their return to Bronygarth, he would need to maintain some distance. Their priority was to find the person responsible for Atticus' death. To ensure Miss Atwood could live life without the constant fear of threats.

Those thoughts proved sobering.

Sobering enough to bring his mind back to the investigation. He still had time to search for Newberry, time to discover why the lord had bedded Larissa, why he was prying into Lucius' affairs. But since deciding to prove Atticus was murdered, something always happened to hinder his plans.

Now, the whisper of his name from the shadows of a carriage house stole his attention. The sibilant sound brought an image of Larissa Sinclair. No doubt the widow had followed him from the house, keen to discover if Miss Atwood was to be his next mistress.

Anger flared anew.

He straightened and stormed across the yard towards the open wooden doors. "What do you want, Larissa?"

The shuffling of footsteps in the darkness preceded the appearance of a woman shrouded in a thick blue cloak. Beneath the raised hood, it was impossible to distinguish her face. The visible black locks should have confirmed his suspicion. Only when she stepped closer did he notice the vivid streak of grey.

"I didn't mean to startle you." The fact the woman's soothing tone was so opposed to Larissa's serpent hiss proved unnerving. She took a hesitant step towards him. "But I could not risk being seen by your friends."

"Do I know you?" Lucius narrowed his gaze.

Her light laugh carried a nervous tension. "I should hope you do, though it has been far too long since I took your hand and sang you a lullaby."

A lullaby?

He stilled. "Is this some wicked devil's trick to confuse my mind?"

"A devil's trick? No, Lucius. It is a mother's way of attempting to greet her son."

Time crashed to a halt.

Shock rendered him rigid.

The word *mother* gripped his tongue with desperate fingers, for he lacked the strength and courage to let it fall.

She edged closer, craned her neck and peered out into the mews before lowering her hood. "My, how you've grown."

His heart thumped so hard he couldn't breathe. How could this be? Julia Fontaine had been murdered in a jealous rage, buried in an unmarked grave in the grounds of Bideford Park.

"I thought you were dead."

The duke had said as much.

Skilled in prophecy, Lucius had predicted Sybil would sneak into his house at night, predicted someone would attack them on their return to Half Moon Street, predicted that at some point he would fall victim to her charms. But he could never have predicted this.

"Is that what your father told you?" His mother remained in the carriage house, and Lucius was forced to join her there. "You poor boy."

Disbelief made him study every facial feature, every blemish, every line. Despite trying to keep his mother's image alive in his mind, the picture had grown hazy over the years. It didn't help that his father had torn down her portrait and slashed the canvas to shreds.

"I'm no longer a boy." He hated that she'd called him that—

the word his father used as a weapon to belittle him, to strip him of his identity.

"No." She released a weary sigh. "It's been twenty years since we last spoke."

"Almost twenty-one."

Discomfort clawed at his shoulders. In his fantasy, he had imagined rushing into her embrace, imagined her stroking his hair, saying that she had never meant to leave him. Everything felt right. Perfect. As if the bond had never been broken. The ties never severed. The love never lost.

"I understand your reticence," she said, and he wondered why her voice was devoid of guilt. "It's been a long time. You must have many questions."

It wasn't the thousand questions that left him fraught with confusion. He had expected to see a young, attractive woman with vibrant eyes and porcelain skin. A perfect image of the woman who'd loved him and left him. *Fool.* This woman's gaunt face spoke of hardship. Her wide blue eyes carried a deep, abiding sadness.

"Have you been living in London all this time?"

Surely not. Despite knowing he was the sole beneficiary of his grandmother's estate, he had searched every workhouse, every brothel, studied every actress in every play. He had stared at every lord's mistress, hoping, praying that his father's cruel words amounted to nothing but rotten lies.

"No. When I left, I went north."

"You were the one who left?" He could not hide his surprise. "The duke didn't have you removed from the house?" In his distant memory, he'd pictured her clinging to the door jamb, begging to stay.

She kicked at the straw strewn over the cobblestones. "I fled in fear of my life. Your father ... he had a terrible temper." She tucked her hair behind her ears, drawing attention to the small scar across her cheekbone. "I'd thought to come back, but the duke ... he made it impossible for me to return."

As a child, Lucius didn't care which parent started the fight. He didn't care who was to blame for their arguments—as long as they were together. A family. Now, he felt the need to punish someone for causing his pain.

But who?

The duke was an invalid on his deathbed.

Julia Fontaine looked to have suffered enough.

"Why seek me now?" he said, shocked at the coldness in his voice. Was this not the woman he had spent years mourning? Was this not the person who could fill the gaping hole in his heart?

"Surely it's obvious." Her watery laugh held no amusement. "I heard the duke is confined to his bed. They say he cannot speak. They say he lacks the strength to hold a nib and scrawl his name."

Perhaps it was Atticus' influence that made him wary and led him to ask, "Who told you of his illness? To my knowledge, few people are aware of the duke's condition."

"Does it matter?" She paused to cough into a handkerchief. "What matters is that after such a lengthy separation, we can be together now. What can he do? He cannot instruct his men to hunt me down. He cannot use devious methods to keep me away."

"Then why are you hiding in the shadows?"

His mother laughed again, though the sound carried mild annoyance. "Must you question everything? Are you not pleased to see me, Lucius?"

He should have been ecstatic.

Yet for some reason, he felt detached.

Despite knowing beyond a shadow of doubt that this woman was Julia Fontaine—his missing mother—he did not feel the instant connection.

"I thought you were dead," he repeated. "It's a shock to find you're living and breathing and not buried at Bideford Park."

She closed the gap between them and gently touched his upper arm. Oh, he wanted to feel that rush of unconditional love —a warm burst of happiness—but it didn't come.

He waited.

Nothing.

He brushed his anxiety aside.

These things took time.

"Perhaps I might come home with you this evening," she said, hope springing in her doleful eyes. "If we must talk of the past, let us do so before the comfort of a warm fire, in the privacy of your drawing room. Away from your father's spies."

He hesitated.

An internal conflict raged. A war between a lonely boy's hopes and dreams and the responsibility that came with being a man. What was he to do? Trust in a fantasy or something tangible?

"I have a prior engagement that cannot be postponed." Nothing, not even the untimely arrival of his mother, would force him to leave Sybil alone at Bronygarth. Nothing would prevent him seeking justice for Atticus, the person who had given his friendship and support. "Give me your direction, and perhaps we might meet tomorrow evening."

Her mouth thinned into a bitter smile. "Don't you trust me, Lucius? Has your father poisoned your mind against me?"

This was where he might have faltered, might have tried to reassure this stranger who had disappeared so long ago. But over the last few years, he'd learned to look at most situations objectively.

Unless the subject was Sybil Atwood.

Then he lost all sense and reason.

"I have spent twenty years wondering what happened to you." He had spent most of that time carrying the guilt, taking the blame. "One more day won't make a difference."

She muttered incoherently, clearly displeased at his response.

"Forgive me if you find my manner a little cold," he said, feeling the need to explain, to make her understand just how her absence had affected him. "But when one has spent so long alone, one develops a need for caution."

His mother touched his arm again. "You don't need to be alone anymore, Lucius."

He should have pictured a family scene, laughter around the dining table where Julia Fontaine spoke of her son's quirky habits as a boy. Instead, he pictured himself in bed with Sybil Atwood, all tangled limbs and clasped hands as they struggled to catch their breath.

Lucius forced a smile. "Are you staying with friends? A lodging house, or hotel?"

"I'm staying out of town. Old habits die hard, and I fear your father will make a sudden recovery and learn of my unexpected arrival." She paused. "I followed you from Brook Street tonight. A friend told me you live there."

Strange that he hadn't noticed her lingering in the shadows. He was usually quite thorough when it came to scanning the street for potential threats.

"I own the house, though have never received an allowance from the duke." Oddly, he had always hoped his refusal to accept the devil's charity would make his mother proud. "I might have bought a commission had it not been for my grandmother's legacy."

Her dull blue eyes widened. "The duchess despised me. I'm surprised to hear she made provisions for you."

"I speak of your mother, Katharine Fontaine, not the duchess."

"My mother?" Her look of surprise turned to disbelief. Perhaps Katharine Fontaine had believed her daughter was dead, too. Perhaps they were estranged. Perhaps Julia knew nothing of his grandmother's gift. "I had not spoken to her for some years before her death."

"I should like to learn more about her when we meet tomorrow." The solicitor had been vague in offering explanations for the bequest. "Come to Brook Street at eight."

She inclined her head. "Until tomorrow then."

"Shall I hail a hackney? A woman should not walk the streets alone at night."

"You're the gentleman your father never could be," she said, her smile barely hiding a terrible sadness. "But my friend is waiting in a carriage on Swallow Street."

"Then I shall walk with you."

"No." She seemed flustered. "It's a short walk. You know how the gossips are. Should anyone see us together, your father will hear of it before the first cockcrow."

"Then I shall have someone else accompany you." Lucius' conscience would not allow her to walk alone. He bid his mother good night, gestured to a groom and paid him to escort the lady to Swallow Street. Upon the groom's return, Lucius asked, "Was there a carriage waiting?"

"Not a carriage, a hackney, sir."

"Did you see if there was anyone else inside?"

The scrawny fellow shrugged. "A man called to the jarvey, but I didn't see him."

Lucius thanked the groom, who was keen to return to his work.

Again, Lucius found himself standing, staring into the dark, replaying what might have occurred in Julia's life during those missing decades. The thoughts were as frustrating as not knowing whether she was alive or dead. Painting his father as the wicked villain was easy. His mother's frightened face and thin frame marked her as the victim. Yet Atticus had advised him not to create stories in his mind to suit his mood or purpose.

Releasing a loud sigh, he strode closer to the brazier, pulled out his pocket watch and glanced at the time. He could go in search of Newberry. A fight would ease the tension in his shoulders. He could go to Bideford Park, barge into his father's chamber and torment him with news of Julia Fontaine.

Instead, he strode out of the mews and headed towards his carriage parked on George Street. Furnis woke from his nap as soon as Lucius opened the carriage door.

"Back to Brook Street, sir?"

"No. I wish to return to Bronygarth. Can you take me to the Wild Hare to collect my horse and be back in time to fetch Miss Atwood?"

He would not leave Sybil waiting with the Wycliffs, worrying about what might have happened. He would not have the Wycliffs think him negligent or tardy.

"Aye, if I drive like the devil's chasing our tail."

"Is there any other way to drive?" Lucius said, recalling Miss Atwood's comment that he should be more reckless.

The coachman snorted. "I don't suppose there is, sir."

CHAPTER THIRTEEN

Typical! On a night when Sybil was more desperate than ever to reach Bronygarth, the journey was plagued by problems.

The storm had broken. A forceful wind whistled through the carriage. The vehicle rocked violently on its springs, swaying as if carried on turbulent waves. Rain lashed down from the heavens, a torrent that swamped the narrow track winding up through the woods to Mr Daventry's haunted castle.

The coachman's cries of encouragement to the horses fought with the roar of powerful gusts and the rumble of thunder.

"Lord above!" Sybil gripped the overhead strap yet struggled to remain seated. She had abandoned all attempts to warm her feet on the bricks.

Rain as hard as pebbles struck the windows like the devil's stoning. Beyond she could see nothing but towering trees, swaying shadows and a never-ending gloom.

Surely Lucius wasn't out scouting the road. She doubted anyone would be foolish enough to follow them in this damnable weather.

Sybil had no time to contemplate the matter further. A loud cry sliced through the wind's mournful moan. The carriage lost momentum, slowing and then stopping as the wheels became bound in the mire.

Minutes passed.

Minutes of shouts and barked commands.

Then the carriage door flew open.

Lucius Daventry stood there, an imposing figure in the darkness, his greatcoat whipping wildly, water dripping from the wide brim of his hat.

"Take my hand!" he shouted through the deafening din. "We'll ride Phaedrus for the last half mile."

The gale seemed to grip the carriage in its mighty arms, tossing it about like a child's toy. Sybil had no option but to jump down to the muddy track. Sodden earth squelched over her dainty slippers, sucking them off her feet as she moved to walk.

Her knees buckled.

Lucius was there, preventing her fall. "Leave them! Hurry!" He wrapped his arm around her, propelling her forward to where Samuel stood struggling to hold the reins of a black stallion. "Climb atop the box with your father, lad. I'll send Jonah back to help."

The boy nodded.

Rain pelted Sybil's face. Hair clung to her cheeks. Soggy and caked in mud, her stockings sagged at the toes, making it hard to slip her foot into the stirrup. Lucius was busy helping Samuel steady the spooked horse, and so she quickly reached under her skirts, removed her right stocking and mounted Phaedrus.

"Lord, this is the devil of all storms," she cried as Lucius climbed up behind.

"Hold me tightly." He took control of the reins. "Some of these trees are two hundred years old and are dangerous in hazardous weather."

Sybil did not object. She pushed her hands inside his greatcoat and threaded her arms around his waist. While she should have been terrified—gripping his soaked shirt for fear of falling —another sensation took precedence.

Hunger.

Raw.

Carnal.

She wanted to devour every inch of Lucius Daventry. She wanted to press her mouth to his neck and taste his earthy essence. She wanted to feel his firm fingers gripping her thigh, wanted to hear him moaning into her mouth in the way that stole her sanity.

With one arm holding her tight to his chest, Lucius rode as fast as the howling wind. While he had taken command of the situation—taken care of her—there was something different about him now. Dare she say he seemed distant. Aloof. It was as if he'd locked his feelings away in the vault under the lake, and this was merely the shell of the man going through the motions.

Did his reticence have to do with their kiss?

Was he annoyed at Mr Wycliff's interference?

"This is dreadful," she said, hoping for some reassurance that the horrible weather had affected his mood.

"We'll be home soon." Despite his abrupt tone, his choice of words eased her fears.

They galloped along the lane in silence. Lucius dodged the flying debris as the wind hurled broken branches and twigs in their path. Mud flicked off the horse's hooves. The wind's icy breath nipped at her cheeks, forcing her to press her face against Lucius' chest.

Holding him—hugging him—brought immediate relief.

When they reached the castle, Lucius rode directly to the stables. Jonah appeared, his wet greatcoat plastered to his broad shoulders, his brown hair fastened at the nape with black ribbon. Were he a footman in a grand house, the mistress might summon him just for the pleasure of gazing upon his impressive physique.

"Robert needs help with the carriage." Lucius removed his hat, shook off the excess water and gave it to Jonah. "He's but half a mile along the track. Take Phaedrus and a length of rope. I'll settle Miss Atwood, then saddle another horse and meet you there."

Jonah nodded. "And if the carriage won't budge?"

"Return with the horses."

"Aye, sir." Jonah mounted the black stallion and darted off into the dismal night.

Lucius turned to her. "We need to get you inside. Get you something warm to drink. Wash the mud off your feet."

Without warning, he scooped her up into his strong arms and

carried her across the cobbled courtyard. Not once did he lose his grip while pushing through the violent storm.

They entered the house near the servants' hall, moved along the dark, narrow passages and past the small chapel with barely room for a pew. Lucius carried her into the drawing room, an inherently masculine space with burgundy furnishings and walnut tables. While the sight of lit candles and the roaring fire warmed her instantly, the low timber ceiling added to the stifling tension.

"Are you still angry with Mr Wycliff?" she said, as Lucius lowered her down onto the blanket spread across the sofa.

"Wycliff was acting in your interests." He stared at her muddy feet though his mind was elsewhere. "For that, I am grateful. Wait here. I shall be back in a moment."

He left the room and returned minutes later carrying a porcelain washbowl and a towel. He knelt before her, placed the bowl of water on the floor and captured her right ankle.

Her breath hitched.

Conflicting emotions clashed in his eyes—sadness, the faint flicker of desire. He exhaled deeply as he pushed the dirty hem of Sybil's gown up to her bare calf and used the linen square to wash away the mud squelching between her toes.

"Are you worried about Robert and Samuel?" she said, watching him as he cleaned her foot as if she were as delicate as a doll.

He glanced briefly at the closed curtains moving back and forth as the wind found its way in through the shutters. "I should go to them," he said, his anxiety evident. Yet he cupped her arch and dripped warm water over the bridge of her foot.

"Then go," she urged. "I can attend to this task."

"You should remove your wet cloak before you catch a chill."

"I will." She offered a reassuring smile. "By the time you return, I shall have clean feet and dry clothes." And she would attempt to discover what had brought about this melancholic mood.

A strange maudlin silence captured him again.

"Lucius, you should help Robert." She snatched her foot from his grasp, bent down and took the linen square. "Samuel is so slight and hasn't your strength, especially in this heavy downpour."

Offering a huff and a mumbled curse, he stood. "Tomas is here and will watch over you until I return." He took the towel and wiped the rivulets of water trickling down from his hair to the open neck of his shirt. "I cannot envisage being longer than an hour."

"Go," she said, laughing lightly. "Before the road becomes impassable."

"You have the freedom of the house. Tomas will prepare supper if you're hungry."

"Go."

Lucius inclined his head, then turned on his heel and strode from the room.

In truth, she hadn't wanted him to go, not in these dreadful conditions. And what lady wouldn't want a handsome gentleman tending to her ablutions? His hands had been as cold as her feet, though she liked the tender, almost sensual way he'd washed her toes.

Indeed, she thought of every soft stroke as she removed her dirty stocking and finished the task. His image filled her head as she slipped out of the wet cloak. Beneath, her dress was damp. She might have gone upstairs to change had Tomas not appeared carrying a tray laden with hot fruit punch, a bowl of lamb stew and a crust of bread.

"A storm always gets the hunger pangs growling, ma'am," Tomas said. Large eye bags and a gaunt face gave the impression he'd not slept in weeks. "And Mr Daventry said you'd need something to chase away the cold."

"Thank you, Tomas." She might have said that a passionate kiss from the master would heat her blood sufficiently.

"Mr Daventry won't mind if you eat here, ma'am." Tomas placed the crude wooden tray on the walnut table. "No one's lit the fire in the dining room, and it's warmer here than in the bedchamber."

The mere mention of the bedchamber brought to mind Mr Daventry's nightmares. Perhaps his anxiety stemmed from a fear of falling asleep tonight.

"Then I shall settle by the fire and eat supper while I wait for Mr Daventry." She wondered if Tomas knew why Lucius had brought her to Bronygarth. But how did one broach the subject? "Did you know my father?"

The man's droopy lids twitched. "I did, ma'am, and a more charitable man I never did meet. If it wasn't for him and Mr Daventry, I'd have met with the hangman's noose."

Pride filled Sybil's chest, not just for her father's considerate actions. "I trust they found evidence to absolve you of a crime."

"They proved Moses Maroney is a devil of a liar if that's your meaning, ma'am. Said I stole three silver spoons when it was him who sold them to pay for his visits to that harlot at—" He stopped abruptly. "Begging your pardon, ma'am. I'm not used to minding my tongue."

Sybil smiled. "Fear not. Mr Daventry can be equally blunt in his delivery. And you needn't worry. I can't imagine I shall remain here long. Mr Daventry is trying to save me from a frightening fate, too."

"Then you're in good hands, ma'am."

"The best," she agreed, having experienced the power and skill in Lucius Daventry's deft fingers. "Thank you, Tomas."

The man bowed and promised to let her know when Lucius returned. And so she sat on the rug near the hearth, ate her meal and dried her clothes. The heat relaxed her cold, tired limbs. The hot punch contained more than a nip of brandy, and it wasn't long before she curled up with a cushion and fell asleep.

The tapping on her shoulder dragged her out of a peaceful slumber. She blinked and rubbed her eyes only to find Tomas looming, wringing his hands and giving a mumbled apology.

"Oh, I thought you were abed, ma'am." Brandy fumes wafted over her as Tomas leaned closer. "What with tending to the horses and making sure Samuel downed his hot toddy, I forgot to come and stoke the fire."

The temperature in the room had plummeted. Sybil glanced at the dying embers, at the candle stubs spluttering in the lamps. She shot up. "Has Mr Daventry returned?"

Tomas grimaced and scratched his head. "About an hour ago, ma'am. He went to wash and change his clothes. I looked in to tell you, but didn't see you lying down there. Mr Daventry thinks you've gone to bed."

"Gone to bed? Oh." Her shoulders sagged in disappointment. "Not to worry. I can speak to him in the morning. The safety of the men and the horses is what's important."

The man chuckled. "Samuel downed his toddy faster than you can say Jack Robinson, though it will do him a power of good, even if he is spouting nonsense."

Sybil gathered her cloak and left Tomas to check the lamps and poke the embers. A mild pang of fear made her pause at the bottom of the dark staircase. Frightful thoughts of hauntings and ghosts raised the hairs on her nape. It didn't help that the leaded windows creaked and rattled like a spectre shaking its chains. But despite the oppressive atmosphere, she felt strangely at home at Bronygarth.

After mounting the stairs, curiosity made her stop outside Mr Daventry's door. She considered knocking, but it was late, and he must be exhausted after spending hours battling in the wind and rain.

No one had lit the fire in her chamber. No one had turned down the bed or placed a warming pan beneath the ice-cold sheets. As the frigid temperature penetrated her bones, she scoured the drawers and the armoire, looking for more blankets.

Of course, she had another purpose for stamping around and making a racket. But after hurrying to listen at the adjoining door, she heard nothing to convince her Lucius was awake.

Knowing she had no hope of sleeping, Sybil lingered at the door before pushing doubts aside and turning the key in the lock.

The hinges groaned as she eased the door from the jamb.

A frisson of excitement sent her heart skipping as she stepped into his bedchamber. She peered through the gloom, hindered by the lack of firelight, the lack of any lit candles.

"Lucius," she whispered, but he was not sitting in the chair near the stone fireplace. The glass on the side table was empty, the decanter full. "Lucius." She stepped closer to the bed, and with trembling fingers pulled back the green hangings.

The bed was empty.

That didn't stop her touching the pillow and stroking the coverlet. She could have spent an hour in his room, inhaling the seductive scent that hung in the cool air. She might have shrugged into his shirt, sipped his brandy, read his book. Such was the depth of her growing obsession.

The sudden thud from the floor above tore a gasp from her lips. She strained to listen, was convinced she heard the rich rumble of Lucius' voice, cursing.

A desire to see him drew her into the gloomy corridor. While her stomach lurched at the prospect of meeting a phantom dressed in Jacobean finery, she took command of her nerves and climbed the narrow staircase leading to the attic.

It wasn't difficult to find the man who intrigued her more by the day. Light spilled from the narrow opening of a door. Sybil crept closer and peered through the gap.

Lucius Daventry was sprawled on an elegant chaise, wearing nothing but a white shirt open at the neck and buckskin breeches. His eyes were closed, and she might have thought him asleep had he not uttered another vile curse.

Without warning, he pushed to his feet and strode over to the bookcase. He scanned the row of cloth-covered books, picked one and studied the recto beneath the light of the standing candelabra.

"Beloved son," the words left his lips on a wind of contempt. And then he hurled the volume at the wall before striding back to the chaise and resuming his relaxed position.

Sensing his distress and having witnessed his pensive mood earlier in the evening, she couldn't leave him alone with his demons. Not when she feared the beasts might turn on their master.

"Lucius," she called softly and pushed open the door.

He didn't reply but lay there consumed by his morbid mood.

"Lucius." Sybil stepped into the room.

Her voice seemed to pull him back from the darkness. He turned his head a fraction and stared at her through tormented eyes. Tortured eyes. Eyes pleading to be dragged free from their miserable prison.

Her pulse pounded in her throat. "I heard a noise, thought I heard your voice."

The intense stare that once roused her anger roused a host of different emotions now—pity, desire, a tenderness so consuming she could barely breathe.

"Tomas said you'd retired to your bedchamber." His sharp gaze softened as he scanned the neckline of her gown. "Clearly he was wrong."

"I was waiting for you," she said, closing the gap between them. She noticed a pile of books discarded on the floor near the bookcase. "I took supper in the drawing room and fell asleep by the fire."

"I ate up here." He gestured to the plate and cutlery under the chaise. "You needed rest, and I didn't want to cause a disturbance." He brushed his hand through his coal-black hair, the action drawing her eyes to his bare chest visible beneath his open shirt.

Heat pooled between her thighs.

So hot.

So heavy.

So damned distracting.

"What do you need, Lucius?" she found herself saying. "Do you need to talk? Do you want to be alone? Can I do anything to ease your discomfort?"

"You shouldn't be here, Sybil." A weary sigh escaped him. "I don't have the strength to fight it anymore. I don't have the strength to keep pretending. Not tonight at least."

"Tonight?" She thought to touch his sleeve, but hesitated. "Did something happen after I left the mews? Is it Newberry? Tell me the devil hasn't called you out."

He gave a weak chuckle, though she sensed his demons prowling, drooling and slapping their chops. "Newberry's no threat. I could finish him with a shot from a rusty musket."

"What then? Does it have to do with abandoning the carriage in the woods?"

"Possessions can be replaced."

"You're not helping me, Lucius."

His gaze turned carnal as he focused on her bare toes. "Then let me help by insisting you return to your bedchamber. Return now, before heightened emotions force us to repeat our illicit encounter in the library."

Was that supposed to send her scuttling back to her room?

Was that supposed to have her hunting for a chastity belt?

"You know I like it when you're reckless," she said in the seductive tone of a skilled courtesan. But these all-consuming feelings went beyond the need for physical pleasure. She would be just as happy to sit and hold his hand.

"Damn it, Sybil. We're on dangerous ground." He pushed his hand into the opening of his shirt to massage his chest muscle, and she struggled to keep her mouth closed. "What I want, and what is right are two entirely different things."

"Are you saying you want me?" Never had she been so bold. But life was precarious. One had to grab these precious moments.

His hand stilled on his chest. "In every way a man might want a woman. I'm like a wanderer lost in the desert, so hot, so parched, so damn thirsty. A single drop from the heavens would prove immensely satisfying. There, is that what you wanted to hear?"

It was exactly what she wanted to hear.

The temptation to reach out and touch him proved too great, but he captured her wrist before her fingers made contact. For a few heartbeats, they stared into each other's eyes.

She gazed deep, willing him to surrender.

Willing him not to predict or plan.

Willing him to be wild and reckless.

CHAPTER FOURTEEN

The emptiness he carried in his chest seemed to dissipate in Sybil Atwood's company. Lucius had been ready to throw on his greatcoat and ride through the thunder and rain until he reached Bideford Park. He was ready to throw Warner against the wall and show him the pencil etching that bore such a striking likeness. He was ready to drag his father from his deathbed and demand to know what the hell had happened twenty years ago.

The mental torment—years of bitterness and anguish—proved too much to bear. But then an angel appeared at his door. An angel in a sumptuous green gown offering a wealth of heavenly delights.

The sensual glint in those emerald eyes told him she had a grasp of the situation. A situation that might begin with raging lust, proceed to immense pleasure, love, marriage. Maybe a full, enriched life beyond his responsibility to the Order.

Lucius brought the lady's hand to his lips, closed his eyes and pressed a long, lingering kiss on her palm. Instantly, his tense shoulders relaxed.

"I saw my mother tonight." The words sounded incredulous. Unbelievable. He drew her hand to his chest and placed it over his heart, let her feel its wild uncertainty beating an erratic rhythm. "She was hiding in the carriage house and approached me not long after you left the mews."

Sybil opened her mouth, but couldn't seem to speak through her shock. Eventually, she said, "Hiding? Why?"

"Hiding from my father's spies." Not that the duke had the power to hurt her anymore. The man couldn't raise a cross word, let alone his fist.

"So she's alive."

"It would appear so."

"Where has she been all this time?"

He shrugged. "Somewhere north of London." Imagine if she had lived in Wetherby or a mile from Bronygarth. "Fear kept her away by all accounts."

Sybil studied him intently. "You don't sound pleased. I thought you'd be happy, relieved to see her again, to know what happened. Did she say something to cause your distress?"

"I'm not distressed." Though he still felt the need to keep Sybil's dainty hand pressed to his heart. "Confused. Sad. Bloody angry." So bloody angry.

"You're suffering from every conceivable emotion, then." She gestured to the chaise. "May I sit?" But before he could move from his lounging position, she promptly dropped down onto his lap.

All thoughts of his parents, of his failure to punish the person responsible for Atticus' murder, of the stranded carriage, abandoned him.

She ran her hand up over his chest to cup his nape. "Ashby had the right idea," she whispered as she pressed her forehead to his, pressed her lush breasts to his chest.

Lucius closed his eyes briefly and inhaled her natural perfume. The aroma teased those deep carnal cravings. It infused his being, touching him in the secret place beyond the material world. A place without maps or coordinates. A place some people denied existed.

"Are you suggesting we follow our hearts, Miss Atwood?"

"That, and I thought you might work your way up to the tops of my stockings while we talk."

For the first time since devouring her mouth in the library, he smiled. "You're not wearing stockings."

"That's merely incidental."

"Well, I wouldn't want Ashby to think he has an advantage."

They stared at each other as their breathing quickened. Lucius saw his desire reflected in those vibrant green gems, saw hope there, too.

"You spoke of wandering the desert," she said, and the minx reached for the dirty hem of her gown and bunched her skirts to her knees. "Perhaps I might quench your thirst. Perhaps you'd like to drink."

Bloody hell!

If he woke to find this was a damn dream, he'd murder someone.

He studied her bare legs, pale and smooth like alabaster, before trailing his fingers slowly from her ankle to her knee. "Convince me this is what you want."

"Can you not hear my need for you in my voice?"

"Convince me, Sybil."

Her light laugh lasted for a few seconds before the hazy veil of desire altered her expression. She placed both palms on his chest, leaned forward and claimed his mouth.

Twice she pressed her lips to his. Two sweet kisses, like the nervous dips of a toe in the lake. He let her test the water before opening his mouth and urging her to jump in. He heard the rush of excitement in her throaty gasp, in her pretty hum, felt it in the way she caressed his chest, in the way she struggled to sit still in his lap.

Tempering the urge to rush, he drew back, nipped at the corner of her mouth, slid his tongue along the seam of her lips. His hand slipped to her thigh, and he gripped the soft flesh, desperate to feel it cushioning his hip as he plunged into her wetness.

"Once my hand passes the top of your imagined stocking," he whispered against her mouth, "I fear I'll not stop there."

She placed her hand on his and edged it a little higher. "Don't stop there."

He swallowed past the surge of euphoria, past the painful

ache of his cock pushing against his breeches. "You wish me to touch you intimately?"

She gave a little shrug and a coy smile.

"Do you want me to pleasure you, Sybil?" Lust had taken command of his voice. "Do you want to feel my fingers moving inside you when you find your release?"

Her eyes widened. "I want you, Lucius." She edged his hand past the point where her stocking might end. "I want you to ease this deep ache, however that may be."

God, his tongue was as thick and as heavy as his cock.

"Once we pass this point, neither of us will be thinking clearly. We won't want to stop." He needed her to understand. "It's not too late to say no."

She sucked on her bottom lip. "May I try something? Something that has my curiosity champing at the bit?"

"You may do what you please with me, Miss Atwood."

She pinned him to the chaise with her sinful smile and playful gaze, guided his hand to the intimate place between her thighs where it was so damn hot and wet.

Fuck!

His head fell back in time with hers.

A moan left her lips, and he moaned, too.

"It's as I thought," she breathed, her eyelids fluttering. "Please, please continue."

It took every ounce of control not to spill himself in his breeches. "Say please again, Sybil. Say please in the way that makes me know you crave my touch."

"Please, Lucius." She arched her back as his fingers slipped slowly back and forth over her sex, caressing her in the intoxicating rhythm he knew would drive her wild. "Please," she begged. "Oh, God, please."

"Touch me," he whispered. "Touch me. Touch me anywhere."

Sybil touched him everywhere. Her hands delved under his shirt. She massaged his chest, stroked his nipples. She writhed in his lap, writhed against his hard shaft. Those vibrant copper curls fell about her shoulders as she bent her head, covered his mouth and slipped her warm tongue over his.

Fuck!

He was supposed to be doing the pleasuring, and yet he was on the verge of losing control. She seemed to be everywhere. Consuming. Devouring. Filling his head with her beguiling essence.

His free hand tangled in her hair, fastening her tight to his mouth. He swallowed her hum of pleasure as he pushed his fingers slowly into her heat. It took but a few more strokes with his thumb, a few slick slides of his fingers until her body convulsed.

A cry of satisfaction escaped her.

A cry accompanied by the needy whisper of his name.

Damn, but she was majestic in her release—all wild hair, glazed eyes and breathless pants. A siren determined to lure him to sin with her sensual song. A siren luring him to break his oath, to forget his vow.

Was this betrayal? Surely this wasn't the protection Atticus had in mind. Still, his mentor was a man who lived for the truth. And the truth was Lucius had fallen in love with Sybil Atwood.

"I want to make love to you, Sybil." He needed to make love to her else he might end up in Bedlam. "But I understand if that's a step too far."

She looked at him through drowsy eyes, eyes heavy with desire. "Make love? Hmm, it sounds divine."

Divine didn't even begin to describe what it was like to watch her shudder in his arms. What it would be like to watch her come while he was buried deep inside her.

"While I expect the experience will be transcendent, taking your virtue is not something my conscience will allow."

She screwed her nose in the pretty way that said she found him confusing. "What if you don't take my virtue? What if I give it freely, willingly? There's a vast difference."

"You can only give it once," he said, touched that she would choose him as the recipient of such a precious gift. "You might meet someone—"

She kissed him again. He was getting used to these sudden bursts of affection. Perhaps she was still dizzy on the heights of her release, for her tongue drove into his mouth with a fervent hunger. Before he could match the voracious movements, she was tugging at his clothes, pushing her hands through his hair, writhing, panting.

All thoughts of vows and blasted promises left him.

I love her, he said silently as if making his excuses to her father, to the Lord, to anyone who was bloody well listening.

"We should return to your bedchamber," he said, as the last threads of logic considered her comfort. "You should be in—"

"Next time," she whispered against his neck. "I like it here on the chaise."

"I don't think you have the measure of the situation," he said for the second time tonight.

She pulled back and looked at him. "You're going to make love to me, here and now. You're going to look after me, tell me what to do, how to please you. I'm going to experience those delicious tingles again. And you're going to mutter curses like you do when you lose control of your senses."

"Yes," he said.

"Good. Now, I'm bound to be nervous. From what Cassandra told me, it might hurt a little, but you're not to think about that. I'm told it soon passes."

He fell silent.

She amazed him on every level.

Now he had taken ownership of the emotion he could not stop the warm waves of love rippling through his chest. Love for this wildly vivacious woman who raised another smile when she said, "Do you think you might help me out of this dress?"

❦

For a man skilled at kissing—extremely skilled at making a lady feel like she is floating amidst the stars—Lucius seemed to be stumbling at the last hurdle. Since kissing him in the library, since feeling the magnetic connection, she knew it was impossible to temper their passion.

Heavens, the man drove her wild with desire. He had seduced her mind from the beginning, seduced her heart with the depth of his devotion, seduced her body with his expert tongue.

Trust your heart, dear girl, her father had said. And her heart said she wanted Lucius Daventry in every conceivable way.

Sybil climbed off his lap, captured his hand and pulled him to his feet. "It occurs to me that the problem is your mind. There's a host of things going on in there and that is hardly conducive to an evening of seduction."

Lucius arched a brow. "A whole evening? There are hours until dawn. I fear once I'm buried deep in your sweet body, I'll barely last a few minutes."

"You should be optimistic." She dragged him out onto the landing. "You might make love to me more than once."

He laughed. "I can hear that damn parrot again, reminding me you don't have the measure of the situation."

"Perhaps," she admitted. "Now, you're to wait out here and empty your mind. Then you're going to count to twenty before slipping into the room as if this were a ball and you're about to make love to your mistress."

"I have never made love to a mistress," he snapped.

"Then you're going to sneak in here to save my reputation, but you're going to lose your mind like you did in the library."

"Sybil, there's no need to stage a scene," he said, pulling her back into the attic room and closing the door. "Just kiss me, and I'll soon forget the rest of the world exists."

"Oh."

His mouth curled into a sinful smile. He gathered his shirt, drew the garment over his head and threw it to the floor. Heat flooded her sex at the sight of his muscular arms, the hard planes of his chest, at every carved contour.

"Impressive." She followed the teasing trail of dark hair leading from his navel and disappearing below the waistband of his breeches. More than impressive.

"Thank you." He gave a confident wink.

Pushing nerves aside, she reached behind and unfastened the small row of buttons securing her gown. Once undone, she tugged the sleeves off her shoulders, shimmied until the silk slipped over her hips to pool on the floor. Her petticoat followed.

Lucius massaged the muscles in his chest and moistened his lips. "Front fastening stays."

"Without the luxury of a maid, it pays to be prepared."

She tugged on the ties, shrugged out of her short stays until left standing in just her chemise. Lord, her body burned. Yet her erect nipples pushed against the delicate fabric.

Lucius grinned. He unbuttoned his breeches and pushed the garment past his lean hips to reveal his jutting erection.

Holy Lord.

"It usually takes me a little time to rise to the occasion," he said, palming the solid length. "Yet I was hard the second you entered the room."

Curiosity had her staring, wondering how she was to take the whole length of him into her body.

Sybil arched a brow. "Equally impressive." Magnificent, to be exact. "Though I have but a pencil sketch as a comparison."

She wished she hadn't mentioned what they'd found in Sir Melrose's library. The last thing she wanted was to remind him of their mounting problems. And so, she swallowed the last remnants of her modesty and pulled her chemise up over her head.

A husky curse escaped him when she threw the garment to the floor. Nerves might have had her covering her breasts with her arms. But she recalled the salacious conversation he'd had with Benedict Cavanagh.

"I heard tell that you've longed to fondle my breasts."

He stared beneath heavy lids, grinned through a mouth made for wickedness. "I've imagined holding you, touching you a thousand times or more."

"Then hold me, Lucius. Touch me."

He closed the gap between them in an instant and claimed her lips in a fierce open-mouthed kiss. Despite the chill in the air, his skin was hot against hers, warming her core. He smelled of leather and soap and spice. Manly. With every deep plunge of his tongue, the fire between her legs flamed.

He broke contact, glanced down at her breasts pressed

against his bare chest. "If this is a dream, don't let me wake now."

Sybil slipped her arms around his waist, gripped his buttocks and gave one cheek a pinch.

"Ow!" He laughed.

"If this is a dream, that would surely have woken you."

"You want to play, is that it?" His hum spoke of sensual power. "You want me to torment you, tease you." His velvet voice fanned lust's flames. "You want me to tell you all the things I want to do with you, Sybil."

Excitement flared. "Tell me."

"By now your sex is throbbing, aching for my touch," he said, taking hold of his erection and pushing his member between her legs. "It's all you can think about, me stroking you, me thrusting hard into your tight body. Us moving together. Us panting and writhing."

Sybil grabbed his shoulders to steady her balance. Oh, she loved the feel of his erection sliding over her sex. Her head fell back, and she moaned. "Don't stop, Lucius."

"I'm going to make you come like this."

"Yes," she breathed.

He gripped her buttock with his free hand, continued to rub the head of his shaft over her sex. Oh, she was getting closer to that delicious peak. Closer. So close she was about to topple off the edge. And then her world shattered into a million sparkling pieces.

"Lucius," she cried, as heat from her climax flooded her core.

He held her close as she shuddered in his arms. "God, love, next time I want to be buried inside you."

Next time? She needed him inside her now.

"Show me how to please you," she said, still feeling as if she were soaring through the clouds. She captured his hand and pulled him to the chaise. "Show me what to do. Show me how to make love to you."

"You want to learn how to love me, Sybil?" he whispered almost incredulously. The warmth in his eyes seemed to penetrate her skin, her flesh, reaching down into her soul.

"Let me give myself to you," she said, fearing he might have a change of heart. "If you're worried because I'm a virgin ... if you don't want me—"

"You're the only woman I want." He glanced at the chaise. "Lie down. Next time will be better than this, I promise you."

Better?

Good Lord. Any better, and she'd lose her mind.

She did as he asked, and he covered her with his hard body, squashing her in a way that made her feel safe. Secure. Loved.

Lucius closed his eyes and kissed her, his tongue slipping over hers in a tantalising rhythm, twining, mating. She could spend eternity kissing him like this—slow, deep, with such intense feeling it was like a silent language. Their language.

Each tangle of their tongues tightened the inner coil. She obeyed the instinctive need to clamp her thighs around him. To hold him tight in a primal embrace.

"Look into my eyes," he said. "I'm going to join with you."

A rush of affection washed over her as he eased inside her.

"You're so tight." He sucked in a breath. "Tell me if I'm hurting you."

"You're not." She gripped his buttocks, loved the way they clenched and released as he pushed a little deeper, withdrew, pushed into her again.

"Oh, God, Sybil." He closed his eyes as he worked slowly in and out of her body.

She didn't want to close her eyes.

Watching every sleek movement proved highly arousing.

He gripped the headrest with his left hand, angled his hips so that with every delicious slide he rubbed against her sex.

"Look at me, Sybil," he breathed, opening his eyes. "Forgive me if this hurts."

She stared into eyes that to some might look plain grey—a shade reminiscent of steel, cold and hard. But they conveyed so much more. The black rims circling his irises embodied the dark, dangerous nature of his character. The flecks of bright blue were as warm and inviting as summer skies and rippling seas.

They were so mesmerising she forgot he was about to push past her maidenhead. He did so with one hard thrust. The slight stinging passed. It took but a few seconds to grow accustomed to the feel of being full, full with Lucius Daventry.

And then he began the teasing thrusts that had her panting and crying his name. Then he began to show her exactly how to love him.

CHAPTER FIFTEEN

Ravenous, Lucius devoured his breakfast with a little less fervency than he had Sybil's delectable body. They had made love for a second time in his bed. Might have made love a third had he not carried her to the adjoining chamber and insisted she sleep.

He had slept for two hours before rising refreshed and ready to tackle his mountain of problems. Anyone witnessing his permanent grin would believe he didn't have a care in the world. Indeed, his men had traded more than a few odd glances, traded more than a few curious questions.

What had happened to drag their master from his dreadful mood? Wasn't it still raining? Wasn't the carriage still stuck half a mile from Bronygarth? Had he finally turned to the bottle to forget his terrible troubles?

Lucius was still grinning as he sipped his coffee, still grinning when the object of his desire strode into the room, bid him good morning and told him to remain seated.

Erotic visions danced in his mind as he scanned her simple green day dress. She had tied her hair back loosely with blue ribbon, but he remembered unruly copper curls spread over his pillow.

He expected to see embarrassment stain her cheeks, thought

she might avoid him while coming to terms with all that had occurred last night. Maybe had regrets.

He was wrong.

"Is that your first helping?" She came around the table, touched his shoulder affectionately and stepped to move past him.

Lucius captured her wrist, drew her close, meant to press a chaste kiss to her lips, but it turned into a lustful melding of mouths, a wild tangling of tongues. He had to break contact before he dragged her onto his lap and let his men see precisely what had caused the shift in his mood.

"The bacon tastes delicious." She licked her lips and moved to examine the platters.

"Let me serve your breakfast."

He pushed out of the chair and met her at the sideboard. What should have been a simple gesture ended in another stolen kiss that might have had them rushing upstairs had they not heard Tomas whistling a country tune.

Sybil placed her palm on his chest. "You wash my feet, serve me breakfast, make love to me with such skill, is there anything you don't do, Mr Daventry?"

"Not where you're concerned, Miss Atwood," he replied, stepping back just as Tomas entered carrying fresh poached eggs.

Jonah arrived to serve Sybil breakfast, and with her approval, Lucius invited both men to sit at the table to discuss what had occurred at the Black Swan.

Before getting to the matter of the coaching inn, Jonah said, "There's something else you should know, sir." He paused and cast Sybil a surreptitious glance, continued only when Lucius gave a curt nod. "Samuel said he saw someone in the garden last night. A floating figure. A ghost."

"A ghost?" Tomas snorted. "The guzzle-guts downed brandy like it was catlap. Happen he saw fairies dancin' on the lake, too."

Jonah's expression remained grave. "When I questioned him, he said he'd gone outside to hurl, said he saw the figure near the lake, said he heard the rattling of chains."

"Good God!" Lucius' pulse raced. "Have you checked the door leading down to the vault?"

Jonah's reassuring nod brought some relief. "The gate's locked. Everything's in order. Everything's secure."

"I think it's fair to assume we had a trespasser, not a damn ghost." Lucius scrubbed his hand over his face. The devil was getting too close for comfort. "Forget any household tasks. Make watching the vault a priority. Keep a weapon and patrol regularly."

Jonah nodded.

"And did you learn anything at the Black Swan?" Sybil said.

Tomas placed a tatty pocketbook on the table and flicked to the relevant page. "I took notes on everyone who came in after you left, ma'am."

"So you remained in the taproom for two hours?" Lucius attempted to clarify. It was the first chance he'd had to speak about the incident. "Did anyone suspect you were there to spy?"

Lucius and his men rarely visited local establishments. People were nosy by nature, and he did not need anyone prying into his affairs.

Tomas shook his head. "A fancy coach came in, and the bluffer took to—"

"Bluffer?" Sybil asked.

"The innkeeper," Lucius said and gestured for Tomas to continue.

Tomas nodded. "The innkeeper took to bowing and scraping while the lord barked orders."

Lucius' heart thumped against his chest. "Did you make a note of this lord's name?" If it was Newberry, he would start polishing his pistols.

"Faulkner. Lord Faulkner. A right old nabob who still wears powder and lace. Had a young bit of muslin with him. A tempting armful."

The lord was a pretentious prat with the brain of a donkey. "I doubt Faulkner is our man. Do you have a list of those who entered after Miss Atwood left?"

Tomas nodded. "A family of three from Grantham who never went upstairs. A handful of people off the stagecoach who had no time to eat and had to fill their pockets with bread."

Tomas continued with the descriptions of two merchants

from Ripon selling spurs, farmhands looking for work and a spinster and her young niece, who had an eye for anyone in breeches.

Sybil looked up from buttering her toast. "Did anyone else approach the innkeeper? Whoever instructed me to come to the Black Swan must have an arrangement with the owner."

Tomas shook his head.

"Perhaps the innkeeper didn't have time to alert our quarry of your arrival," Lucius said. "Unless the devil is staying at the inn."

Silence ensued.

Then Tomas gasped. "A woman renting a room upstairs came down and passed something to the bluffer. I took her for a light-skirt, thought she was paying by the swell if you take my meaning."

"Perhaps it was the woman who warned me off the stew. The one staying opposite room number five." Sybil dropped a sugar lump into her coffee. "She did look world weary, so could be what some call a Bird of Paradise."

Tomas smiled. "A ladybird."

"If so, I imagine she would have warned you off the sausages, not the stew." Lucius laughed, and Jonah sniggered. "Did you notice anyone else visiting the upstairs rooms?"

Again Tomas shook his head. "Other than the woman with the ghostly streak, only one—"

"Ghostly streak?" Lucius froze. "That's an odd description."

"Tomas is referring to her hair," Sybil said, sipping her coffee. "It was as black as yours but with a shocking streak of grey."

Lucius flopped back in the chair. His blood turned cold. Were they talking about Julia Fontaine? The rational part of his brain scrambled to find another explanation. Having a streak of grey hair was hardly a strange anomaly.

"What is it?" Sybil's deep frown spoke of his own apprehension. "What's wrong?"

"The woman, was she thin with wide, sad eyes? Was she a little shorter than you, Miss Atwood? Did she have a scar running across her cheekbone?"

"I'm not sure about the scar," Sybil said. "I barely took much notice. But she is as you describe. Why? Is it someone you know?"

"It's someone I hardly know at all." Darkness threatened to devour his good mood. Soon the storm would break to unleash a torrent of confusion, guilt and despair. He glanced at Jonah and Tomas. "That's all for now. We'll remain here and study Atticus' notes for a few hours." He daren't risk going down to the vault, not with spies lurking in their midst. "Patrol the grounds. Be vigilant."

Both men nodded and took their cue to leave.

When alone again, Sybil said, "Shall we move to the drawing room so you can tell me about this woman?" There wasn't a shred of jealousy in her tone.

"I'm not sure that's wise. Talking to you in relaxed surroundings stirs the devil in me."

"If you're the devil, then I was born for sin."

He managed a smile, resisted the urge to round the table, kiss her and slip his hand under her skirts. "While the need to stroke your stockings burns in my veins, I fear this is a time for the pragmatic thinker. You must learn to like the judicious gentleman as much as the reckless lover."

Her eyes brightened with amusement. "Make no mistake, Mr Daventry, I admire the whole package."

Merciful Mary. This woman would be the death of him. He could barely raise a coherent thought when in her company. "Must you persist in being such a tempting distraction, Miss Atwood?"

"I would rather be a tempting distraction than an annoying one," she said, reminding him of his comment at the auction. "Is it always like this?"

"What?"

"Desire. I'm curious. Does it grip you at every inopportune moment? Does it consume every ounce of your being?"

"Are you saying you want me, Sybil?"

"I wanted you the moment I opened my eyes this morning. I can't seem to calm the energetic thrum."

This lady had no problem speaking the truth. It was a rare quality. A quality he admired.

"Lust can be all-consuming." But he was in love with her, and that meant he had to focus on saving her life not devouring her body. "Let us return to the task at hand." Indeed, he had almost forgotten about Julia Fontaine. "Tonight, I shall worship you in the way that makes your toes curl."

A delectable hum left her lips, and her eyes turned soft and dreamy.

"Where were we?" he said.

"Attempting to focus. You were going to tell me about the woman you hardly know who's staying at the Black Swan."

"You mean Julia Fontaine."

"Your mother?"

"Indeed." It had to be her.

Sybil frowned. "I fear it might not be a coincidence."

"No."

"Does she know you own this house?"

Julia had made no mention of Bronygarth, only the house in Brook Street. "I cannot see how she could know. The duke makes it his business to know everything, but he hasn't seen Julia Fontaine for twenty years."

Silence ensued.

"Well, she's not the person who sent the threatening letters demanding I bring the journals to room five."

"No."

"Then she must know you live close by." She paused and glanced at the open journal. "In terms of finding the villain, we're back to where we started."

"Yes," he mused, but Atticus had urged him to look for connections where there weren't any. When one started piecing together parts of a puzzle, an obscure picture soon became clearer. "Or maybe not."

The lady arched a curious brow. "You have other suspicions?"

"I just find it hard to accept that these random pieces of information aren't connected."

She smiled. "You sound just like my father."

"That's a handsome compliment."

"One wholly deserved."

The need to confess what she meant to him surfaced. The need to tell her that he had loved her for so long. The need to say that loving her was the only thing that made him feel whole.

By way of a distraction, he said, "What's it like?"

"Desire?" she said, confused.

"No. Loving your parents."

The words carried the weight of a burden he'd lugged around for years. The guilt he bore for his lack of feeling. The crippling sense of inadequacy, the belief that he was somehow to blame.

She pursed her lips and took a moment to answer. "I suppose I always took our love for granted. But I couldn't have wished for a better childhood, couldn't have wished for better parents."

He could sense emotion welling before water filled her eyes.

"I didn't mean to make you cry," he said softly. "I was there the night your mother died. I was there hiding in the shadows when you came running downstairs, when you collapsed into your father's arms."

She blinked back her tears. "You were the person who came to see my father in his study?"

"We often met late at night, for obvious reasons." He sighed. "Your pain has stayed with me. It made me feel normal. Everyone suffers. Those who are loved and those who aren't."

She dabbed at her eyes. "There is no love between you and your parents?"

"None." Guilt tightened its noose around his neck. "When I saw my mother last night, I didn't embrace her. I didn't welcome her, didn't say how I'd mourned her absence. I'm no longer the lonely child. Can't be the loving son she lost."

Sybil pushed out of the chair and came around the table. "Is that what was troubling you?"

He shrugged, but when her soft hand slipped into his, he clasped it tightly. "The irony is we have no control over who we love or who we don't."

"No." She placed her other hand on his shoulder. "When it comes to your mother, perhaps you should give it some time. Let things develop naturally. It must be difficult to focus on anything when we have so many other matters demanding our attention."

"Yes," he said.

But he was a man of predictions and premonitions and prophecies. He knew beyond doubt that no other woman would speak to his soul like Sybil Atwood. He knew he was but one clue away from solving the riddle of Atticus' murder. And he knew that Julia Fontaine was not what she seemed.

CHAPTER SIXTEEN

Sybil was supposed to be reading through her father's notes, but she was too busy watching him across the dining table. Lucius Daventry. Watching the way his lips moved as he read silently from a journal, remembering the earthy taste of his mouth, the feel of his tongue, the heat. Watching the way his strong hand gripped the pages, remembering the sensual way it had slipped over her sex, rousing pants and pleas and moans of pleasure.

She silently sighed.

With skill, the man had worked his way in and out of her body. He had used the same expertise to work his way into her heart. She could no longer distinguish between longing, lust and love. She was addicted to his company, to passionate kisses, to the softening of those grey eyes as he cradled her in his arms.

"Have you discovered anything of interest?" he said, looking up to meet her gaze.

Only that I think I've fallen in love with you.

"The scribbled notes have faded," she said, gathering her wits. "The words are difficult to decipher. But Mr Cribb must have been a man of means."

"What makes you say that?"

"Logic says the first point of call when investigating someone is to visit their home, then their place of work. My father had written the word *work*, but the space beneath is blank."

"A man of means doesn't rent a room above a china dealer in Saffron Hill."

She considered the point. "I only wish my father would have listed the suspects. There's a record of those he questioned at the market, but little else. So, your reason for suspecting Sir Melrose and Lord Newberry stems from their desperate need to purchase the journals?"

"My gut says both men are guilty of a crime."

She had to agree, particularly in the case of Lord Newberry.

Silence ensued, and they continued studying the journals.

While musing over the text, a low hum left his lips. Heavens. It brought to mind the sweet sound of satisfaction when he found his release. Oh, he had looked magnificent then, so relaxed and untroubled.

"My father never spoke to you of his suspicions?" A pooling of heat between her thighs made it hard to sit still. Lust was the devil's distraction. "I find that strange considering you were so close."

His sigh, and the way he brushed his hand through his hair, told her he thought the same. "Atticus insisted on working with Proctor. In the interest of safety, those working on a case are sworn to secrecy."

"I would have thought it safer if all members had access to the information. It is more difficult to murder eight men than two."

"Even the most trustworthy men are open to temptation. Open to acts of betrayal." His gaze roamed over her face. "It was a rule your father made. A rule that was supposed to protect lives."

And yet both men working on the case were dead.

"May I ask how you came to find Mr Proctor's body?"

Lucius sat back in the chair. "I received a note to meet him on Bishop's Walk, Lambeth, near the church. A wall and an avenue of trees block the view of the path. I arrived at midnight as requested, found him slumped on the bank with a knife protruding from his chest."

"Someone stabbed him?" Shock made her state the obvious. She winced, not wanting to imagine the harrowing scene. "Was he already dead?"

Lucius nodded. He closed his eyes and inhaled a deep sorrowful breath. "I pushed him into the river. What else could I do? Then I fled, fearing someone sought to frame me for his murder. It was the night your father died. I visited Proctor's lodgings, looking for his notes on the case, but found nothing. Then I returned home and drank myself into oblivion."

Despite the burning need to offer comfort, touching him would only rouse lustful thoughts. Lucius needed her help, needed her to focus.

"In his note, did Mr Proctor say why he wanted to meet you?"

"No. Only that he had discovered something important, something he thought I should know."

"And you have no idea what?"

"No."

"And why there?"

"He lived but a stone's throw away on Stangate Street." The perfect lines of his face twisted into a grimace. "Had I woken your father and informed him of what had occurred, had guilt not consumed me, had I not drowned my sorrows with brandy, I might have saved your father's life."

Shock, that there might be some truth to his words, that he could have prevented the tragedy, was swept away by logic and her growing love for this man.

"You don't know that's true, Lucius. Did you not heed my father's advice? Did he not say that you can torture your mind with stories that have no basis in fact?"

He stared at her with grateful eyes, stared for the longest time.

The clatter of china preceded the arrival of Tomas carrying the tea tray. He set the tray down on the table, explained that Robert and Samuel had freed the carriage. He placed the plate of Shrewsbury biscuits next to Sybil, gave a nudge and a wink and urged her to try one.

"And Furnis delivered these to the Wild Hare this morning,

sir." Tomas handed Lucius a pile of letters. "Robert collected them a half hour ago."

The man left them to their tea, and Sybil poured while Lucius broke the first seal and read the missive.

"An invitation to attend Mrs Crandall's masquerade." He screwed up the card, reached behind him and threw it into the fire. The next was a letter from Mr Warner, and Lucius blurted, "Damn fop. I've been instructed to make an appointment should I wish to visit the duke in future. We shall see about that."

"I fear Mr Warner has suffered from a terrible lapse in judgement."

Lucius grinned. It was good to see excitement dance in his eyes. "I shall relish the prospect of informing him of his blunder." He threw that letter into the fire, too. "Damn," he said upon scanning the next note. "It's from Wycliff. I don't know whether to curse or jump for joy."

Whatever the reaction, Sybil was impressed by Mr Wycliff's prompt response. "Does he have news from Mr Flannery?"

Lucius shook his head and laughed. "Wycliff knows how to make a man feel inadequate."

"Trust me," she said, smiling over the rim of her teacup. "There is nothing inadequate about you, Mr Daventry." She spent a few seconds remembering just how competent he was. "What does Mr Wycliff say?"

"Only that Flannery gave him the address of a private club called Gorget's Garrett. He said he's meeting Flannery this afternoon and will have other information to impart. He invites us both to his house on Bruton Street tonight."

"Then we shall attend."

He pursed his lips and exhaled deeply. "I agreed to meet my mother in Brook Street at eight. It's supposed to be a night of explanations. And I have a burning desire to know why she's taken a room at the Black Swan."

Perhaps his mother knew he owned the castle and merely wished to stay close while attempting a reunion. "Maybe I could call on the Wycliffs while you return to Brook Street. Then we will achieve both—"

"No."

"No?"

"After Newberry's threat to have you carted off to an asylum in the dead of night, I don't want you venturing to town. Put the idea from your mind. It's safer here. Safer if we remain together."

"You forget, sir, that I do not respond well to orders." She knew his assertiveness stemmed from fear—fear for her wellbeing. But if their relationship was to flourish, they had to work together.

He arched a brow. "Was it an order?"

"You might have phrased it differently. Not been so blunt."

"Forgive me." A smile played on his lips. The blue flecks in his eyes glistened. "I ask, I beg, that you remain by my side. I cannot lose you, Sybil. Not because of a promise made, but because I need you in my life."

The words touched her heart. She couldn't imagine a life without him, either. "Then we shall visit the Wycliffs together. You can leave a note with Bower asking your mother to meet you tomorrow."

His smile broadened. "That's settled then."

"Yes." As they stared at each other across the table, she knew his thoughts mirrored her own. Knew one kiss would lead to an afternoon spent in bed. "Let us return to the task at hand," she said, repeating his earlier statement. "Tonight, I shall worship you in the way that makes your toes curl."

"Minx," he said, still watching her while he broke the seal on the last letter. "How is a man to concentrate when his mind is imagining all the delightful things you might do?"

His gaze dropped to the missive. He read a few lines, then his amused expression faded. Wearing a heavy frown, he studied the letter with a look of confusion, surprise, then elation.

Sybil fought the urge to ask a host of questions while she waited patiently for him to finish reading.

"It's regarding the letters Atticus sent to India," he eventually said. "This is addressed to your father from a Messrs. James & Sons solicitors in Guilford Street. Blake must have delivered it to Brook Street."

"From a solicitor? Not from the man my father believed owned a share in the mine?"

"It simply says that Mr Dobson is deceased, that he died of a tropical fever eighteen months ago, and that any questions regarding his estate should be addressed to his cousin." Lucius shook his head, laughed and uttered, "The conniving devil."

"Who?" Sybil was almost out of her chair in anticipation.

"Newberry. Mr Dobson is cousin to Lord Newberry."

They both sat in silence for a moment, absorbing the important revelation. She had known Newberry was guilty of something. Why else would he offer such an extortionate sum when he lacked the mental capacity to understand scientific theories?

"Come. We're going to town." Lucius slapped the table and pushed out of the chair, but then hesitated. "Would you care to accompany me to town, Miss Atwood?"

"I would be delighted, Mr Daventry. What are your intentions?"

A wicked grin replaced his elated smile. "First, we shall call on Newberry and drag a confession from his devious lips. Then we shall visit Wycliff before returning home to Bronygarth where you will make good on your promise to make my toes curl."

Heavens, she could hardly wait.

"You omitted one minor detail."

"Oh? And I'm usually so thorough."

Sybil arched a coy brow. "On the way to town, you might like to examine my stockings."

CHAPTER SEVENTEEN

"There is no evidence to suggest Lord Newberry is the mystery third owner of the mine. No evidence to prove he conspired to bring about its collapse. Or that he killed my father because he was getting close to the truth."

"No evidence at all," Lucius agreed as he watched Sybil brush her skirts and straighten her jaunty hat. "Only conjecture. But I can be rather persuasive when I want something."

"Very persuasive. Still, you cannot barge into a peer's home and accuse him of murder." She fastened the buttons on her dark green pelisse and relaxed back in the carriage seat. "There. How do I look?"

"Composed. Confident. Like a woman ready to tear the truth from the devil's lips."

She smiled. "Not like a woman whose lover has examined her stockings?"

Her lover? Oh, he wanted to be so much more than that. "The pleasure gained from your release has left an indelible glow I find utterly captivating."

A light laugh left her. "I admire your honesty."

And yet he had not been totally honest. Navigating unfamiliar territory left him nervous, unsteady on his feet. How did a man tell a woman he had fallen in love with her? How did he explain what she meant to him?

"I'm glad," he said, shifting his thoughts back to easing his physical ache. "In the name of honesty and equality, you won't mind pleasuring me on the journey home."

Her eyes widened. "A lady with a hunger for knowledge welcomes new experiences."

They might have continued their salacious banter had the carriage not stopped outside Lord Newberry's house in Cavendish Square.

"Lucius, I'm not sure this is a good idea." She peered through the window at the façade that bore the same air of grandeur as its master.

"Don't be afraid. Newberry won't dare threaten you in my company." Indeed, Lucius was more concerned with how he might keep calm when he wanted to rip the lord's head off his shoulders.

Despite not having an appointment, the liveried footman hurried down the steps to open the carriage door. It would be a battle getting past the butler. Lucius thought about ditching his measly arrows and loading the trebuchet, but he had the perfect weapon with which to enter.

Indeed, he handed his card to Newberry's pompous servant, said he had come to discuss terms relating to the sale of Atticus Atwood's journals. A brief conversation with the lord resulted in the sprightly butler ushering them into the study.

After a tepid greeting and an exchange of the usual glib phrases, the smug lord positioned himself behind his desk, relaxed back in the chair and grinned with gleaming satisfaction.

"Well, Daventry, I'm glad you've seen sense at last." The lord looked down his nose at Sybil. "Let me start by saying I forgive your pitiful attempt to slander my good name, Miss Atwood. Fanciful notions and fairy tales scream of desperation, do they not?"

Lucius was forced to interject. "Moderate your tone when speaking to Miss Atwood." Else he was likely to fly over the desk and drive his fist down the arrogant lord's throat.

"I think you'll find most fairy tales are based on reality," Sybil countered. "Every story has a villain. A wicked devil who professes loyalty and kindness but in truth is a vain creature obsessed with his own self-importance."

Lucius cast her a sidelong glance. He couldn't be prouder.

Newberry's jaw firmed. "Then this is a subverted tale, my dear. Greed wins over morality. Daventry is no fool. Money can help insignificant men rise in the ranks."

"And the truth can bring haughty, overweening prigs to their knees," Lucius countered. "Make no mistake, Newberry, I'm here to see justice prevails."

Newberry straightened. His blue eyes shifted suspiciously. "Why do I get the impression you're not here to sell the books? You have no intention of accepting my offer." He frowned. "If this is about what happened with Larissa—"

"I don't give a damn about Larissa."

"What then?" Newberry's gaze darted back and forth between them. "Have you come to warn me over the way I spoke to Miss Atwood?"

"Warn you?" Lucius snorted. "I want to kill you for frightening her with threats of kidnapping and asylums."

Newberry gave a derisive snort. "So, you've taken Miss Atwood as your mistress. You say this isn't about money, yet you had her appear at the auction to force men to up their bids."

Lucius was losing patience. "Miss Atwood is not my mistress." It was not a lie. She was the woman he loved. The woman he would marry once this dreadful business was over. Assuming she'd have him. "Her father was my friend. A man who trusted me with information he'd discovered about certain men in the *ton*."

Newberry seemed to consider his reply carefully before saying, "So, you've come to blackmail me over an imagined misdemeanour. Is that it?"

Lucius sighed and decided to fire the trebuchet. "I received a letter this morning from the solicitor dealing with Mr Dobson's estate." He grinned. "You know Mr Dobson, of course. He's your cousin and was one of the owners of a mine near Wigan. Along with Lord Talbot, you were a partner in the venture."

Guilt turned Newberry's face chalk-white. He drew his handkerchief from his coat pocket and dabbed his brow. "What the devil are you talking about, Daventry?" He gulped nervously in spite of his belligerent tone. "Wigan? Don't be absurd. Do I look like a man who frequents northern towns?"

Lucius noted the lord's visible anxiety. But how was he to extract the information without evidence? Most crimes stemmed from greed or family loyalty. Why would a man living in India invest in a mine thousands of miles from home? Unless he'd fled to India, having arranged the collapse.

"If you're not here to sell the damn journals, I suggest you leave." Newberry stuffed his handkerchief back into his pocket.

"Don't be so hasty. You can have the journals for our agreed sum of seven thousand pounds." Lucius was aware of Sybil's frantic gaze shooting in his direction. "There's nothing in them but theories on magnetism, on electric circuits and isolating metals. You said you can settle today. Excellent. I can wait while you gather the funds and sign the notes."

Newberry appeared confused.

The tension in the air was palpable.

The silence proved deafening.

"It baffles me why so many men are interested in mathematical equations and quantitative reasoning," Lucius added. "I fail to appreciate their value myself."

Newberry sat forward and gripped the desk. "What about my written statement of intention?" Unease coated every syllable.

"As you said, insignificant men need money." He paused, let the silence stretch until the atmosphere proved suffocating. "And it's Atticus Atwood's notebooks that interest me, not his journals."

"Notebooks?" Newberry developed an odd facial tic. "More theories?"

"Precisely. Theories on the devious deeds committed by privileged men. You might wish to bid for them, too, considering they make mention of your cousin Mr Dobson causing the collapse of a mine near Wigan. It's said that's the reason he fled to India."

"Theories are not fact," the lord countered.

"No, but there are fascinating accounts from witnesses. And Messrs. James & Sons were accommodating when I called at their office this morning. It seems poor Mr Dobson had a mountain of debts," Lucius lied. "Desperate men do desperate things, Newberry."

Sybil cleared her throat. "As I said, I have read my father's books and know of the damning statements."

After another clawing silence, Newberry said, "There is nothing to prove I had a share in the mine. Nothing to prove I had anything to do with the tragic accident."

No, because all records had been mysteriously destroyed.

"I think we all know it wasn't an accident," Sybil said gravely.

Lucius tempered his anger. "That's a matter for the authorities to decide. As well as the deaths of those who perished in the mine, there's the question of Atticus Atwood's murder to address." Proving any of it would be an impossible feat. "The magistrate is interested to hear of anyone with a motive."

"Murder!" Newberry shot out of the chair as if the pad were on fire. "Good God, Daventry. I swear, I knew nothing about Dobson's plans in Wigan. The man was a bloody idiot. I packed him off as soon as he confessed to evicting the tenants and having a buyer for the land."

"You were his partner in the venture."

"I just lent him the damn money in exchange for a thirty percent share." The lord dragged his hand through his hair, then reached into the desk drawer. He removed a silver flask and gulped the contents. "As for Atticus," he said, throwing the flask back into the drawer, "yes, he asked me about Dobson owning the mine, but as God is my witness, I didn't kill the man."

"His death must have brought some relief," Sybil countered, the pain of losing her father hiding in her voice. "Admit it was convenient timing."

"Damn it, no! Atwood was willing to negotiate, to drop the matter if I agreed to abide by certain conditions. Then he died, and I discovered Daventry had inherited his damn books." Newberry flopped into the chair, released a weary sigh and turned to Lucius. "I've been waiting for months for your blackmail note. When you said you were selling Atwood's work, I seized the opportunity, would have paid anything to obtain them."

Lucius sat quietly, debating the information.

He knew Atticus well enough to know what he would have demanded from Lord Newberry. Justice. Justice for the poor families who had lost loved ones and a means of income. Even with evidence, he doubted a man of Newberry's standing would ever be committed for trial.

"I think I have a solution," Lucius said, "but allow me a moment to confer with Miss Atwood."

"You ask as if I have a choice." Newberry pushed out of the chair and stomped from the room.

Lucius explained his plan to Sybil, reminded her of their lack of evidence. Sometimes justice meant making compromises.

"Newberry's an arrogant fop, but instinct says he's innocent of Atticus' murder," he said, his heart heavy with regret, for he was desperate to blame someone. "Cowards threaten women. It takes a devil to suffocate a man in his bed."

Sybil's eyes widened. "Heavens, do you think that's how my father died?"

He captured her hand and stroked it gently. "I believe so." There had been nothing to rouse the coroner's suspicions.

She looked to her lap before meeting his gaze. "Do what you think is right." Tears welled, and she inhaled in an attempt to keep them at bay.

Lucius leaned forward and pressed a chaste kiss to her lips. Love filled his heart. "Trust me. The person responsible will pay. Newberry is guilty of negligence, maybe arson, of being a damn fool, but I'm confident he didn't kill Atticus." The lord was hardly the sort to enter a house uninvited, let alone have the skill to pick the lock.

Sybil cupped his cheek with a tenderness that stole his breath. "I trust you with my life, Lucius. I trust your decision regarding Lord Newberry. And let me say that there is nothing insignificant about you."

He kissed her again, released her before Newberry sauntered back into the room.

"So, what do you intend to do, Daventry?" Newberry took his seat behind the desk. He appeared to have reclaimed his right of entitlement during his brief absence. "Bind my legs and hurl me into the Thames? Nail my tongue to the pillory?"

"You deserve nothing less," Lucius said. "No, I intend to give you Atticus' notes relating to the incident at the mine. But only under certain conditions."

"What conditions? What do you want? Blood?" Newberry mocked. "Nomination to my club?"

"I would rather eat my own eyeballs." Lucius snorted. "No. Your solicitor will find the families of all those who died in the mining accident. They will all receive the sum of a thousand pounds as compensation. Those evicted from their homes will receive five hundred pounds. I don't care if the sums are given anonymously. But I want proof before handing over the evidence."

Newberry gritted his teeth. "You're talking about sixty families, about forty-five thousand pounds."

Lucius stood and tugged the sleeves of his coat. "The choice is yours. Now, I'm sure you would like to see the matter concluded quickly, lest I have another change of heart."

And with that, they left the lord to his business.

CHAPTER EIGHTEEN

"Miss Trimble is to manage my husband's home for destitute ladies," Mrs Wycliff said, keen to explain the presence of an elegant woman who had just passed Sybil in the hall. "The refurbishments have taken a little longer than expected, which means we might have to postpone our trip to Italy."

"We won't need to postpone." Mr Wycliff crossed the drawing room, thrust a glass of brandy into Lucius' hand, a sherry into Sybil's. "My father can oversee things for a few months while we're away."

"Your father!" Mrs Wycliff couldn't hide her shock. "Heavens, he does nothing for himself. He hires people to arrange his extravagant parties. Hired a man with the same measurements to visit his tailor. What does he know about ladies down on their luck?"

"It will give him a sense of purpose. And Miss Trimble will keep him in check." Mr Wycliff swallowed a mouthful of brandy before dropping down onto the sofa to sit next to his wife. "We can discuss this later. Daventry hasn't come to hear about my father's faults."

"No," Lucius said, "though I doubt the list is as long as my father's failings."

"It's said the duke is a heartless devil."

Lucius sighed. "That would be an accurate assessment."

Mrs Wycliff's gaze softened. "And yet you appear to have a huge heart, Mr Daventry. Your need to protect Miss Atwood is commendable."

"I swore an oath to her father, and I always keep my word."

They were seated together on the sofa opposite the Wycliffs. Lucius was but a foot away, yet Sybil longed to reach out to him, to take his hand and hold it tight.

Mr Wycliff cocked his head and smiled. "People are quick to judge, me included. One would think experience would make me wiser, yet cynicism is hard to master."

"We are all guilty of cynicism." Sybil had thought the worst of Lucius Daventry in the beginning. "I imagine it would surprise people to learn that the dangerous Damian Wycliff is benevolent."

Mr Wycliff laughed. "Sometimes life brings unexpected opportunities, does it not?"

"Indeed," Lucius agreed, glancing at Sybil.

Silence descended.

"Flannery didn't disappoint," Lucius said. "I'd heard he excelled in gathering information, but I didn't expect results so quickly."

"Men desperate to reclaim their vowels can be extremely forthcoming." Mr Wycliff swallowed another mouthful of brandy. "When Flannery offered to wipe a debt in exchange for information, one desperate lord revealed all he knew about Gorget's Garrett."

Lucius sat forward. "Tell Flannery I shall reimburse him for any expenses incurred while making enquires."

Mr Wycliff gave a dismissive wave. "It's been dealt with."

"Paying my debts is as important as keeping my word."

"Very well. You owe Flannery two thousand pounds."

Lucius nodded. "Tell me about Gorget's Garrett."

It was an odd name, Sybil thought. Not that of a person or place. It could be an alehouse, tavern or coaching inn. The term *garret* suggested an attic and her mind raced back to the quaint loft room at Bronygarth and her night of passion with Lucius Daventry.

"The Garrett is a select club." Mr Wycliff's tone suggested something indecent, something illicit. "A club catering to men who prefer to wear gowns and garters. Ribbons and rouge."

"A molly-house?"

"The cynical me would assume so, but I'm told the men simply like to pretend they're women. Lust and lechery play no part in their clandestine meetings."

"I'm not so sure." Lucius withdrew the lewd sketch found in Sir Melrose's secret cupboard. He leaned forward and handed it to Mr Wycliff. "We came across this while searching Sir Melrose's library. There must have been ten or more hidden in a box. The cynical me says Sir Melrose prefers bedding men. Perhaps he justifies his preference by choosing those with a fetish for wearing women's clothes."

Sybil found the hypothesis fascinating. So fascinating she had been absently sipping her sherry and had drained the glass.

"Then the drawings are a catalogue of sorts," she said. "A selection of men one might find at the Garrett. Men willing to dress as women and take a male lover."

"One might assume so, Miss Atwood." Mr Wycliff sniggered as he studied the portrait. "Just because a man has a large chin, don't presume the rest of him is in proportion."

Sybil waited for Lucius to mention the likeness to the duke's steward, Mr Warner, but he didn't. "So we know what Gorget's Garrett is," she said. "And we presume Sir Melrose has specific tastes in the bedchamber. But what has any of it got to do with my father's journals or the death of Mr Cribb?"

Mr Wycliff returned the sketch to Lucius. "Flannery's men spoke to another tenant living above the china dealer."

"Mr Davies?" Lucius sounded intrigued. "I spoke to him myself, but he told me nothing of interest."

Mr Wycliff grinned. "I imagine he wouldn't tell me anything either. But Flannery's men are known on the streets. Flannery's men command respect amongst the lower classes."

"I sensed Davies feared he might incriminate himself were he to reveal anything about Mr Cribb," Lucius explained.

Mrs Wycliff came to her feet and offered Sybil another glass of sherry. Her husband apologised for neglecting his duties, for not being attentive to her needs. The lady responded with a smile that spoke of a love so deep Sybil couldn't help but stare. She trailed her fingers over her husband's shoulder as she moved past—a sensual action brimming with silent promises.

Sybil turned and locked gazes with Lucius. She wondered if he could see the same depth of devotion in her eyes, if her insatiable need for him was evident in her mannerisms, too.

The slight curl of his lips said their thoughts were aligned. Thoughts that would leave them racing from the Wycliffs, keen to indulge in a wild night of pleasure.

"Most of Flannery's men have a checkered history." Mr Wycliff watched his wife as she crossed the room to hand Sybil a second glass of sherry. "Most have had some dealings with the criminal fraternity."

"I assume Davies needed a little gentle persuasion."

Mr Wycliff gave a wicked smirk. "Something like that. It seems Mr Cribb had a few friends. Men who visited at odd times during the day and night. Men who visited on the same day each week. Mr Cribb had no means of employment though he regularly purchased new clothes and was never in arrears with his rent."

"It's obvious how he earned an income," Lucius said.

"The shopkeeper said Cribb was an educated man who thought himself above his peers. He professed to have a foolproof plan, said he would soon be living in a house in Mayfair, not lodging in Saffron Hill."

"Logic suggests the plan involved one of two things," Sybil said, before sipping her sherry. "Mr Cribb was going to blackmail one of his gentleman friends, which means the victim is wealthy, or he was going to become a rich man's companion."

The room fell silent while they contemplated the information.

It did not take a genius to put the puzzle pieces together. Sir Melrose liked men. Mr Cribb liked men and was set to blackmail a wealthy gentleman. Her father was investigating the possibility that Mr Cribb was murdered. And Sir Melrose was desperate to purchase the journals.

Sybil repeated her account aloud. "But all we have is gossip.

Nothing substantial. Nothing to suggest Sir Melrose killed my father." Indeed, she could not imagine a man of his status entering a house at night to commit such an evil deed.

"We have various leads now," Lucius reassured her. "We have the sketch of the man with which to blackmail Sir Melrose. We can visit Gorget's Garrett. Have Flannery's men question all the witnesses from Smithfield Market."

They continued to debate various methods of gaining evidence.

It struck Sybil that while she wanted to punish the person who had caused her father's death, the longer the investigation took, the longer she could remain at Bronygarth with Lucius Daventry.

How many more nights would she have to indulge her desires?

A thousand would not be enough.

How many more days would she have to converse with him during breakfast? To see him smile? To ease the ache in his heart? To let him know that someone loved him?

A lifetime would not be enough.

They dined with the Wycliffs, talked of the couple's upcoming trip to Italy. Lucius expressed a desire to travel, too, and Sybil wondered if his work for the Order would always keep him close to home.

When it came time to leave, Mr Wycliff took Lucius to one side, and the gentlemen conversed privately.

Mrs Wycliff stole the opportunity to draw Sybil into an embrace. She insisted they use their given names, surprised Sybil by saying, "I think you should tell Mr Daventry that you've fallen in love with him."

Tell Mr Daventry!

Heavens. She wanted to tell the entire world—such was the depth of her affection—but she wasn't sure how or when to make the declaration.

"He has too much on his mind at present," Sybil said, unable to argue with Mrs Wycliff's assertion.

"To know you're loved can have a positively profound effect. His concerns for other people are commendable. He's willing to risk his life to protect you, but who takes care of him? Who nurtures his soul? Who gives his life meaning?"

Sybil's heart ached at the thought. Lucius Daventry had lost two close friends. His family lacked the capacity to love him. Did his nightmares not stem from childhood fears of abandonment?

My demons appear when I'm at my most vulnerable.

"I know what it's like to feel unloved," Mrs Wycliff added. But before she could say anymore, the gentlemen finished their hushed conversation and rejoined them.

Denied the opportunity of explaining the depth of her feelings for Mr Daventry, Sybil embraced Mrs Wycliff again, and said, "Thank you for your hospitality and your insightful comments. I shall certainly bear them in mind."

With that, they bid the Wycliffs farewell. When Lucius' hand settled on Sybil's back, she sensed he was as eager as she to spend time together in his carriage.

"Wycliff said to call on him should we need further assistance."

"The gentleman has proved most helpful."

"Indeed. I should recruit him to the Order."

"Perhaps you should recruit Mr Flannery," she said with some amusement. "He's the one with a skill for snooping."

Lucius opened the carriage door but didn't usher Sybil inside.

"Did my mother arrive at the appointed time?" Lucius asked his coachman, who had been tasked with returning to Brook Street to gather information while they dined with the Wycliffs.

Oh, please say yes, Sybil silently pleaded.

Furnis nodded. "She asked to use your study to write a note."

"Good God!" Lucius exclaimed. "Tell me Bower didn't agree." Mistrust rang loud.

Furnis squirmed. "The lady started crying. Was upset you weren't there, sir. Bower stayed with her while she wrote the note."

"Do you have it?"

"Aye." Furnis reached into his greatcoat pocket, removed the unsealed note and handed it to Lucius who peeled back the folds and scanned the missive beneath the light of the carriage lamp.

"Robert is waiting at the Plough. Take us there," Lucius said, thrusting the note into his coat pocket. He gave no sign he found the woman's words distressing. Yet Sybil feared he would soon sink into a solemn mood. "When you return to Brook Street, inform Bower he's to watch Sir Melrose Crampton. He's to keep watch on his mansion house on Maddox Street. I want to know where he goes, what he does, who he speaks to."

"Aye, sir." Furnis sounded a little flustered.

Lucius assisted Sybil into the vehicle. Once inside, he rapped on the roof, and they were soon trundling through the streets.

She watched him in the darkness. Frustration and a host of other emotions took turns to distort his facial features. He hung his head and pressed his fingers to the bridge of his nose.

Fear took command of her then.

What if his demons consumed him?

What if Julia Fontaine had not come to atone for her mistakes?

Sybil removed her hat while she waited for him to speak. Despite the cold, she unbuttoned her pelisse, for she had a sense he would need to hold her close tonight.

The act of undressing captured his attention. "It's bitterly cold. You should gather the blanket, not remove layers."

"Colder than it was in the attic." The last time his demons were tugging on their leash. "Do you want to talk about what your mother wrote in the letter or would you prefer I pleasure you first?"

He studied her intently as she pulled down the blinds. "It takes but twenty minutes to reach the Plough."

"Then we haven't a moment to lose." Doubt crept into her mind. "Unless you would rather sit in silence."

Fire flashed in his eyes as he scanned her body. "I am but a slave to your wants and desires." His voice was suddenly thick with lust.

Her mind scrambled over this unfamiliar terrain. This wasn't about desire, about one being the master, one being the slave. This wasn't about finding release. This was about two people who needed love in their lives.

The truth was one's best friend, she reminded herself.

"I want to feel close to you, Lucius." She swallowed down her nerves. "I want to sheath you, hold you so tight you can hardly breathe. I don't want to feel empty anymore. I want to feel full, full with you."

"Come here," he said, the words a husky growl.

Sybil crossed the carriage. She hoisted her skirts and sat astride him. "Bury yourself in my body, Lucius. Let me love you."

His warm mouth covered hers in an instant. He didn't have to tease her lips apart. She opened for him, needed this wanderer to drink deeply. He did. And heaven help her, he was so thirsty, so parched. Their tongues mated, stroking, caressing, loving as their greedy moans filled the small space.

Desire and love fused to make the inner ache unbearable. "Lucius," she breathed. "Don't wait. I need you now."

In desperation, he fiddled with the fall of his breeches, gripped his erection and pushed into her body.

Sybil groaned aloud.

Oh, God. It was so exquisite she almost cried.

His head fell back against the squab as she sank down on his solid length. A deep hum left his lips. "God, love, you always know what I need."

"Fill me," she muttered. "Fill me again and again."

He wrapped his arms around her waist, locking them together. "We're joined in the most primal way, yet our connection is more than physical."

"Yes," she said as his hands moved to grip her hips, to help her find a slow, intoxicating rhythm. "You were right." She sank down, sheathing him to the hilt.

He sucked in a sharp breath. "Love, you're so hot, so wet, so damn hungry for me. Right about what?"

"When you said I would never give myself to a man I didn't love."

He stilled, held her impaled. "What are you saying?"

She hummed. "That I'm in love with you, Lucius. I love everything about you. Your strength. Your devotion. The streaks of blue in your eyes that sparkle when you're amused." She rocked on his erection. The slightest movement flooded her body with waves of pure pleasure. "I love the way you kiss me, the way you care for me, the way you drive hard into my body. I love you."

Lucius stared at her, his slow smile spreading. "You love me?"

"More than I could ever explain."

His eyes shone with emotion, every beautiful blue fleck filled with joy. He responded by threading his hands into her hair, anchoring his mouth to hers.

He broke contact on a gasp. "God, Sybil, I've loved you for so long. When I saw you on the stairs that night, you stirred something inside me. Something so profound, I've held you in my heart ever since."

A rush of happiness made her lean forward and kiss him softly on the mouth. But then a sudden urgency overtook them —the need to show their love in the physical act that brought such immense pleasure.

One minute she was astride him, the next she was bent over the opposite seat as he pounded into her sex with a fervency that spoke of love as much as lust. The slapping wasn't loud enough to convey the depth of her feelings. The whimpers and moans weren't deep enough. The rocking not wild enough.

When the muscles in her core convulsed and clamped around him, she cried, "I love you, Lucius."

"God, I love you," he gasped. "More than I could ever explain."

CHAPTER NINETEEN

L ucius gathered Sybil closer to his chest and pulled the blanket up over her shoulders. She slept soundly, breathing softly, despite the wind rattling the leaded windows in his bedchamber. The bed hangings swayed as if a spectre stood tapping from the other side. That, coupled with the chill air, served as an ominous warning of what was to come.

Unlike him, Sybil had been unperturbed when he explained that his mother wanted to meet him at the Black Swan. One would expect the reunion to take place during the day, over a meal and a tankard of ale. Where his mother would produce a hundred heartfelt letters written to her son, but never sent. What reason could Julia Fontaine have for insisting he come under cover of darkness?

She must be terrified of the duke, Sybil had said.

Yet Lucius suspected a sinister motive.

Instinct said his mother was the missing piece of the puzzle. A puzzle he was desperate to solve. After twenty years, her sudden arrival couldn't be a coincidence. Surely her choice of coaching inn, and the place she had made her first appearance, carried some significance, too.

Sybil stirred at his side, and her hand came to rest on his chest.

God, he loved her.

He was so in love with her, his heart ached.

It took strength of mind not to imagine a bright and glorious future. He would marry her, raise a family, be a loving husband and father. But what about his loyalty to Atticus? What about his work for the Order?

"I'm sorry, Lucius. I must have fallen asleep." Sybil's gentle voice reached out to him in the darkness. "I promised to stay awake until it was time for you to leave."

He kissed her forehead and stroked her hair. "I'm going soon."

She came up on her elbow and looked at him. "Won't you let me come with you? I can sit quietly in the corner and read beneath the candlelight while you speak to your mother."

"I want you to stay here. I need you to stay here." He planned to delve deep into his mother's history, planned to pick apart her account of the tale until he found the truth. He couldn't do that while worrying about Sybil. "Tomas and Jonah will keep guard during my absence. There's a pistol in the nightstand drawer. I can load it before I leave."

"A pistol? There's no need." She stroked his chest, the soothing caress making it harder to leave. "I shall be fine here."

Lucius nodded, confident there was no place safer than Bronygarth.

Reluctantly, he slipped his arm free from her warm body, drew back the coverlet and climbed out of bed. He could feel the heat of Sybil's gaze as he dressed. Indeed, it took immense effort not to shout to hell with his mother and jump back into bed to satisfy the woman he wanted for his wife.

The cautious part of his nature made him load the pistol. Despite Sybil's reassurances, he tasted the nervous tension in her kiss. Dismissing a strange unease, he promised to return in an hour before insisting she lock the door.

He gave his men specific instructions. Made them swear to protect Sybil with the same unwavering loyalty they did their master. Then he mounted Phaedrus and rode through the merciless east wind until he reached the coaching inn.

The Black Swan.

The metal sign creaked as it swayed wildly. The image of the black bird was there to aid the illiterate, yet the creature stared at Lucius with its evil eye, marking him the enemy. Some said a black swan was a symbol of suffering, or a metaphor for shocking surprises. Some said it spoke of Machiavellian schemes.

Lucius feared all explanations were true.

Dismissing his unease, he rode Phaedrus under the wide archway and into the yard. A lit lantern and a roaring brazier confirmed the inn was open for business. The wind played havoc with the brazier's flames, threatening extinction before giving a sudden reprieve. He, too, felt whipped into uncertainty, tormented by a higher power.

A young groom approached, said he was waiting for the mail coach from Edinburgh, that the driver always stopped for his supper before continuing to town. Lucius flicked the lad a coin and left Phaedrus in his care before marching to the main door of the inn.

Tucking the sheathed blade into his boot, he straightened his shoulders and entered.

The taproom was empty but for an Irish wolfhound curled by the fire. Lucius approached the oak counter, but there was no sign of the innkeeper. He waited. The creak of hinges forced him to turn towards the rear of the room. His mother stood in the doorway. Her red dress hung off bony shoulders, looked to have been made for a much larger woman. Indeed, her frame was more skeletal than trim.

"Lucius. You came." Her welcoming smile barely masked her apprehension. "Forgive the rather crude surroundings, but I prefer it here to town."

His mind struggled with the sudden onslaught of questions.

Had his overtly suspicious nature led him to misjudge her?

Was her arrival nothing more than a coincidence?

"Such things matter not to me." He preferred a shabby castle in the woods to an elegant townhouse. "Forgive my absence earlier. A matter of great importance prevented me from keeping our appointment."

"I understand," she said evenly, and yet Furnis had said she'd sobbed upon finding him away from home. Evidently, she had overcome her distress. "Come through to the private parlour. No one will disturb us there."

Lucius crossed the room and ducked his head to clear the low lintel. His mother directed him to the long table positioned near the open fire. He shrugged out of his greatcoat, waited for her to sit before dropping into the crude wooden chair opposite.

Should a reunion be this difficult?

Should it be so fraught with tension?

"You must have many questions." She snatched the stoneware pitcher and filled two matching mugs with ale. "Ask me anything."

Twenty years' worth of whys and wherefores surfaced. The need to interrogate, to challenge, to attribute blame, left him wondering where to start. He swigged his ale. An old ale. A pale, well-hopped brew too good to be served in a roadside inn.

"I was in love with your father in the beginning," she said to break the long, drawn-out silence. "But the pressure for him to marry and sire heirs caused a terrible rift between us."

"And yet he never married."

"No. I fear the duke's obsession with me poisoned his mind. I left because it became intolerable, because I feared for my life. One cannot remain in a destructive environment."

In the dim light, it was hard to see the scar on her cheek-bone. *She has not aged well*, he thought. He wanted to believe it stemmed from the distress of leaving her son. He wanted to. But couldn't.

"I begged him to let me take you away, too," she said, yet her tone lacked conviction. "But you belong to the duke—"

"I belong to no one," Lucius snapped.

If anyone had a right to make such a claim, it was his friend and mentor. The person who taught him how to be a man. Or Katharine Fontaine. The stranger who had enabled him to prosper.

"Tell me about my grandmother." Many times, he had tried to form a mental picture of the benevolent lady. "What was she like? How did she come by such a fortune?" Why had such a generous woman allowed her daughter to become a courtesan?

Julia Fontaine looked as if he'd asked her to name every

Home Secretary since William Petty. She opened her mouth, mumbled incoherently before saying, "I'm not sure where to start."

"Was her hair as dark as mine? Did she think of me? Why did she not attempt to visit?" He had a catalogue of questions.

She pursed her lips and seemed to consider her answer carefully. "I don't remember her," she finally admitted. "My mother sent me to live with an uncle when I was five."

Lucius fell silent, lost in a moment of confusion.

"She died a year later," Julia added.

"Died?" Lucius reeled from the shock. "That's impossible. She died a month before my eighteenth birthday. My inheritance was held in trust until I reached my majority."

"Lucius, Katharine Fontaine was destitute when she died."

"Destitute?"

"She was buried in a pauper's grave."

"Then who in blazes left me a fortune?" As soon as the words left his lips, he knew the answer. A conniving, manipulative devil, that's who. A father who couldn't give love or affection but could give money freely.

"It can only be the duke," she said, echoing his sentiment. "He has the means to trick you. He would see it as his duty to provide for you financially."

"His duty to control me, to prove I need him," Lucius corrected. Hatred raced through his veins. He might have sat there and let animosity fester. He might have plotted and planned a way to repay his father. And he would repay him. But the urge to get this meeting over with and return to Bronygarth, to Sybil, led him to say, "On the subject of manipulation, you said the duke made it impossible for you to return."

She cradled the mug between dry, cracked hands and stared at it for a time. "Melverley chased me from town. Ensured no one extended me credit. Had me barred from every social event. Prevented me from becoming another man's mistress. Indeed, no man dared make me an offer."

Oh, Lucius knew the bitter, domineering devil only too well.

The duke would do anything, anything to get his way.

He studied the frail woman before him, all limp limbs as she sagged in the seat. He found it rather ironic that the picture on the wall behind was of a weeping willow. The drooping foliage dangled close to the water. His mother's hair hung loose, the ends an inch from her full mug of ale. And yet another image invaded his musings—that of a woman sobbing by a lake.

Sybil!

A shudder of fear shook him to his core.

He needed to get this meeting over with.

Every nerve in his body said he needed to leave the Black Swan.

"So you went north," he said, though his mind was elsewhere now.

"Yes, to Scotland. There's something about crossing the border that makes one feel safe. Free."

Scotland?

Why did the mere mention of the country set him on edge?

"Whereabouts in Scotland?"

"Whereabouts?" She looked at him as if the answer was of no consequence. "Moffat. It's renowned for its mineral-rich spring water. They say the medicinal baths have healing properties."

"Moffat?" His heart thumped in his chest. His stomach churned. "In Dumfriesshire?"

"Indeed."

Suspicion didn't just flare—it blazed.

"And you felt you could return to London now the duke is on his deathbed." His cynicism was evident in his tone. "Why?"

Would she have the gall to say she wanted to be his mother?

"There is nothing to fear anymore." She paused to cough violently into her handkerchief. "I received word of your father's condition and came on the first stagecoach."

Liar!

His father's health had deteriorated this past week. No one knew. So how the devil had someone sent word to Scotland? How the hell had she got to London so quickly?

Lucius downed his drink and refilled the mug. Ale splashed onto the wooden table as his hand shook from suppressed anger.

Keep calm.

Extract the information.

"I'm curious to hear about your life there. Have you other children? Did you marry?"

"No. No other children. We tried." She looked at the ale in the mug as if the liquid represented every tear shed. "My husband was desperate for an heir. It seems to be a recurring theme in my life."

"So you did marry. You're no longer Julia Fontaine."

"No." Her weak smile faded quickly. "My married name is Dunwoody. It's not as elegant as Fontaine."

Dunwoody?

Bloody hell!

It took the control of a saint to remain seated in the chair. His stomach roiled. Every puzzle piece appeared in his mind. Laid out before him. The solemn Scot watching his house, stealing the journal, hiring thugs to kidnap Sybil. The vowels in the name of Dunwoody. Her vowels, not her husband's. The deeds to the property in Dumfriesshire. Cribb. The sketch of Warner.

Warner?

Is that how she knew his father was sick?

Did Warner know she lived across the border?

Yet the steward had only served his father for five years.

Think! Damn it!

He downed another mug of ale as a means of stalling while he assembled his erratic thoughts. There were so many confusing elements, so many pieces of information to slot together. Indeed, his mind seemed suddenly heavy, woozy, as he tried to make sense of it all.

Still, Sybil's words penetrated the chaos.

Don't fire a measly arrow.

Load the trebuchet and hurl a fireball.

"I agree," he said. "Fontaine is of medieval origin, the name given to those who lived by water." A weeping willow who sheds false tears. "Dunwoody rings of a debt-ridden devil willing to sell her soul to reclaim her vowels."

The fireball hit with an imaginary bang, sending his mother shooting back in the chair.

"What baffles me," he continued, trying to ignore the sudden need to sleep, "is how you know the steward."

"The steward?" She glanced at his empty mug.

Why would Warner know where his mother lived?

Ah, because the duke's obsession demanded it so.

"Mr Warner. The duke's steward." Hell, his head started spinning. "The friend who told you he was sick. The confidant who told you I lived in Brook Street." The fop who surely knew he owned Bronygarth, too.

Sybil!

"Mr Warner," he repeated. The urge to hurry, the urge to return home thrummed in his veins. "The servant who t-tends to my father while ... while colluding with you." The last comment was an educated guess. Melrose was the person who held the marionettes' strings. But there could—

Damn.

Lucius shook his head and fought the need to lie down.

"Lucius? Are you unwell?"

Hellfire!

He could hardly keep his eyes open. He looked to the woman seated opposite. Concern was not the emotion etched on her gaunt face. Relief brought a faint smile to her lips. What the hell had she done to him?

"Angus!" she called. "Angus!"

Lucius vaguely recalled the parlour door opening, caught a hazy look at the solemn man in black, heard his mother say, "Forgive me, but there was no other way" before plunging into darkness, into oblivion.

CHAPTER TWENTY

The sick roiling in Sybil's stomach told her something was wrong. The tightening of her chest and a trembling trepidation forced her out of bed. She hurried to the window, dragged back the heavy curtains and stared out.

Dark blue waves of sunlight weaved through black clouds.

The morning sun would soon breach the horizon.

Lucius had been gone hours—far too long.

The logical part of her brain said reunions were complicated affairs. More so after a twenty-year separation. Indeed, how did one condense their experiences into a short conversation? Heightened emotions complicated matters. There would be anger, tears, heartfelt explanations. Blame. Remorse.

So why could she not calm her mind? Why did gut instinct scream for her to dress and ride to the Black Swan?

Trust your heart, dear girl.

Trust your intuition.

Her father's words spurred Sybil into action. She raced to her room, washed in cold water that had been in the bowl at least a day. There was no time to worry about stays. A chemise and petticoat would suffice.

Jonah wasn't keeping guard outside her door.

Did he have similar fears for Lucius, too?

Were they under attack from an intruder?

Had the floating ghost found its way into the tunnel?

Sybil hurried down the dark staircase, followed the sound of raised voices and came upon Tomas and Jonah arguing in the narrow corridor near the chapel.

"Ma'am?" Tomas said, his grave tone conveying her worst fears.

"Something has happened to Mr Daventry," she said, her voice determined, assertive, for she would not have them think her a flighty female. "Something is wrong. We must go to the Black Swan at once. You'll not persuade me otherwise."

"You see. What did I say?" Jonah towered over Tomas. "Mr Daventry wouldn't make us swear to protect Miss Atwood and then stay away this long."

"No, he would not," Sybil agreed.

Lucius had been reluctant to leave. For heaven's sake, he was so worried about her safety, he had loaded the pistol. Such a lengthy absence was out of character. And he had been suspicious of his mother's motives.

"Happen his mother had some explaining to do," Tomas countered. "It doesn't mean there's any havey-cavey business. I can't see Mr Daventry leaving with half a story, with anything less than the truth."

"In Mr Daventry's absence, I am mistress of this house," she said, "and I am telling you I want a horse saddled for I intend to ride to the Black Swan."

Tomas shifted uncomfortably. "Mr Daventry will string me up from Bloody Bridge if I let you leave, ma'am."

Sybil straightened her shoulders. She knew the poor fellow was only following orders, knew Lucius could be rather insistent, but she couldn't shake the feeling something dreadful had happened.

"Tomas, I am the most reckless woman ever to make Mr Daventry's acquaintance. He told me so himself. I am stubborn, obstinate to the point of being unreasonable. I'm going to the Black Swan and woe betide anyone who attempts to stop me."

Tomas threw his hands in the air in frustration. "Then we must go, too. But who will protect the vault?"

"I don't care about the vault." It came as no surprise to find she valued the master of the Order over the volumes hidden in old chests. "I care about Mr Daventry."

Tomas heaved a sigh.

"This could be a trap," Jonah said cautiously. "A ploy to lure us away from here so the intruder might break into the vault."

Sybil was about to speak when Samuel came bursting through the servants' door at the end of the corridor. "There's a letter for Miss Atwood." The boy waved the paper in the air and skidded to a halt.

"For me?" Sybil shuddered.

No one knew she was staying at Bronygarth. She snatched the note from the boy's grasp and broke the seal. With trembling fingers, she gripped the paper and read the precise list of instructions.

"Is it from Mr Daventry, ma'am?" Tomas said, wringing his hands.

"It's about Mr Daventry, though not written by his hand." Her legs buckled as a wave of despair stole her strength.

Both men rushed to her aid.

"Take your time," Tomas said. "Samuel can read it if it helps. Mr Daventry taught him his letters and numbers."

"No, it's fine." Heavens, Lucius needed her. She couldn't fall apart now. "Samuel, who delivered the note?"

"A girl named Fanny. Said she works at the Black Swan and a Scottish cove paid her two shillings to bring it before dawn."

"Scottish?" Sybil's mind raced to the solemn-looking man who had stolen the fake journal from the auction. So, Julia was not working alone.

"What news of Mr Daventry?" Tomas asked again.

"The letter is from his mother, Mrs Dunwoody." Merciful Lord. The puzzle seemed so much clearer now. "She has taken Mr Daventry hostage. In exchange for his safe return, she demands all evidence relating to the riot at Smithfield Market."

Tomas frowned. "Mr Daventry, taken hostage? By a woman?"

"The Scot is her accomplice. They must have used some devious method to capture him." Tears threatened to fall, but Sybil kept them at bay. "I'm to gather the evidence and meet her in Lambeth tonight, at midnight. I'm to take the Lambeth

Church steps and follow the path to the boat builder, Godfrey and Searle."

Mrs Dunwoody wanted to meet a short distance from Bishop's Walk, where Mr Proctor was killed. That did not bode well. Julia Fontaine—or Julia Dunwoody, as she was now called—had no loyalty to her son. What was to stop her taking the evidence and killing them both? Was she so desperate to reclaim her vowels from Sir Melrose?

Tomas and Jonah exchanged nervous glances.

"What do you want us to do, Miss Atwood?" Jonah said.

Tomas shook his head. "Someone has to stay. Someone has to protect the vault."

Mother Mary!

She wanted to shout to hell with the vault. Damn the blasted journals. Who cared about solved cases? Who wanted to read about fraud and treachery, old cases without sufficient proof of the offender's innocence? Her beloved father had died because of his obsession. Lucius might die, too.

No! Sybil stamped her foot. *No!*

She would not lose him.

The world needed strong, honest men like Lucius Daventry. Men who fought to protect the innocent. But the journals were important to Lucius, and she had to consider that point when deciding what the devil to do.

"Lucius' mother insists I go alone."

Tomas gasped. "Oh, ma'am, you mustn't go alone. That woman is here to do the devil's work."

Sybil struggled to think through the chaos.

"Just give me a moment." She turned and paced the corridor while mentally assessing her options. After a minute of tense silence, she swung around to face the worried servants. "Tomas, you and Jonah will wait here. Patrol the grounds. Protect the vault. Be vigilant. Robert will ride to town and deliver a note to Mr Wycliff."

"Mr Wycliff?" Jonah asked.

"A friend as skilled in combat as Mr Daventry." Yes, Mr Wycliff would know exactly what to do. She would ensure he knew to come at once. That it was a matter of life and death.

"Mr Wycliff will take me to the Black Swan where we will question the innkeeper."

"You'll want to threaten him, not question him, ma'am."

"Thank you, Tomas. Yes, we will ensure he spills his guts." She had a loaded pistol in the nightstand drawer to use as a means of intimidation. "All being well, I shall return to town with Mr Wycliff and make plans to meet the devil at midnight. Under no circumstances are you to leave your posts here. Is that understood?"

"Yes, ma'am," both men said in unison.

She turned to Samuel. "I want you to help me copy information from a journal. I assume Mr Daventry taught you to write as well as read."

"Yes, Miss Atwood."

"Good. Run and tell your father I wish to see him at once and then wash your hands and meet me in the dining room." Sybil paused to catch her breath. "So, do we all know what we have to do?" No doubt she had missed something vital. She excelled at snooping, but trapping a cunning murderer was a different matter.

They all nodded.

Samuel hurried away to fetch his father. Jonah went to check no one had attempted to break into the tunnels while they had been distracted.

Tomas lingered. He studied her for a moment and said, "You know, ma'am, I think he'd be mighty proud of you right now."

Touched, Sybil placed her hand on her heart. "Who? My father?"

"No, ma'am, Mr Daventry. Happen a reckless, stubborn woman is exactly what the master needs."

⬦

On a foggy night, and when travelling in the dark confines of a hired carriage, one street looked like another. A man relied on spotting landmarks when attempting to establish his direction. A mansion house. A public building. A bridge. In this instance, it was Westminster Bridge, with the blurred image of the House of

Commons to the right. That meant they were heading to Lambeth.

Slumped in the carriage seat, Lucius let his head loll forward. He moaned and muttered incoherent nonsense to convince Julia Dunwoody he was still under the influence of laudanum. Hell, he could grace the stage with his performance.

The woman who gave birth to him did not deserve the title *mother*. She had plied him with ale, knowing she'd added enough milk of the poppy to render him unconscious. He wasn't sure how the solemn brute Angus managed to carry him to the carriage. Perhaps the innkeeper had offered his assistance. Indeed, once Lucius had dealt with these disloyal rogues, he would visit the owner of the Black Swan.

Julia Dunwoody—for he refused to refer to her as anything else—reached out from the seat opposite. She captured his chin and lifted his head, stared into his eyes.

"Lucius?" The woman huffed in frustration. "You should be alert now."

Twice, since first stirring from his drug-induced slumber, she had made him drink an opium tincture. Enough to keep him subdued. Twice, he'd held the liquid in his mouth. Had spat it into the pad of the seat when he'd slumped forward. He might have easily escaped, but he was getting too close to the truth.

"Lucius. I need you to walk." She grabbed him and slapped his face. The attack was the culmination of years of neglect, spoke of genuine disdain for the duke and her son. "Wake up."

If she wanted him more alert, he would oblige.

"Walk?" he said, swaying in the seat like a maudlin drunk. "Walk where?"

"We're to meet Miss Atwood near Stangate Street."

Sybil!

His heart lurched. She must be worried sick. Terrified.

It took strength not to jump up from the seat, howl and thrash about like a madman. But his hands were bound at the wrists. The devil woman had taken the blade from his boot. And only a fool charged into a fight without assessing the scene.

Patience. Patience.

"If you harm a hair on her head, you'll rue the day you came back into my life." He let her feel the full force of his wrath.

"So, you are more alert than you would have me believe."

A sudden coughing fit had her dragging a handkerchief from the pocket of her cloak. She covered her mouth, spat blood into the white linen for the second time in the space of an hour.

"And you're frailer than I thought." Mixed emotions clashed swords in his chest. He had every reason to hate her. Yet the lonely boy didn't want to lose his mother to a dreaded illness. "Your husband should be in here, taking care of you, not sitting atop the damn box."

"My husband?" Confusion marred her brow.

"Angus. The Scot with the miserable face. You have a habit of attracting wretched men."

"Angus isn't my husband." She wiped spittle from her mouth. "He's my cousin. I told you, my mother sent me to live in Scotland with an uncle when I was but five years old. Angus is like a brother."

So she had the capacity to love someone.

"Angus often took the beatings meant for me," she added. The comment roused disturbing images, conveyed a painful history.

"And where is Mr Dunwoody?" he mocked.

"In Scotland. I left the day he moved his mistress into my home. The day I was relegated to the role of housekeeper."

"You've had more than your share of hardship." There it was again—the child in him grasping at any reason to account for her deplorable actions. "That doesn't excuse what you've done. Let me reiterate my earlier point. I would die to protect Miss Atwood. No one is more important to me than her. Now, would you care to explain what the hell is going on?"

"Miss Atwood is bringing the evidence her father gathered about the riot at Smithfield Market. She is going to exchange it for your safe return."

"And that's all? That's the reason for this whole damn charade? You want the journals so you can claim your vowels back from Sir Melrose?"

"If Miss Atwood values you over her father's work—" She

stopped abruptly and coughed into her handkerchief. The wracking sound filled the small space. "Then ... then everything should go to plan."

"You didn't just arrive," he said, for she presumed too much about his relationship with Sybil. "You've been in London for weeks. You sent Miss Atwood threatening letters in the hope she would bring the journals to the Black Swan. You've followed her home on many occasions. You've watched us closely."

She gave a curt nod. "You visit her in Half Moon Street almost every night. You've been lovers for some time."

"Not quite."

And he visited the butler, not the love of his life. He scouted the area, checked the premises, conversed with Blake. He kept his oath to Atticus in the only way he knew how.

"Are you so desperate to reclaim your vowels that you must resort to frightening a young woman, to kidnapping your son?"

"I don't care about the vowels," she said, shocking the hell out of him. "I care about the deeds to Angus' property. He tried to help me, and I betrayed his trust. I cannot rest until I make amends."

It was both a relief and some form of cruel torture to discover she loved someone enough to go to this much trouble. To save Angus, she was willing to sacrifice her son.

"You have a gambling problem," he said as the carriage rumbled to a halt on what he presumed was Stangate Street. Again his heart lurched at the thought of Sybil waiting alone on a dark, lonely stretch of the river.

"Your father has paid my gaming debts for years, on the proviso I remain in Scotland. Mr Warner stopped making the payments some months ago, though I doubt the duke knows of his duplicity."

So Warner was in contact with Julia Dunwoody.

"We're here." The woman shuffled forward. "Don't blame Angus. He is just trying to help me, just trying to play the older brother, as he always has." She stared at Lucius for a time. "I did so want to be a good mother, Lucius. Perhaps in the next life, I'll have a chance to try again."

The time for conversation was at an end.

Angus opened the carriage door and gave Julia his hand to assist her descent. He reached into the carriage and gripped Lucius' arm, helped him to the pavement, too.

Angus snatched a carriage lantern, and after a brief argument with the coachman, told the fellow to wait. Then the Scot spoke quietly to Julia. The woman cupped his cheek, and they talked as if saying their final goodbyes.

Lucius was somewhat surprised when the Scot accompanied them down the Stangate Street steps. Julia walked as if she had the weight of the world on her shoulders—hunched, more shuffling than full strides. Through the fog, they followed the river past the boat builders before stopping on the narrow path. They waited for a few minutes, the silence broken by the Scot's heavy breathing and Julia Dunwoody's hacking cough.

Two people approached from the direction of the State Barge Houses. A woman in a cloak. *Sybil!* A man in a greatcoat and hat, though Lucius could not identify him from such a distance.

Julia seemed mildly perturbed. She stared at Sybil and muttered, "I told her to come alone."

"I wish she hadn't come at all," he added.

Angus turned to Lucius, and in a broad Scottish accent said, "Nae harm shall befall the lass. Nae harm shall befall ye, lad."

Lucius found the comment oddly comforting. Perhaps because the man spoke with the fondness of kin. Perhaps because he had called him lad, not boy.

CHAPTER TWENTY-ONE

O nly a woman out to rescue the man she loved dared venture along a narrow river path on a foggy night. The heavy white veil hung low, hovering above the water, obscuring the view of the opposite bank. Boats and buildings were but black shadows hiding amidst the gloom. Eerie noises drifted out from the mist. Creaking oars, the slapping of water, the flutter of a sail, the muffled voices of boatmen going about their nightly business.

No wonder this was a hunting ground for thieves and pickpockets.

Sybil drew her cloak across her chest, though the stench of the river made one forget about the chill in the air. Ahead, she saw the faint glow of a lantern, and like a moth to a flame moved closer.

Three hazy figures stood waiting in the dark.

A powerful rush of emotion brought tears to Sybil's eyes when she recognised Lucius. He looked so tired, so downcast.

Beside her, Alcock carried the satchel containing the journal with statements from those at Smithfield Market. A notebook with letters written by Samuel, another written by Sybil but made to look as if a witness could place Sir Melrose at Gorget's Garrett. And a loaded pistol.

As they came to a halt a mere ten feet away, Mrs Wycliff's coachwoman peered at the solemn-looking Scot and whispered, "Just say the word, ma'am, and I'll knock that tall blighter into the river, make no mistake."

Mrs Wycliff had warned Sybil about Alcock's penchant for violence. "I'm sure it won't come to that."

She prayed it wouldn't come to that.

"The quiet ones are the worst," Alcock said, her opinion of the Scot drawn from Sybil's description of a morbid man.

"Did I not tell you to come alone, Miss Atwood?" the worst mother in history said.

Tears welled again when Sybil locked gazes with Lucius. Not because his hands were bound at the wrists. Not because she was scared of the Scot. No. A man as loving as Lucius Daventry did not deserve to be treated with such disdain. Not by his kin.

"It's not safe for a woman to walk this path alone," Sybil countered. "My coachwoman came merely to ward off thieves and to carry the evidence you requested."

Lucius studied the coachwoman, and the corners of his mouth twitched. Sybil had brought Alcock because she worked for the Wycliffs, and so Lucius would know not to worry, would know help was at hand. Indeed, somewhere in the ghostly gloom, Mr Wycliff and his friends were lying in wait. She only wished she knew where.

"My son thinks highly of you, Miss Atwood," Julia Dunwoody said, narrowing her gaze as she focused on Alcock's face. "I trust you won't disappoint."

"I have what you asked for if that is your meaning."

And once Mrs Dunwoody gave Sir Melrose the journal, he would discover that a witness could place him at the Garrett. That would give Lucius an opportunity to set a trap, to exact his revenge.

All they had to do now was survive the next few minutes.

Sybil was about to insist they settle their business quickly, when the sound of a mumbled conversation and the clip of booted footsteps echoed along the path.

"Ah, right on cue." Julia paused to cough. "Here come the real villains in this game. The night would not be complete without a dose of revenge."

Villains?

Revenge?

Was this woman not behind the evil machinations?

But no, two men burst through the enveloping fog.

Sir Melrose Crampton came to a crashing halt. Shock, then fear held him rigid. Sybil was more taken aback by the arrival of Mr Warner.

"What the devil is going on?" Sir Melrose's frantic gaze darted to Lucius, to Sybil, and then back to Julia Dunwoody.

Mr Warner's face turned ashen. He looked like he might cast up his accounts. He clutched Sir Melrose's arm with an intimacy that belied their positions. "Good God. You said we were coming to collect the j-journal." The weasel waved a finger at Lucius. "Why the hell is he here?"

"Warner, you conceited arse." Lucius' face was granite hard. "Know that as soon as I'm free of my restraints, I'll throttle the last breath from your deceitful body."

"Why are you so shocked, Sir Melrose?" Julia's slow smile built. "You wanted Atticus Atwood's journal in exchange for the vowels and the title deed. I'm here on your orders. To reclaim the documents you used to blackmail me."

Sir Melrose's hollow cheeks quivered. "I assumed you had the journals in your possession."

"Yes, I am about to make the exchange." Julia spoke as if her son were a mere commodity. A pawn to barter. "Am I to blame for your early arrival?"

"But ... but." Sir Melrose couldn't find the words to contradict the panic etched on his face. He sucked in a deep breath and seemed to regain his composure. "Yes, well, the Royal Society will be grateful to you, Mrs Dunwoody. Though I'm confused." The man's beady eyes settled on the satchel gripped by Alcock's meaty paws. "I thought Mr Daventry possessed Atwood's work."

"Miss Atwood had access to her father's journals. I merely used my son as leverage to force her hand."

Cold-hearted hag!

Lucius muttered an obscenity.

"How you obtain the journals is your affair," Sir Melrose replied. "You serve national interests, madam. It's only right the work of an eminent scientist is held by such a prestigious academy as the Royal Society."

"Ballocks!" Lucius shouted.

"Ballocks, indeed." Julia covered her mouth but suppressed another cough. "What my son means, Sir Melrose, is that everyone here knows you're a liar. You mention the Royal Society's need to obtain the journals, yet you specifically asked for one journal. The one containing details of a riot in Smithfield Market. One look at Miss Atwood's satchel confirms the lady has brought but one book."

"Not just one book," Sybil corrected.

She was beginning to understand the woman's reason for bringing everyone together. Now, Sybil didn't have to wait for Julia to give Sir Melrose the notebook with the fake evidence. She could have her own revenge.

"Yes, I have the journal containing witness statements from those at the market," Sybil continued. "And I have a notebook with letters confirming Sir Melrose is a member of a select club known as Gorget's Garrett. I understand it's a molly-house."

Warner inhaled sharply. "Damnation. We should leave." He tugged Sir Melrose's sleeve again. "We don't need to listen to this nonsense."

"That's right," Lucius countered. "Listen to your lover. The man whose naked picture we found in your library. The man whose likeness is drawn on the reverse of an invitation card for the Garrett. I've seen the proof that confirms Mr Cribb was also a member. You remember Mr Cribb. The man who was murdered in the market."

"We also have Mr Proctor's notes." So much for the truth being one's best friend. Lies after more lies tumbled from Sybil's mouth. "Before being savagely murdered, he discovered the late-night habits of the Duke of Melverley's steward. That gives you a motive, Mr Warner."

Why else would Mr Proctor have asked to meet Lucius?

"And now you have a dilemma," Lucius said. "We all know the truth, Sir Melrose. You've already murdered three men—Cribb, Proctor and Atticus Atwood. How do you propose to keep us silent?"

Sir Melrose turned deathly pale. "Look, I may be guilty of blackmail, but—"

"The fact you're willing to go to extreme lengths to obtain the journal is proof of your guilt," Lucius pressed.

"Warner is equally guilty," Julia said, but this time her cough made her retch. The Scot patted her back until she could breathe easily again. "Warner withheld my allowance from the Duke of Melverley. Warner is the one who suggested you use me in your scheme. Knowing of my weakness for the tables, he employed a card sharp. He made sure I ran up debts, made sure I had no choice but to return here and steal the evidence of Sir Melrose's crimes from my son."

Sir Melrose looked like he might retch, too. He scrubbed his face with his bony hand and whimpered. He exchanged nervous glances with Warner, who suddenly shuffled backwards and bolted.

"Peregrine?" Sir Melrose shouted at his accomplice. Panic turned to anger. "Don't leave me to answer for your crimes!"

"Hellfire!" Lucius thrust his bound hands at the Scot. "Untie me quickly, before Warner gets away."

"I'll catch the devil." Alcock thrust the satchel at Sybil, forgetting there was a loaded pistol inside, and gave chase. Mere seconds passed before she burst back through the misty gloom. "Mr Wycliff and his friends nabbed him by the boathouse."

Mr Wycliff appeared, hauling Warner behind him by the scruff of his neck. His friends Mr Trent and Mr Cavanagh followed behind to join the crowd gathered on the narrow path. The men were dressed in tatty breeches, poorly fitted coats, coarse shirts and blue striped neckerchiefs.

"I believe you have a runaway," Damian Wycliff mocked, dragging the weasel forward. "Let's hear the fop's confession, shall we?" He released Warner and gave him a hard shove.

Warner almost plunged headfirst into the river. "There's nothing to confess. Can a man not help a troubled friend?"

"Don't blame me for this debacle," Sir Melrose countered.

"Who else should I blame? Had you been scrupulous when picking your lovers, none of this would have happened. Mr Cribb was hunting for a goose ripe for the plucking. And you're a damn goose."

"Keep your mouth shut!" Sir Melrose turned to Mrs Dunwoody. "This is your fault. If you'd just given me the journal as I asked." He raised his arm as if ready to strike the woman.

The Scot stepped forward. Lucius did, too.

Everything happened quickly then.

"God, I'm tired of this game." In one fell swoop, Lucius lunged, threw his bound hands over Warner's head and yanked the rope against the man's windpipe. "Confess to the murder of Mr Cribb."

Warner choked and spluttered. His face turned beetroot red as he struggled to breathe. He thumped Lucius' arm, kicked and tried to wriggle free.

Lucius gritted his teeth. "I warned you I'd take your last breath. Now bloody confess."

Warner stabbed his finger at Sir Melrose and croaked, "He k-killed Cribb."

"Liar!" Sir Melrose cried. "Warner killed Cribb, and the runner who lived on Stangate Street."

Lucius choked Warner again, much to the delight of Alcock, who appeared as excited as if she were watching acrobats and tightrope walkers at Astley's Amphitheatre.

Warner's knees buckled. He batted Lucius' hands, begging to speak. "I'll confess—" He gasped for breath as Lucius released his grip. "I—I killed Proctor ... but ... only because he knew about the Garrett, knew Melrose and I were ... were—" Warner pointed to his lover. "He killed Cribb."

"Silence, buffoon!" Sir Melrose's gaze shifted to the path.

Mr Trent and Mr Cavanagh moved to block all means of escape.

"Which one of you devils killed my father?" Sybil choked back a sob. She didn't want to think that one of these vile men had entered her house while she slept. Had murdered a man who lived only to do good deeds.

Both men looked blank when she repeated the question.

Alcock stepped forward. "Answer the lady else you'll get my fist down yer measly throat."

Sir Melrose denied any involvement.

"I—I might have silenced the man," Warner wheezed, "had he not saved me the trouble and died in his sleep."

Both men were liars. Yet every instinct fought against the idea that her father was murdered. There had been no sign of a struggle. No scratches. No bruises. Nothing to suggest foul play.

Because of the delicate nature of their work, and because of Mr Proctor's death, Lucius had assumed the worst. Perhaps grief had formed the basis of his quest for vengeance.

"I am tired of this game, too," Julia Dunwoody said. She walked calmly up to Mr Warner, though her shoulders were hunched and her cloak trailed the ground. She spat blood-stained spittle in his face. "I hope you rot in hell."

"Step back, Mother." Lucius sounded nervous. "He's liable to kick you into the river."

The woman smiled. "You're a good person, Lucius, not like me." She cupped his cheek with a surprising level of tenderness. "I'm sorry I'm not the mother you needed. But I know what these men are capable of, and I'll not have them threaten you again."

Julia stepped away and hugged the Scot. Then she whipped a knife from a sheath strapped to her calf and turned on Sir Melrose. "Give me the deed else I shall gut you like a fish." She pressed the tip of the blade to the man's chest. "Now!"

With shaking hands, Sir Melrose reached into his coat and withdrew the folded papers.

"Angus, take the deed and check the information."

The Scot obeyed. He snatched the papers and scanned the script. "Aye, this is the deed for Millhouse."

"Take it and leave," Julia said, but did not lower her weapon.

"I'll nae leave now."

"We agreed."

"I'll nae leave ye."

Julia gave a resigned sigh. "Remember how helpless I was as a child?" She coughed again. "I'm not helpless anymore, Angus." She stared into Sir Melrose's eyes. "I can take only one of you with me," she said, bitterness coating every word as she plunged the blade into Sir Melrose's chest. "And Warner has less chance of escaping the noose."

For a few heartbeats, everyone gawped in stunned silence.

Julia grabbed hold of Sir Melrose as he sagged forward, his mouth and eyes wide with shock, with pain. With surprising strength, she held on to him as she plunged into the river.

"No!" Lucius cried. He relinquished his hold on Warner, instructed Wycliff to take the steward prisoner and dived into the river after his mother.

"Lucius!" Fear chilled Sybil to the bone. "Lucius! Merciful mother! Someone help him!"

How did a man swim with his hands bound?

How did a man swim with cold limbs?

Bower appeared through the fog. She had forgotten he'd been tasked with following Sir Melrose. The butler stripped off his coat without uttering a word and dived into the Thames.

"Trent, hold Warner." Mr Wycliff shrugged out of his shabby coat and entered the water, too.

Angus dashed tears from his eyes. "I'd help, lass, but I cannae swim," he said, his voice shrill with horror as he held his lantern aloft. "Julia hadnae thought the lad would follow."

Despite her parting comments, Julia Dunwoody knew little of Lucius' character. She didn't know of his abiding loyalty, of his determination to see justice prevail. She didn't know that his need to feel loved had him clinging on to the thinnest shred of hope.

From the depths of the fog, someone surfaced and gasped.

The cries of boatmen rent the air, followed by shouting and violent splashing.

Terror held Sybil in a stranglehold.

Lucius was her life, her love.

She couldn't lose him.

"I can't see him," came a distressed voice from the misty gloom.

A scuffle behind resulted in Alcock giving Warner another swift punch to the gut.

"You there!" came another call from the darkness. "Grab his arm. Drag him out."

A minute passed, maybe two.

"Cavanagh!" Mr Wycliff cried, grabbing hold of the low bank. "Give me your damn hand."

Mr Cavanagh raced forward, and with Angus' help hauled Mr Wycliff from the river.

"Lucius, where's Lucius?" Sybil's body shook more than Mr Wycliff's cold, tired limbs. "Did you find him?"

Oh, Lord, please say you found him.

Mr Wycliff bent his head and gasped for breath. Mr Cavanagh practically tore the man's sodden shirt from his back, demanded Alcock give up her greatcoat and draped the garment around Wycliff's trembling shoulders.

"Where's Lucius?" A sob caught in Sybil's throat.

With a shaky hand, Wycliff gestured to the river. "In ... in a boat."

The giant wave of relief lasted mere seconds before another terrifying thought took hold. "Tell me he's alive."

"Yes ... he's alive."

"Thank God. And Bower?"

"The other man? A boatman dragged him out."

Angus stepped forward. "And Julia?"

Mr Wycliff closed his eyes and shook his head. "She s-sank as if she had a lead b-ball strapped to her ankle."

"Nae a ball, weights sewn into the hem of her cloak. She nae had but a few weeks left and wanted a quick end."

Anger flooded Sybil's veins.

Julia had worked out the perfect plan for revenge. Yet again, she had failed to consider how her actions might affect her son.

"I need to go to him, to Lucius," Sybil said. Before his demons surfaced and gnawed through their leash. "What shall we do with Mr Warner?"

Damian Wycliff rubbed his arms in a frantic bid to keep warm. "We need to deal with the matter now. I—I suggest we go straight to P-Peel. We all heard Warner's confession."

Warner blubbered and pleaded for clemency. He tried to shake free from Mr Trent's grasp, and so Alcock punched him again.

"You're coming, too," Sybil said to Angus. "We need everyone to make statements regarding tonight's events. It's the least you can do for Mr Daventry." She turned to Mr Wycliff. "Where will they take him, the men in the boat?"

"To the boathouses."

"Then I must hurry. I'll meet you there." She thrust the satchel at Benedict Cavanagh. "Take care of the evidence." She had more important things on her mind. "Perhaps remove the pistol before we hand it to Peel."

And without further ado, she picked up her skirts and darted along the path.

❧

Sybil found Lucius in a boathouse, free of his bindings, wearing the crude, colourful garb of a navvy, his wet clothes in a pile on the floor. He sat before a brazier, staring into the flames. Sybil thanked the two men who had pulled him from the river.

"Don't scare me like that again." She touched his shoulder and drew her hand through his wet hair. When he met her gaze, she said, "For one awful second, I thought I'd lost you."

"Forgive me." His chin trembled from the cold. "I wasn't thinking clearly."

"No, you were not." Upon hearing her raised voice, the boatmen made themselves scarce. "What if you haven't been as careful as you claim? We've made love many times. What if I am with child? I don't want to raise your son on my own."

Her father once said that to live for the future was to live for a fantasy. Yet one could not underestimate the power of optimism.

The blue flecks in his eyes sparked to life. "The reckless man in me hopes I have been careless." He pulled her between his legs, wrapped his arms around her waist and pressed his cheek to her abdomen.

She hoped he'd been careless, too. A perfect fantasy appeared in her mind, them living together at Bronygarth with a rabble of reckless children.

"I'm sorry, sorry that's how your mother met her end. Sorry that you had to witness the distressing event." Sybil suppressed her anger by running her hands through his hair as he hugged her. Julia Dunwoody was a selfish woman who caused suffering with her thoughtless actions. "Angus said she'd sewn weights into the hem of her cloak, that she had but a few weeks left to live."

A brief silence ensued.

"It's strange," he said, meeting her gaze. "For twenty years, I've struggled with the thought she was dead, buried at Bideford Park. And yet now I feel oddly at peace."

"Perhaps because she's not the helpless mother you imagined. She could have contacted you, could have eased your fears. It seems she had her own demons to battle."

"Yes." The word escaped him on a sad sigh.

"Mr Wycliff will be here in a moment. He suggests we take Warner to see Peel tonight, that we explain everything."

"I'll not tell Peel about the Order."

"There's no need. We will tell him exactly what we told Damian Wycliff. Though I shall have to confess to forging some evidence."

A weak smile touched his lips. "I did wonder about the witness placing Sir Melrose at the Garrett."

"Once Julia had the journal and notebook, I assumed she would visit Sir Melrose and claim back her vowels. As soon as Sir Melrose read the letters, I knew he would hunt for the witness."

"You thought we could set a trap?"

"That was the idea. But it's all over now."

After a brief pause, he said, "Do you believe them? Warner and Sir Melrose? Do you believe they're innocent of Atticus' murder?"

Sybil cupped his cheek. Heavens, she wanted to kiss him, wanted to rub the warmth back into every inch of his body. "I'm inclined to believe my father's heart gave out. That he died in his sleep. He looked so peaceful when I found him."

After a moment's contemplation he said, "Yes. I have to believe you're right."

Bower burst into the boathouse, water dripping from his hair and clothes. The boatmen hurried to his aid. Mr Wycliff appeared, too, and while they all warmed themselves by the brazier, the conversation turned to justice, to punishing Warner.

Taking Mr Trent's and Mr Wycliff's vehicles, they left Lambeth in search of Peel. They called at his home in Stanhope Street. With his wife and children staying at Lulworth, they found the Home Secretary working late in his office.

Peel was extremely interested to hear her father's views on the cause of the riot at Smithfield Market. He listened intently to all the evidence, to the sworn testimonies from four illegitimate sons of powerful aristocrats. Listened as Lucius spoke about the corruption at Bow Street. Peel ordered a search of the river near Bishop's Walk, had Mr Warner taken into custody. Promised to keep them informed.

Outside the office, Lucius thanked Mr Wycliff, Mr Trent and Mr Cavanagh for coming to Sybil's aid. Before leaving, Angus gave Lucius his direction should he ever find himself north of the border. Finally, Sybil and Lucius were alone in a hackney heading to Brook Street.

Lucius stared out of the window, though there was nothing to see but passing shadows in the gloom. There was no need for her to return to Bronygarth now. That thought roused a pain so intense she fought to breathe.

"You're quiet," she said, waiting for a sign of encouragement, a sign to say he wanted her to dart across the carriage and fall into his arms.

He turned to look at her. "I'm so tired. Tired of living in the past. Tired of chasing devious devils."

"Tired of me?"

His gaze softened. "Sybil, I could never tire of you. I imagine you'll still excite me when I'm in my dotage." And there it was, that warm, sensual tone that said he needed her. The words that spoke of a long and happy future.

It gave her the courage to be bold.

"When you're old and frail will you still pull me into your lap? Will you still examine my stockings? Will you still make love to me with such passion, such skill?"

"Trust me. I shall pleasure you until I draw my last breath."

"Might you have the strength to examine my stockings now?" She studied his labourer's clothes, the dark stubble covering his strong jaw, and found the rugged Lucius Daventry just as appealing. "Might you reassure me all is well?"

He reached out to her.

Her heart lurched upon noting the rope burns circling his wrist. But she slipped her hand into his and came to sit astride him.

This time, their kiss spoke of a different hunger. A need to feed the soul-deep ache. A need to nourish the beautiful dream. He made love to her mouth in the slow, tender way that had her holding him tight, never wanting to let go.

"Marry me," she said, breaking contact. "I don't want to return to Half Moon Street. I want to stay with you at Bronygarth." She swallowed down her nerves. "I want to be your wife, bear your children. I want to love you for the rest of my life."

Water welled in his eyes, and he swallowed so many times she lost count. He clasped her face in his hands. "You're the love of my life. The only woman I have ever wanted. I'd planned to ask you the same question, but you beat me to it, impatient minx."

"Does that mean you accept my proposal?"

"Love, I'd marry you right here, right now, were it possible." His open-mouthed kiss curled her toes. Indeed, she needed to feel him filling her body, needed to feel locked in his primal embrace. "I can apply at the registry for a common license unless you wish to wait and marry in St George's."

"Whatever is quickest. I don't care about pomp and ceremony."

He kissed her again, so deeply his earthy essence infused her being. "God, I'm so in love with you. Though when Atticus asked me to take care of you, I'm not sure this was what he had in mind."

Sybil suspected things had developed exactly as her father had planned. "My father was obsessed with the truth. Perhaps he always knew we would suit."

"Perhaps he hoped for something better for his daughter," he said, yet his sinful smirk said he was teasing. "After all, who wants to fight for the truth and chase villains across town? Who wants to marry a scandalous rogue and make passionate love in a haunted castle?"

Sybil smiled. "Who indeed?"

EPILOGUE

BRONYGARTH - TWELVE MONTHS LATER

Lucius held his son close to his bare chest and rocked him gently as it seemed to bring them both comfort. "You're like your father," he whispered. "You like being held, like the warm feeling that comes with knowing you're loved." He kissed the babe's head, crossed the room to glance into the other crib. "Come, see how peacefully your brother sleeps."

Love filled his heart as he stared at his son, Atticus, sleeping with the calm spirit of his namesake. A man could ask for nothing more than one healthy child. Sybil had given him the gift of twins.

"Mrs Timms thinks you should leave Lucius to cry in his crib." Sybil's soft voice drifted through the darkness.

He glanced up and saw his wife standing at the adjoining door, dressed in nothing but his shirt, her copper curls cascading over her shoulders. Lovelust flared. That was his name for the overpowering mix of emotions that took command of him whenever their gazes locked.

"Mrs Timms thinks our sons should sleep in the east wing, too." He placed his namesake gently into the crib. "I have a mind to tell the nursemaid to dunk her head in the horse trough. The woman thinks love is an affliction."

"Not everyone thinks as we do," she said as he closed the gap between them. "But you should get some rest. We need to leave for Bideford Park at eight. We said we would be there when the first boys arrive."

The Duke of Melverley had died within days of Julia Dunwoody. The same day the steward was found mysteriously dead in a cell in Newgate. The entailed estate in Surrey and the townhouse in Grosvenor Square went to the duke's coxcomb cousin. Lucius inherited everything else, numerous properties, jewels, paintings, a stable of Arabian stallions and the dreaded Bideford Park.

"You've spent months hiring the right tutors, the right house-masters," she continued, "forward-thinking men who will embrace the illegitimate sons of the aristocracy, not belittle them. It's only right we show our support tomorrow."

And they would.

He'd been ready to raze the house to the ground. But Sybil said that the measure of a person was how they dealt with difficult situations. Turn the nightmare into a dream, she had urged. And he had. He had opened another school, too, one for lost and lonely boys left to wander the streets. He'd used his father's money to support men who wished to train as doctors and solicitors. And there was still so much more to do if he hoped to make his sons proud. Make his wife proud. To leave a positive mark on the world.

But for now, he wasn't interested in what tomorrow would bring. Now, he wanted to make love to his wife.

"I like it when you wear my shirt," he said, dismissing the call to let sense prevail. He slid his arm around her waist, feeling every soft curve through the fine lawn. He kissed her deeply, his cock hardening as she slipped her warm tongue over his.

"I don't suppose you know what's significant about today." She arched a brow as she pulled away from him. "It doesn't matter if you don't remember."

Damn. Mild panic fluttered in his chest.

He knew he hadn't forgotten her birthday.

"Think." Sybil placed her hand on his bare chest, the tips of her fingers gliding over his left nipple, teasing it to peak. "What were we doing this day last year?"

"It's not our anniversary. That's in ten days."

"Not our wedding anniversary, no."

From the playful glint in her eyes, from the intimate way she touched him, the answer became apparent. "You gave me the first of many precious gifts a year ago today," he said.

"Indeed."

"Does that mean you wish to celebrate?" Hell, he did. He reached under the shirt to clasp her bare buttock lest she mistake his intention.

"It's past midnight. We have to leave for Bideford Park at eight." The husky tone of her voice said she wanted him.

"If I remember rightly, this time last year we barely slept at all. The next day, we still managed to visit Newberry, the Wycliffs and make love in a carriage on the way home." And she'd professed her love in the dark confines of his vehicle. Oh, that was another anniversary to celebrate.

"Hmm. We did." She pursed her lips as she continued massaging his chest. "Would you indulge me? Would you mind if we played a little game?"

"Love, I would walk over hot coals if I thought it would make you happy."

She giggled, barely able to contain her excitement. "Then put on your shirt." Unabashed she drew the shirt over her head and gave it to him. "Wait for me in our attic room."

God, she was beautiful. Her breasts were heavier now, but he had no complaint. "You present me with your naked body and expect me to leave?"

She pushed him towards the door. "If you want to make love to me, Mr Daventry, you will have to pander to my whims."

Lovelust burned in his veins. He threw on his shirt, padded from the bedchamber and climbed the attic stairs.

On Sybil's instructions, nothing in the room had changed. Jonah had brought up an ottoman filled with pillows and blankets, and Lucius had placed the books back on the shelves. Everything else remained the same.

He relaxed on the chaise as he had done on that stormy night a year ago. Then, his thoughts had been dark, angry, confused. After the heated kiss in the library, he'd been battling with his conscience. After meeting his mother in the mews, he had not been able to calm the rage.

And then an angel had appeared to soothe him with her celestial body. An angel who brought light to his life, a light that had never dimmed.

He glanced at the door, wondering what kept her.

Tonight brought another anniversary of sorts. A year had passed since he had trusted Damian Wycliff and accepted Dermot Flannery's assistance. Sybil had convinced him of the need to share the burden of the Order. There were ways to focus on the truth without keeping secrets. And so he had rented an office, hired four ruthless gentlemen to investigate cases where clients lacked the funds to pay. Men whose grievances with the aristocracy gave them a hunger for justice. Dangerous men eager for a challenge.

"Lucius." Sybil's voice drew his gaze to the door. She entered the room, looking exactly as she had that night. Indeed, his heart skipped a beat as erotic memories flooded his mind.

"I see this is an accurate representation," he said, his hungry gaze sliding over the green silk gown, moving to the swell of her breasts and the teasing pearl choker.

"Not quite. The gown is a little tight."

"I find I'm rather obsessed with your curves."

"And I thought to focus on the one thing missing from our first passionate encounter."

Masculine pride forced him to say, "Trust me. I missed nothing. There wasn't an inch of your body I didn't pleasure." God, he'd been so damn ravenous.

With a gentle sway of her hips, she walked towards him. "May I sit?"

He didn't attempt to move from his lounging position. "Yes. You may sit on me."

She dropped into his lap. "You must be thirsty."

"Parched."

"I'm told Ashby has the right idea."

"I wouldn't know." Ashby and Miriam had resigned their positions, and with a little financial assistance had opened a servants' registry.

Sybil gave a cheeky grin as she raised the hem of her gown to reveal white silk stockings. "They're extremely expensive. Would you care to examine them?"

Lucius struggled to contain his raging lovelust. "It's only right I do. A husband must determine if his wife is frivolous."

She captured his hand and brought it to rest on her thigh. "Your wife is frivolous and downright reckless, sir."

"Reckless and utterly adorable."

She edged his hand up past the top of her stockings. "This is the moment where I kiss you. The moment where you rouse those delicious tingles."

"This is the moment where we add something new to the memory." He'd known he was in love with her when he first thrust into her body, but hadn't the courage to say the words. "The last year has been the best of my life."

She smiled. "Mine, too. And we shall have many more to come."

"Words cannot explain how much I love you. You saved me from a miserable existence."

She cupped his cheek and kissed him softly on the mouth. "You're everything I could want in a husband. Know that you're loved beyond measure."

The warm glow in his chest radiated. "I don't think we have any worries about arriving on time tomorrow. I'm so damn hard for you, this will be over quickly."

"You should be optimistic, Mr Daventry," she said, sliding his hand between her damp thighs.

"Optimistic?"

"You might make love to me twice."

THANK YOU!

Thank you for reading ***The Mystery of Mr Daventry.***

Sadly, that's the end of this series ... but not the end for Lucius Daventry or the four unconventional men he hired to solve new cases.

Meet the first intrepid hero and the woman who sends his world spinning in ...

Dauntless
Gentlemen of The Order - Book 1

Coming soon!

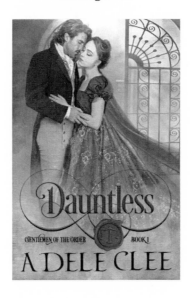

Books by Adele Clee

To Save a Sinner

A Curse of the Heart

What Every Lord Wants

The Secret To Your Surrender

A Simple Case of Seduction

Anything for Love Series

What You Desire

What You Propose

What You Deserve

What You Promised

Lost Ladies of London

The Mysterious Miss Flint

The Deceptive Lady Darby

The Scandalous Lady Sandford

The Daring Miss Darcy

Avenging Lords

At Last the Rogue Returns

A Wicked Wager

Valentine's Vow

A Gentleman's Curse

Scandalous Sons

And the Widow Wore Scarlet

The Mark of a Rogue

When Scandal Came to Town

The Mystery of Mr Daventry